MW00961919

Tin

K.S. Thomas

Published by Never Did Point North Publishing, 2015.

Table of Contents

For every 'Quinn'.

CHAPTER ONE

RIKER

I fucking hate my life. Really. Fucking. Hate. It. I'm pretty sure the only reason I'm even still here is because no one else is left to live it. It's not even my life anymore. Just pieces of everyone else's. Shit they left behind that couldn't be sold or handed off to strangers. Responsibilities. Land that's been in this family for generations. And that motherfucking horse. Nox.

He was my grandfather's pride and joy. Pretty damn sure he loved that horse more than he loved any of us. Although I don't see why. That four-legged asshole has done nothing but cause problems for the ranch since my grandfather's been gone. Three years now, he's been busting through fences, tearing up stalls, and scaring off pretty much anyone who's willing to get close enough to feed him. Which leaves me. But it's all good. In the grand scheme of things, Nox is but a minor listing on the billboard of reasons I fucking hate my life.

• • • •

QUINN

I glance down at my black leather boots. They're not faring well in the muck and mud, but after last night's rain, I expected as much. Once upon a time, I had proper clothes for this stuff. These days, however, most of my wardrobe consists of skinny jeans and ballet flats. And I'm not complaining. I'm just not prepared. But then how prepared do I need to be today? It's my niece's birthday party, and even though she's about to get up on a horse, it's not likely I'll be getting anywhere near one. Still, I wish I had my old boots.

1

"This was a great idea, Kirsten. I think the kids are having a blast." I take my seat next to the other moms on the bench outside the riding arena. Automatically, I scan their footwear, then smile internally. At least I still knew better than to wear opened toe sandals.

My sister's friend, C.J., leans forward to see past the two moms sitting between her and Kirsten. "Sophie is doing awesome. Is this her first time on a pony?"

Kristen smiles. "It sure is. And no shocker there. Look at who her aunt is." She gently nudges me in the ribs. "Sophie was probably born with some sort of special pony DNA."

I laugh. "Are you implying your child is part pony? And that she inherited this pony-part from me?"

"Maybe not a pony gene, just your pony sense." She's grinning. She's the only one who's been around long enough to remember.

C.J. cocks an arched brow in my direction. "You ride, Quinn?"

"Used to." Another lifetime ago.

C.J. shrugs. "I didn't know that." And it's clearly really bugging her. C.J. likes to be in the know. And we all like it when she is, because she spreads "the know" around. In a totally "non-gossipy, just informing every one of the current events like I'm a newscaster and it's my job" sort of way. And really, where would we be without the news? Especially since I've only just moved here. Meeting C.J. has really gone a long way in getting to know everyone else. Even if I haven't actually *met* everyone else yet.

Right now she's staring back and forth between my sister and I, shaking her head, and I can't tell if it's because she's so distraught over having been left in the dark about my little riding habit or if we've done something else to offend her. It's possible. I love C.J. and all, but that girl is high maintenance.

"Sometimes I really don't see how the two of you are even sisters," she says.

Ah. That thing. Yeah. We knew about that too. Which is why Kirsten whips back her long, perfect, platinum-blonde curls and laughs while I tuck a strand of my dirty-blonde waves carelessly behind my ear and offer up an awkward smirk. It's the best I can do sitting next to life-size Barbie.

Feeling properly motivated to move this conversation along, I point out the six girls straight ahead, just bobbing along on their ponies. Well, they're horses. But everyone here's been calling them ponies and I don't want to be the asshole who corrects them now.

"Anyway, how long are they going to make the girls just walk around in circles? I mean, this is a lesson, right? They should be teaching them stuff."

Kirsten gives me a look, and I know I'm annoying her already. I do it a lot. But today it's in record time, and I feel all at once slighted *and* impressed with myself.

"They're only five, Quinn. They're stoked just to be up on a pony."

And now I kinda *do* want to correct her. But I won't.

"I'm just saying. You paid for a lesson. A lesson implies learning stuff," I grumble as I slide off the bench. As much as I'm trying, I still don't fit in with Kirsten and her friends the way she'd like me to. I don't really know what she thought would be so different this time around. We certainly never hung around with the same crowd when we were kids.

Even with the age difference meaning less now at twenty-two and twenty-seven, we still couldn't be less alike. If anything, the last three years have probably put more distance between us than ever. But I know Kirsten, and she'll never accept that. She needs us to be close. She needs us to be perfect and sisterly. Because she's perfect. Only I'm so far from it, perfect looks like a speck of dust from where I'm standing.

I overhear C.J. make a comment about my sudden exit, but I don't turn around. Instead, I head toward the barn to try and absorb some of the scents. Maybe if I just stand inside an empty stall for a while and then don't shower for a couple of days, I can pretend my life hasn't turned into the shithole it is. I realize, of course, Kirsten would never let me stink up her house like that—not with horse or myself. So this very moment is an act of playing pretend already, but I'm getting good at that. Playing pretend. It's my thing. I'm the Master of It.

Rounding the corner to the front of the structure, I'm suddenly face-to-face with a riderless horse running straight at me in a full gallop. Without even thinking, I stretch out my arms and step directly into its path.

"Whoa. Whoa, now." It's the most gorgeous Friesian stallion I've ever seen, and he slides to a stop just a few feet in front of me. Double-checking to make sure I'm right about this boy business, I take a step toward him. He shies away, backing up, and I can tell he's seriously considering bolting again. "Easy, boy. It's okay. You're okay." Keeping my eyes averted as I walk slightly sideways, I continue to approach him until I'm standing at his side. "There you go. That's a good boy." Careful not to startle him again, I slowly brush my hand along his neck, then pat him gently before grasping a handful of his mane near the withers. Considering he's not wearing a halter or a bridle, there isn't much else I can hold onto right now, and letting him roam the property while kids are present doesn't seem like the most excellent idea. Of course, now that I've got him by his mane, I'm not really sure what to do next.

"Nox. You *sonofabi*—oh."

I turn toward the deep voice and realize I'm standing face-to-face with the second most gorgeous thing I've seen today. Except while the first one was scared, this one looks pissed.

"I take it this guy is with you?" I walk toward him, clicking my tongue to let my new horse boyfriend know we're moving.

"He is. Or he was." The guy is still scowling, and I'm already starting to take back the gorgeous thing.

"You know horses." He says it like a statement, but his expression suggests it's more like a riddle spoken by the Mad Hatter in Wonderland, like the idea is completely absurd.

"I know horses," I confirm. Then, because I'm tired of holding back every little thing that might offend someone, I add, "Judging by the way he came racing over here to see me, you don't."

But he just ignores me. Or ignores my comment, anyway. The way he's staring, piercing me with those devastatingly blue eyes, he's definitely not ignoring *me*. "What's with the boots?"

"Excuse me?" Except I kinda know exactly what he means, and that only pisses me off more.

"Your boots. They're sure as hell not made for being out here. Just seems odd that someone who knows horses wouldn't know that." The following "you're just another city girl moron" glare leaves little room for interpretation.

"Not that it's any of your business, but I came here to watch my niece ride. If I had known I'd be bailing your ass out, believe me, I would have dressed more appropriately."

He surprises me by actually breaking into a smile. And I'm back to believing in his natural beauty. Fuck me, the man is hot. And even though we're both being assholes, I can tell I'm entertaining him. Which in some sick sort of way is completely satisfying.

"Tell me, Boots. You always this argumentative?"

I shrug. "I don't know. Are you always such a dick?" I have to bite back a smile. Because, damn. That felt good. And, call me crazy, but I kinda think he liked it too.

His mouth opens, and I'm ready for round two when the sound of Kirsten's voice cuts through our moment like an ax. A big, ginormous, chop and hack my moment with hot grumpy cowboy guy to bits ax. My sister never goes small. Knives. They're small. Kirsten comes in with an ax.

"Quinn? Holy hell, what are you doing with that horse? Give it back. Right now." Her perfect porcelain skin seems to lose another shade of color. I didn't even know it could do that.

"Jeez, Kirsten, relax. I wasn't taking it. What, like I'm going to stick it in my pocket and try to sneak it out of here?"

Out of the corner of my eye, I catch the way grumpy-but-hot Cowboy's lips twitch. I like it. I want to do that again. "Here," I say. "You better take Nox before I use my shrinking potion on him and attempt to squeeze him into my sister's Beemer without her noticing." And there it is again, that smirk. Maybe I should keep talking. Because now that he's standing right next to me, I wouldn't mind seeing that little smirk up close and personal.

"Potion, huh? So you're a witch? Well, that explains the boots. And the hair." His voice drops even lower now that he's so close. I doubt anyone else can even hear him. I face him and immediately notice the fine lines at the corners of his eyes. There's a mischievous youthfulness about him, but it's misleading. He's probably close to Nate's age, which would put him at right around thirty.

He slides a halter over Nox's muzzle and behind his ears, purposely ignoring me the whole time. I catch his eyes dart in my direction once, gauging my reaction.

Rather than doing something super clever and confident, I reach up to touch my ends, which are purple. A delightful contrast to the dirty blonde, I always thought, but based on the disgusted curl of his lip as his gaze sweeps my hair, Cowboy disagrees. Or at least he wants me to think he does. That is the kinda thing we have going here.

"My hair is awesome." Yeah. That's the best I come up with as he walks away, leading a reluctant Nox back into the barn.

I'm still standing here, debating whether or not it would be weird to hurl another insult his way even after he's out of sight, when I feel a stabbing pain in my side from where Kirsten has pummeled me with her pointy little elbow.

"What was that?"

I don't even need to turn and look at her to know she's not happy with me. That tone said it all.

"What was what? Me and the horse? It got loose. I was just helping out. Doing my part to keep your little birthday troop from getting stomped into the ground. You should be thanking me." Total bullshit, by the way. Most horses will go out of their way *not* to step on a human being. But Kirsten doesn't know that.

"I'm not talking about the horse. I'm talking about the guy."

I make the mistake of facing her and regret it instantly. Both her hands are in tiny fists, propped on her hips, and she's got that expression I swear my mother must have passed down to her in some sort of welcome to motherhood ceremony when she popped out a baby herself. Because she didn't ever have it before Sophie.

"You mean the asshole who couldn't handle his horse? Why are we talking about him?" I do my best to match her pose, but I'm a far cry from motherly, so it's a pretty sad effort, and Kirsten totally bypasses it without so much as acknowledging it. Instead, she narrows her eyes a little more until they're itty-bitty slits, then scans me from head to toe. I wonder if Mom taught her this x-ray vision shit as well.

Finally her arms drop to her sides and her eyes open up to normal eyeball status again. "Sorry. For a moment there I was worried."

I shake my head. "Nothing to be worried about. Trust me." I don't trust me. But Cowboy is gone and not coming back out after me. And that I can trust.

I follow my sister back to the arena where the girls are still riding their "ponies" around in circles. I'm hoping I was gone for most of their hour lesson, but I'm thinking it's really only been like five minutes.

"There you are. We were wondering what happened to you." C.J. is up on her feet. She's got her camera out, and I'm guessing she's gotten every angle imaginable at this point of her daughter on that sluggish appaloosa.

"Leave it to my sister to attract a runaway horse and a loser to go with it under any circumstance," Kirsten announces loudly, accompanying the whole thing with a dramatic eye roll.

"Excuse me?" But no one is paying attention to me. They're all laughing at my sister's little display of—I don't even know what to call it—sisterly concern? Total bitch? I'm going to settle somewhere in the middle on this one and call it good.

Fine. There's no denying that my ability to attract douchebags is frighteningly impressive. And the horse thing? Whatever, *that* part I like. Not that I'm putting forth any effort in either department. Men and I are done. Whatever entertaining notions I enjoyed while fucking with Cowboy were exactly that. Entertaining.

I don't want more. I'm not capable of more. More would mean feeling. Would entail wanting. Desiring. And a slew of other emotions I haven't experienced in over three years. And it's not due to any stupid naïve intention of trying to keep my heart from breaking, nor is it as a result of having it broken by some poor slob who should have known better.

I can't feel. I don't have a heart. Period.

Torn between wanting to wander off again and worried I might run into Cowboy once more, resulting in attracting more unwanted attention from my sister, I stay standing in place and stare blindly into the riding arena. I want to be a better aunt right now, but I can't watch this farce of a riding lesson a moment longer without jumping the fence and taking over.

Thankfully, it doesn't come to that, because all of the horses have suddenly come to a unanimous stop.

"What's happening now? It hasn't been an hour already, has it?" I'm still no good at judging time. You can't spend years forcing yourself to lose track of it and then turn around and have a feel for five minutes versus fifty. It's all the same to me.

"It's thirty minutes of riding and thirty minutes of horse play," my sister informs me, still flaunting a noticeably snide undertone.

"I'm sorry. What exactly is horse play?" It sounds like torture. For the horses.

"Oh, the kids will get to groom one of the horses and then I think they dress him up or something." The delight on my sister's face is almost disturbing. She never was much of an animal person. Of course the one thing that would draw her interest would have to include a makeover of sorts.

"Dress him up?" I'm still sorta hoping she misunderstood something as simple as placing a blanket on a horse as putting a dress on it. I'm probably wrong, though.

"Yeah. They have tutus for him and party hats and stuff. I saw pictures from other birthday parties. It's totally adorable. Wait til you see!" Only Kirsten would get this excited over a tutu.

"Sounds fantastic." I resist the urge to twirl my finger in the air for added emphasis on my sarcasm. It came across plenty already.

"Lighten up, Quinn. This is a kid's birthday party. Not some barrel racing event. You keep taking everything so seriously, you're going to ruin this for everyone, including your niece." The mommy glare is back, and I get it. Time to check myself. This *is* a kid's party. I *do* need to lighten up. I just don't have a fucking clue about how to do that anymore.

"Sorry, Kirsten," I mumble as I fall in line behind her. Everyone is headed back to the barn to begin the horse play portion of the party. I guess I should find solace in the fact that they're no longer calling them ponies.

Of course, as luck would have it—and I'm referring to my type of luck, the unlucky kind—Cowboy is standing right there in the aisle with Nox. When he sees the troop of five-year-olds being led inside by their fearless leader, a fifteen-year-old who probably spends her time mucking out stalls and doing every dirty job around here imaginable in exchange for whatever scrap of riding time she can get, he quickly unties the stunning black stallion and leads him into one of the nearby stalls.

But it's too late. Kirsten's seen him. "You. Here." She orders me to her side like I'm one of the freaking five-year-olds she's responsible for.

"Yeah, okay." I nod and purposely walk in the opposite direction. Treating me like a kid is only going to make me want to act like one.

I take my place as far away from the scene as possible and lean against one of the full-length stall doors. Its inhabitant is busy munching away on leftover hay and couldn't care less about my presence.

Meanwhile, Kirsten isn't at all satisfied with my lack of involvement and promptly takes me from one extreme to the next. First dragging me away from the dangers of socialization, then practically throwing me to the wolves.

"My sister. Quinn." Kirsten points directly at me as she calls out to the fifteen-year-old leading the pack.

"What about your sister?" What could she possibly be announcing about me now?

"They asked for a volunteer." She's smiling broadly as she waves me back over, satisfaction gleaming in her eyes. "You know about this stuff," she says to me. "Go help your niece."

I swallow a sigh and start walking in their direction. When Cowboy comes out of the stall and takes the lead rope from the fifteen-year-old tour guide, I can't help but snort loudly. Kirsten's little stunt just backfired on her, big time.

"I can see why they requested a volunteer now. I wouldn't trust you to handle this horse on your own either." I pat the petite bay mare on her neck. She reminds me of my Jazz, but I try not to think about that now.

"The volunteer isn't for the horse," he grumbles, then nods at the crowd of five-year-olds. "It's for them. I don't do kids."

No shit.

"Well then, we're in big trouble," I whisper back. "Because I don't either."

Remembering my sister's evil glare and my niece's innocent smile, I do my best to get a grip. Maybe I'm not cut out to wrangle an entire party, but I know my way around at least one of these little minions.

"Sophie, come on up here with me." I'll just make her my guinea pig. Whatever Cowboy has planned for the kids, she'll do first and I'll wing it with the rest. No one will ever have to know that the anxiety of this encounter is repeatedly bringing me to the brink of peeing my pants.

CHAPTER TWO

RIKER

"You want to tell me what the hell that was earlier today?" I shake my head at Nox, just in case he can't tell from my tone how seriously disappointed I am in him right now. "What? You think she's cute or something? Like the way she smelled? Or maybe you just want to nibble on her soft skin a little."

I'm mocking him.

I'm not mocking him.

He's a fucking horse. I'm mocking my damn self.

"Well, whatever the hell it was, you better forget about it." I lean against the wall of his stall and watch him continue to grind his grain between his teeth like I'm not even here. It's all he ever does. Pretend I'm not here. And I'm the one he hates the least. Until today. Until her.

"I mean it, Nox. Whatever ideas are floating around that big-ass head of yours, let 'em go. Because she's already gone. And she ain't comin' back."

● ● ● ●

QUINN

"You're being awfully quiet." Kirsten's always had a thing about pointing out the obvious. It's kind of a family joke. One she's not aware of, so I'm super bummed I have no one to chuckle with right now. Not that I'm in the mood to chuckle. Not much in the mood to talk either, hence the being quiet, but I have a feeling my sister's going to override my desire for silence.

"Just winding down. All those kids and moms all afternoon was a lot to process." I stare out the Beemer window and hope this'll be the end of it.

"We were barely there for three hours. How strenuous could that have been, Quinn?"

I'd really like to point out that Sophie is crashed out in the back seat right now, so I'm clearly not the only one who found the day to be exhausting, but then I realize comparing myself to a five-year-old is the sort of thing Kirsten would love to do for me, so I really won't be doing myself any favors by doing so.

"Kirsten, I don't want to go over this with you again. Mostly because I don't know how many different ways to explain it to you." Begrudgingly, I shift around to face her. "I understand that you mean well, I really do. And I appreciate everything you're doing to include me in your group of friends. But it doesn't matter how nicely you dress me up or how often you tell everyone about my time doing 'missionary work overseas.'" I use my fingers for quotation marks on that one. I'm still stunned every time I hear her tell *that* story. "I'm never going to fit in. And, frankly, pretending to is exhausting. But I do. I do it for you. I know how important it is for you that people think I'm just your normal, run-of-the-mill girl, so I pretend. I act as normal as I can. But you have to know that *your* normal is not normal for *me*. It's never going to be. Ever again."

"Don't say that." Her pointy little nose scrunches up in disgust. "It's only been a few months. Just give it some more time."

"No. You're not listening to me." I bury my face in my hands. "That girl you think is going to make a reappearance after enough of an adjustment period? She's dead. She doesn't exist anymore. This"—I stab myself hard in the chest with both pointer fingers—"this girl, this anti-social, swears too much and can't ever say the right thing anymore girl, is all that's left. And you need to either accept it or tell me you can't."

My sister is staring straight ahead at the empty road. "And what if I can't? Huh? Then what? You leave? I can't lose you all over again, Quinn." A tear trickles down her cheek. *Shit.* This is the last thing I wanted. "I'm sorry if you feel like I'm putting too much pressure on you, but you're my sister. Whatever hell you went through while you were gone, it was hell for me too. And I get that you came back all jaded and broken and . . . and lost. But I don't see why that has to be a permanent condition. You're twenty-two for Christ's sake. You have your whole life ahead of you." She sniffles and presses her lips together. "So I don't care if you've given up. I don't care if you think this, this semi-lifeless 'the whole world is gray' Quinn is all that survived. You're wrong. And I'm going to keep having faith that the old you is still in there. And when she's brave enough, she'll come out again."

I want to tell her she's fooling herself. Truthfully, I want to scream it. But I don't. I just nod and let her think I'm agreeing with her, or at the very least considering the possibility, and then I go straight back to gazing blankly out the window. It's been two months and watching the constant greenery fly by still fascinates me. The simple things. Those are the only things that matter to me now. Everything else just leads to trouble.

True to the roots of our relationship, Kirsten and I spend the remainder of the drive home in silence. It's the only way we can both convince ourselves we each won the argument, and we're both okay with that.

Thankfully, it's just a ten-minute cruise up the main drag before I see the driveway that winds its way up to the Bernheimer mansion. I'm not exaggerating, either. The place has seven bedrooms and nine bathrooms. And when they bought it a year ago, there were only three of them: Kirsten, Sophie, and Kirsten's husband, Nate.

But I know my sister. The second Nate came home with the promotion and the news that they'd be moving back to his home state, she undoubtedly got online, found the most obnoxious, most expensive house she could find, and made it part of her negotiations. Because leaving Calabasas, California, for some rinky-dink beach town in North Carolina would have seemed an unbearable sacrifice. She would have made sure she got something out of it. Even if it was something she didn't actually want or need. Like this big-ass house.

I'm not complaining, though. It took me all of twenty-four hours to figure out how to move around the place without ever having to cross paths with anyone if I didn't want to. And that was definitely a plus in my book.

Kirsten pulls the car into their massive six-car garage and sighs loudly. Just in case I forgot how much I'm wearing on her. I didn't.

"I'm going to take Sophie inside and let her finish her nap on the sofa in the family room. Think you can manage bringing in the stuff from the trunk?"

I nod. "No problem. Where do you want it all?" We're talking piles upon piles of horsey-themed presents that inexplicably all have the color pink in common.

"The den will work. That way I can get to work on the thank you cards right away." She's already out of her seat and walking toward the back to retrieve Sophie, who's sleeping in such an odd position I can only imagine the cramp she's going to have in her neck when she wakes up.

"The den it is." Because we wouldn't want to fall behind on doing proper things like sending out thank you cards. I shake my head and shudder ever so slightly. Honestly, I don't even know who this old Quinn is that Kirsten is so desperate to get back. Even in my most unscathed and undamaged condition, I was never anything like this girl she's trying to revive now.

It takes me ten minutes to unload everything and stack it along the den's back wall. When I wander into the kitchen, Kirsten is already in full dinner mode. She's wearing an apron and everything. I don't know where she gets it from. The only one who ever wore an apron around our house growing up was our dad when it came time to break out the grill. And it was a highly inappropriate one he won at some stupid game during my uncle's bachelor party. My mom always hated it. But that never stopped him from wearing it.

"Sophie still passed out?" I don't know why I'm asking. It's pretty clear from the deafening silence around here that she's sleeping.

"Sure is. All that ranch work today wiped her out. I don't know how you used to do it day in and day out. I got tired just watching the kids ride for half an hour today." She chuckles as she snaps the end off another green bean.

I crinkle my nose, trying hard to stay focused and not get derailed on the million and one arguments I'd like to make. Starting with the fact that the kids weren't actually riding as much as they were sitting while being led around in circles, and ending with an exasperated *"You're tired? After the shit you gave me in the car, you're tired?"* But I let it all go and smile instead. "Well, if you don't need my help with anything else right now, I think I'm going to head down to the sand and go for a run. Maybe clear my head a bit."

Kirsten just gives me an open-ended nod, which is meant for me to interpret. She likes those. Makes her feel like she's giving me the freedom to make the right decisions for myself. Or at least what she believes the right decisions are. This move never really works in her favor, though. Just because I know that what she wants for me to say is *oh, never mind, let me strap on an apron and help you snap the ends off those green beans while I study your every move so I can become Suzie Homemaker for myself one day*, does *not* mean I'm going to do it.

"Alright, then. See ya." I wave and take off for the stairs leading down to the basement. I picture her standing behind me, jaw dangling, but I don't turn around to see.

As soon as I reach the last step, I fling open the door and Harley comes jumping at me. I hate that this is the only part of the house Kirsten deems dog approved, but I have no room to complain after everything she did for him while I was gone.

"Hey, boy." I tousle the long hair around his neck and give him a good scratch behind his left ear where he likes it. "Wanna go for a run?" He barks loudly. Call me crazy, but my dog understands me better than most humans do.

"Let's do it." He barks again and follows me across the large room, doing his little kangaroo hop. Harley lost his left front leg a few years ago after an accident that nearly killed him. He's made a full recovery since then, and even without the leg, he gets around just as well as he did before. Sometimes people are shocked when they see him down at the beach and realize he only has three legs. When he's running at full speed, you can't even tell.

The entire lower level is essentially my domain now. Kirsten complains that it smells of wet dog, so she only comes down here when she absolutely has to. You'd be surprised how often that's the case. The space was initially designed to be some sort of a man cave/game room, so it's got all sorts of little perks, like a fully stocked bar and a mini kitchen. Not to mention the pool table, the pinball machine, and the big-screen TV complete with every video game ever made. I think Nate's pretty bummed I live down here, actually, but it's where Kirsten put Harley, so it's where I am. Unfortunately, all the fancy extras are going completely to waste on me. Not counting the use I make of the TV and my sister's Netflix subscription.

I dig through the dresser in the corner and pull out my shorts and tank top. Then, having lost any sense of privacy and inhibition, I change right there in the center of the room with the wall of windows leaving me completely on display for anyone who might be walking by outside. It's a private beach, though, so even if I was shy, I wouldn't be too worried.

Last but not least, I grab a cold bottle of water from the fridge behind the bar and head out through the back door leading directly to the sand.

I've been going for daily runs out here since I arrived. They've been my escape. My temporary checkout from life. Reality. I know it seems odd to Kirsten that I need to take these breaks from the lavish lifestyle she's providing me, but this lap of luxury I've been dropped in is mostly like constant sensory overload. Some days I think I almost miss the way things were before. But that's not real either. It's just a broken mind thinking broken thoughts. So, I run. To keep from thinking altogether.

Usually, I turn left and head straight for the inlet. There are fewer houses along that stretch of sand, which generally translates into fewer people. Today, however, a crowd of at least fifty occupies the beach just a few places down from Kirsten's. They've got tents set up and a volleyball game going. And there are kids running wild between the water and what appears to be some sort of a sand village they're all working on.

"I don't know about you, Harley, but I'm not feeling all that." I gesture in midair as if I can somehow wipe out the scene. "Guess we're taking an unexplored route today." I turn right. As always, there are a few scattered umbrellas straight ahead, but they seem a lot more manageable than they did yesterday.

I reach into my pocket for my earbuds and insert them into my ears. Scrolling through my playlist, I tap the first song that has enough bass to drown out the world and then blast it. Harley's still sitting at my feet, just waiting for me to give him the go-ahead.

I nod. "Let's do this." And together, we take off.

CHAPTER THREE

RIKER

I run my hand over the railing. The wood is splintering in places from all the wear and tear of the salty, wet winds that swirl sand across these boards day in and day out. I can't even remember the last time I treated the panels with a fresh coat of stain and sealant, plus I'm pretty sure just from glancing at it that the post on the corner is completely rotted out.

"This place is turning into a real shithole," I mutter to myself. I do that a lot these days. And it's not like anyone's around to stop me, or even notice. Not that it would affect people's opinions of me. For the most part, everyone around here thinks I lost my damn mind four years ago. Fuck it. Maybe I did. "I *am* standing here talking to my goddamned self."

Still resting my hand on the wood, I start tapping my fingers, a nervous habit I acquired right around the time I lost everything else. I take a swig from my bottle of beer and tilt my head into the breeze. It's unusually warm already for this time of year, but I'm not complaining. I close my eyes and zero in on the loud rush of the wind as it dances over the crashing waves until they're the only things I can hear. Slowly, the rest of the world disappears until I'm surrounded by a numb nothingness, and for a moment being alone isn't so unbearable.

Until the sound of a dog barking loudly forces me to yank my eyelids up again.

• • • •

QUINN

"Hey! You!"

The man's voice carries, even over my loud music. Still, I clearly have my earbuds in, so he doesn't have to know that. I could easily keep running and completely ignore him. I go with that.

"Hey! I'm talking to you!"

He sounds closer. Shit. Is he following me? Considering I've only been running for about a mile, I could easily outrun most anyone right now. But I'll have to come by here on the way back, and I won't be as energized then. So I come to an abrupt stop and spin around, prepared for a fight. What I'm not prepared for is Cowboy. Or the fact that he wasn't expecting me to come to a crashing halt midstep—made entirely obvious when he literally runs me over.

"What the fuck? Get off of me!" I'm pummeling him in the chest as hard as I can, but he's so startled to be lying facedown on top of me that he's having a hard time getting reacquainted with his feet.

Finally, he makes it onto his knees. Brushing the sand off his bare chest, he scowls at me. "What the hell did you do that for?" Then, squinting because the sun is in his eyes, he takes a second look at me. "You?" He doesn't even wait for me to answer. Just drops his head back and shouts to the sky, "Come on!"

Apparently, twice is his limit, because his eyes travel in wide circles just to avoid landing on me from then on. He doesn't even offer an apology or, God forbid, a helping hand to get me off my ass and upright again. He just stands up straight, pats the sand from his board shorts, and growls, "Dogs aren't allowed on this beach."

"Are you fucking kidding me? That's why you chased me and tackled me to the ground? Because of my dog?" I scramble to my feet, fueled by an onset of fury I am only capable of when someone goes after Harley. "What are you, the fucking beach police? Why don't you mind your own damn business? You don't own this stretch of sand."

Then he does something that shocks me. He laughs. Like he's laughing at me. Like I said something hysterical, only I have no freaking clue what that might be. And I kinda hate that feeling. I hate it so much I'm temporarily stumped. A dangerous thing when you're standing across from a guy like Cowboy. Especially because this time around he's not covered in nice-fitting jeans or that long-sleeved button up flannel shirt, both of which made him look like he jumped straight out of a country outfitter's catalog.

No. Now he could easily have come flying out of a Ron Jon's Surf Shop billboard. With his board shorts hanging low on his hips, revealing way too damn much by the way, and his seamless tan that makes his mass of muscle body only that much more fascinating, I can barely swallow my saliva fast enough to keep from drooling. And can we talk about the tattoos? Holy hell. The man is covered in some beautiful ink. I understand the conservative shirt from earlier so much more now. He has full sleeves on both arms, reaching up over his shoulders and down his chest. He has another pretty large piece on his left thigh, and who knows what's happening on his back.

If Kirsten thought he looked like a loser in his dirty jeans with his two-day-old scruff and shaggy blond hair before, she would have a slew of new unpleasant terms for him now. So do I, incidentally. None of which my sister would be pleased to hear.

I wipe the corners of my mouth because, mentally, I'm drooling all over him. My eyes travel leisurely past his collarbone and up to his face. And. I. Want. To. Die.

He's staring straight at me while I'm still busy staring at him. And he isn't laughing anymore. He's smirking. Which makes me both weak in the knees and dizzy from the heat rushing to my head.

"Funny. You suddenly don't seem pissed off at me anymore." He glares at me smugly. It's like he can see straight through me with those deep-blue eyes of his. With the evening sky glowing behind him, they look eerily dark, like there's a storm brewing inside them. Or maybe it has nothing to do with the sky. Maybe it's just him.

"Oh, I'm still plenty pissed," I scoff, but my attempt at anger fails now that it's lacking in aim and motivation.

"Clearly." He folds his arms over his chest, and I have to swallow an actual whimper at the sight of his muscles in motion. *Damn him.*

"Whatever, dude. If we're done here, I'm going to take my dog and go home." I motion for Harley to get up. He's been lying in the sand, quietly watching us from about three feet away. "Come on, Harley."

"What happened to his leg?" Cowboy drops down to a squat to get a better look at my dog.

"Why do you care? You hate dogs, remember?" I place my hands on my hips, mostly because I don't really know what to do with myself right now. Then I have a flash of Kirsten in the exact same position and instantly drop them back to my sides.

"I never said I hated dogs." And Cowboy shocks me for the second time. He looks genuinely offended and even slightly hurt.

"You fucking tackled me because of my dog." Since my arms have no real job right now, they're just sort of flying around dramatically, trying to move with my emotions. Which are all over the place right now, so, you know, I'm sure I look pretty ridiculous.

"I didn't tackle you. You tripped me. And it wasn't because I hate dogs. I just . . . fuck it." He exhales loudly. "I was in a shit mood, and I was looking for someone to blame. Then your dog barked and interrupted the only moment of peace I've had all day, and I went with it." He glances back up at me over his shoulder. "I'm sorry. It was an asshole move. And contrary to popular belief, I'm actually not an asshole. All the time."

I twist my lips back and forth to keep from smiling. I don't know what Cowboy's deal is, and I don't want to know. But damn it all to hell if he keeps making me do involuntary things with my mouth.

"I didn't trip you." Because being stubborn is all I have left right now.

He chuckles. "Fine. You didn't trip me. You're right. I tackled you. On purpose. Now will you please tell me why your dog only has three legs?"

This time his charm doesn't make my panties want to dematerialize. On the contrary. His question about Harley's leg makes my blood run ice cold, and all the feelings I had mere seconds ago freeze with it.

I look at Cowboy one last time, then pat my thigh to cue Harley to start walking. "No."

I start jogging back toward the house. I'm still fumbling with my earbuds, so I can hear him moving in the sand behind me.

"What the hell is your problem now?"

I spin back around, this time careful not to cut into his path again. "You are. In case you missed it, I was out here running. With earbuds. I wasn't trying to make small talk. I was trying to blow off some steam."

Cowboy takes a step toward me. And another. Until he's standing so close I can feel another whimper climb up my throat. Jesus Christ, what is this man doing to me? I feel like I'm running a fever the way I'm going back and forth between chills and hot flashes.

"You're right. Small talk really isn't working for us." His voice drops two octaves again like it had when he was standing annoyingly close to me outside the barn.

"No shit." I force myself to hold his stare. The storm in his eyes is clearer than ever. I'm not the only broken person standing here. He's just as fucked up as I am. And even though that thought alone should make me break into a sprint toward home immediately, it doesn't.

"You really wanna blow off some steam?" His deep voice rumbles past my ears along with the wind.

Still feeling the pierce of his eyes as they keep me locked into place, all I can do is nod. I don't have to ask what he has in mind. The tension between us is roaring louder than the ocean behind us. I should be terrified. Scared of drowning in it. Of drowning in him. But I'm not. Because you can't drown when you're used to being at the bottom of the ocean. The waves don't scare me. They're just a welcome promise of change. And I go with them.

Following him up the private boardwalk up to the house, I'm suddenly having second thoughts about this whole thing. For starters, I'm disgusting. Meanwhile, he looks like he just jumped out of the shower. Not me. I'm not only drenched in sweat and covered in sand, I'm still walking around with several layers of dust and grime from hanging out in the barn all afternoon.

The fact that none of this seems to be an issue for him tells me one of two things: either he finds me irresistible beyond reason, and any and all senses that would give away my current condition—e.g., sight and smell—have been completely dulled because of it, or his standards are so ungodly low that even a nasty, dirty, soulless girl like me can meet them, in which case I should probably turn around and walk away right now, because if he's willing to sleep with me . . . well, let's be real, *I* wouldn't be willing to sleep with me.

Sad fact is, it's probably the latter, which brings me back to my second thoughts, and now third because for some unknown reason I'm still following him.

"This is your place?" It's bigger than Kirsten's. I wonder if she knows there's a house this size within a three-mile radius of hers.

Cowboy points at the small, washed-out door beside the garage. "This is my place."

Ah. Yes. This makes way more sense.

"You the caretaker or something?"

He just grunts in response as he leads the way inside. I close my eyes, bracing myself for whatever I'm about to find. Then I remember the places I've been and the things I've seen and realize nothing inside this multimillion-dollar beach house could possibly be all that terrifying, and I open them again.

It's about what I expected. A studio apartment with a mishmash of old furniture. Two wicker patio chairs around a glass table make up the dining area, he's got a mattress with faded brown sheets for a bed, and in the corner there's what appears to be an old recliner doubling as his dresser. Or dirty clothes hamper. I really can't tell which. So, it's probably both.

Off to the left there's a narrow door I'm assuming leads to the bathroom, and then to the right of us there's a small kitchen, the distinct scent of his supper still lingering in the air.

I grin. "Ramen noodles?"

He drops his head and shakes it sheepishly. "I don't like to cook."

It's about what I figured. "Can I take a look at your fridge?"

He cocks his head back. "Why?"

I shrug. "Just want to see if I'm right or not." I'm already walking toward the kitchen. He's not moving, so I'm taking it as a yes. "Oh, yeah. Here we go. Leftover Chinese takeout and three pizza boxes. All of which have . . . wait . . . exactly one slice and two crusts in them. Why don't you eat the crust? It's the best part!" I let the fridge door fall back into place and then return to where I left Cowboy standing in the middle of his small apartment.

"I agree. Sometimes I save a few pieces for the seagulls." He tips his head to the side and his mouth twitches up into a half grin. "And then I forget."

He's being cute. Too cute. And he's sharing. My fault, but still. This isn't what I came here for. I glance briefly at Harley, who's already found a pile of towels to curl up in, and then I just go for it and pull my tank top right over my head.

When Cowboy doesn't react, I toss it across the room and start to shimmy out of my shorts. "Are we doing this or what?"

"I don't know. Did you want to check out my medicine cabinet as well? See if I'm fully stocked in condoms and dollar store toothbrushes for my overnight guests?" His voice has dropped again, so he's not really trying to be funny.

"All I need is one condom. And I'm not staying overnight." I kick my sneakers off into the corner. There's nothing left but my sports bra and panties. I'm about to reach up to take off the bra when Cowboy comes for me.

In one smooth motion he's got me off the ground, both hands firmly under my ass, my legs wrapping tightly around his waist. He presses my back flush against the wall, his rock-hard dick pushing up through his shorts and against the thin material of my underwear. I already have to fight the urge to roll my eyes into the back of my head.

"You'll need at least three. And I won't be done with you until morning," he growls into my mouth, just before his lips crush mine.

In my entire life, I've never been kissed the way I'm being kissed at this very moment. It's almost like Cowboy is gasping for air and breathing me in with each connection our lips make. Only it's exactly the opposite for me. He's leaving me completely breathless. Suffocating me with the intensity of his lips on mine, the way his tongue plunges into my mouth and completely takes over. His kiss. It's all-consuming. Like hunger. And sleep. And I'm starving and exhausted.

Still holding me tight to him, he moves us away from the wall and toward the bed. Or mattress. Let's not romanticize this.

Considering the mattress is less than a foot off the ground, I'm expecting to drop my legs and lower myself, rather than tempt fate and risk bodily injuries while he does the impossible and balances my entire body weight along with his own as he tries to lean forward and lie down.

Wrong. Again. Cowboy's got this. Damn, he's got it good. One arm wrapped snug around my back, holding me to him, and the other stretched out in front, guiding us both safely to ground level, all the while never once breaking our kiss. Which is good, because I'm pretty sure, at this point, both of our lives depend on it.

No longer needing to physically hold me in place, he untangles his arm from around my waist and uses his free hand to undo his shorts. As soon as I notice, my own hands come back to life and I stop pressing them into his chest so I can reach down and help him get out of his pants. He's not wearing anything under them, and *holy Mother of God.* If I wasn't already out of breath from kissing him, I would stop breathing altogether right now.

I can't even blame the fact that it seems like an eternity since I last saw a penis. If there was ever any question about whether God was a man or a woman, Cowboy is all the proof I need that she's female. Only a woman would know to build a man this perfectly. And I mean . . . perfectly.

He drops his entire weight onto my body and moans deeply into my mouth. It's the sexiest damn sound I've ever heard. Between that and the way he's rubbing against my underwear again, not to mention the way his kisses are making my head spin and the fact that my entire body feels like it's about to experience some sort of euphoric overload from merely touching, I'm pretty sure the only decent thing to do is tell him to slow down or I won't have any need for that condom after all. At the rate he's going, I'm going to have an earth-shattering orgasm within the next twenty seconds, and after that I'm not really going to have much use for him anymore.

But I don't say anything because words are a little beyond my realm of capabilities right now. Instead, I place both palms on his chest and push up with all the strength I can muster. Which is peanuts, really, but he notices anyway.

"What's wrong? Am I hurting you?" Actually, now that he's stopped, he kind of is. My body literally aches for his kiss. An act of betrayal I can barely comprehend, which makes me want to ram my own head into a brick wall just to override my body's new and unfounded urges.

"You're not hurting me. Trust me." I can already feel myself turning red for what I'm going to say next. I feel like a fucking thirteen-year-old about to hand over her v-card to the high school football star. "It's just . . . I haven't done this in a while and it's not going to take a whole lot to finish the job here. So you may want to cut any and all foreplay and get right to the main event, because I'm not the kind of girl who's going to stick around and worry about whether or not you got all you were hoping for from this experience."

He drops his head to my shoulder, grazing it with his lips as he chuckles. When he raises his eyes to meet mine, his disheveled hair is hanging down into his line of vision and I have to fight the desire to tenderly swipe it away.

"I don't need you to worry about whether or not I'm getting all I was hoping for from this experience. I don't need you to worry about *me* at all. I *do* need you to stop trying to fucking rush me, though. I know what I'm doing. So just close your eyes, lie back, and shut the fuck up so you can enjoy it."

For the first time in more than three years, someone telling me what to do actually results in my doing it. I don't know why. Maybe because I'm about to get something I want. Maybe because I'm telling myself he's clearly a glutton for punishment, because he is going to have the biggest case of blue balls when I strut out of here after I get mine. Or maybe, maybe, it's because for the first time ever, I'm being told to do something that is actually in my own best interest.

I take a deep breath and get situated again on the bed. Closing my eyes and readying my lips, I'm expecting him to pick up where we left off before I stopped him. Only this time Cowboy has other plans.

Instead of landing on my mouth, his lips trail their way down the side of my neck to my shoulder and across my collarbone. The soft scruff on his jawline tickles my skin, magnifying the tingling feeling his lips leave as they trace my chest.

I sink deeper and deeper into his mattress. It's probably all mental, but if it were possible to literally melt, I'd be doing exactly that right now. In fact, I'm such a puddle that my body is nearly limp when he tug at my arms, bringing me into an upright position while he sits on top of me, straddling me.

I keep my eyes closed as ordered, as he peels my sports bra over my skin and pulls it over my head before gently letting my body slide back onto the pillow behind me.

Holding himself up with the arm he has resting beside my head, he uses his other hand to cup my breast, gently massaging it with his palm while his mouth moves to the other, tantalizing me with each meticulous flick of his tongue across my nipple.

My fists curl around handfuls of his sheets as the mind-bending pleasure begins to mount, sending my body into new and uncontrolled spasms, unable to contain all it's experiencing.

I'm so focused on what his tongue is doing, I barely notice when his hand moves down from my chest, softly caressing the skin on my stomach before sliding under the rim of my panties. I'm pretty sure I'm about to completely lose it when his fingers slide down the front of me. His thumb instinctively seeks out the most sensitive part of my entire body, moving in small circles, gradually increasing in pressure and speed and then letting up again.

I've almost come like ten times already, but somehow Cowboy has more control over my body than I do. It's the exact moment I realize this that his finger enters inside me, and I want to scream. I do scream. I've been screaming. It's like a freaking prayer circle up in here the number of times I've shouted "oh my God" in the last three minutes.

He moves in a second finger, and I feel myself tighten around him. Only this time he doesn't take it away. He just keeps giving me more. More. And more. Until I'm gasping for air and my body shudders and shakes under him from the release.

CHAPTER FOUR

RIKER

I close my eyes to the sun. I'm not ready for daylight. I'm not ready to go back to my life. For some reason, even the uninterrupted sounds of the isolated early morning beach aren't enough to quiet my mind right now.

Well, if nothing else, Sid'll be pleased her condom run didn't go to waste. I thought she'd been nuts when she showed up here two days ago with an armload of condoms and toothbrushes, making her grand speech about how I was still alive and how it was about damn time I acted like it. I wasn't really sure how that translated into safe sex and oral hygiene, but she assured me it did. And maybe it does.

Three condoms and five orgasms for her later, and I'm feeling more alive than I have in a long time. I'm sure it would shock her to know I got more out of the two I gave her than the three we shared. It's been so fucking long since I've put anyone else's needs above my own, doing something that was completely about someone else for a change was becoming a foreign concept. It gets tiring being a selfish son of a bitch all the damn time, but what else am I supposed to be when I live in a hole, isolated from the rest of the world with no other living, breathing being around? Except on the rare occasion that Sid still comes by. And it's my own damn fault she doesn't show up more often than she does. I wouldn't want to be around me either.

But Quinn did. And even though she's gone for now, I have a feeling she'll be back. Of course, I'm giving Quinn something I'm not about to give Sid. She's getting something out of being here with me. Sid gets shit. Because I love her. And she loves me. And that's what you do when you're a selfish son of a bitch. You give those you love the worst of what you have. And Sid's the only one left, so she gets the worst of it all.

• • • •

QUINN

Still feeling the waves of embarrassment after having woken up in Cowboy's bed after specifically making a point of promising a "wham, bam, thank you ma'am" kind of experience, I'm doing my best to sneak back into Kirsten's house.

The sun's already coming up and I'm still dressed in my running gear. I can easily make an argument for having just returned from an early morning run if I get caught, but I've never been all that good a liar. It would take Kirsten all of three seconds to deduce I was out all night with some scumbag who would only get me into trouble. And then I'd grin like an idiot remembering the night I've had, and it would be all she'd need to seal the deal on her conclusions.

Thankfully, I make it back into my downstairs living quarters without a hitch, and Harley and I climb into my bed to spend what's left of the night sleeping there. I know the less gross thing would be to shower first. But I'm exhausted. And strangely, not nearly as disgusted with myself as I ought to be.

It's nearly eleven by the time I come crawling out of my cave and greet the rest of the family. It's Sunday, so Nate is actually home for a change.

"There's trouble," he says. "I heard you tried to steal a horse yesterday."

Only his eyes are visible over the Sunday paper, but I can tell he's laughing at me.

"Seriously, Kirsten? I head for the fridge and pour myself the biggest glass of OJ I think I've ever had. I'm parched. Three guesses why. "You're so freaking dramatic about everything."

"Oh, I'm the dramatic one now? You're the one who pouted all night because of our little talk in the car. You even missed dinner." My sister frowns. "I made chicken pot pie. From scratch."

I'm sure this means something significant to her. I hate chicken pot pie, so it means squat to me.

"I'm sorry. I didn't mean to ditch you. I just went for a run . . . and by the time I got back, I was exhausted and went straight to bed." It's totally true. Minus one major detail. Cowboy. "Which reminds me, do you know there's a house like twice the size of this place less than a mile down the beach?"

Kirsten's mouth twists into a grimace that reminds me of the face she used to make when we were kids and dared each other to eat lemons. "It's not twice the size. It's just laid out differently so it looks bigger." She places a bowl of oatmeal in front of Sophie, who's quietly coloring in her coloring book at the breakfast bar.

Nate clears his throat. "Well, the layout isn't the only reason. The Shepherdson place has like a thousand square feet on this house."

I don't know why I care. I shouldn't care. "Shepherdson? Is that who owns it?"

Kirsten puts a bowl of oatmeal down in front of me as well, and I smile politely. I know she means well. She even musters a smile of her own, in spite of the conversation I've started. "The Shepherdson family practically owns this whole town. Apparently, they settled out here a gazillion years ago and claimed every kernel of sand before anyone else got here."

Nate chuckles. "That's not entirely accurate, hon. Earl Shepherdson came out with his family back when there was nothing but open country out here. They settled inland. Made their living from raising cattle. Later, his son William took over. He's the one who took the land they owned and turned it into a fortune. By the time his son and grandson came along, the family business was booming. And yeah, now they own damn near every vacation rental between here and the moon. Including the place you're talking about."

I experience one of those light bulb sensations. "Hey, was that Earl Shepherdson's ranch we were at yesterday for Sophie's party?" I'd seen the sign. Just hadn't really registered it. Until now. If it was the Shepherdson ranch, it would make sense.

"It was." Nate puts down his paper, giving up on it for good. "His son Willie—William—lived there his whole life. Right up until he died about four years ago. Supposedly the ranch went to family. His grandson'd be my guess, but as far as I know, no one's doing much with it these days. Other than just keeping it running."

I slurp some oatmeal from my spoon. Sophie giggles. Kirsten shoots a dagger from her eyeballs straight for my face. I slurp some more. "So who's this stupid grandson of his letting the place go to waste?"

Nate's trying hard not to smile. Not because he thinks slurping oatmeal is funny, but because his daughter does, and her little laugh is nothing if not infectious. But then, so is my sister's scowl. "James Shepherdson. And I don't know that I would call him stupid."

I cock my brow. "Really? If you ask me, anyone who has access to a place like that and then just sits on it sounds pretty damn stupid to me." My whole life I fantasized about owning a ranch like that one someday. I spent hours upon hours just dreaming up all the things I would do with it. Horse-related services I would offer. Training facilities I would set up. The list went on and on.

But Nate doesn't get it. Why would he? He's a suit and tie guy who probably hasn't ever stood close enough to a horse to even know what one smells like.

"You know, for someone who has a pretty interesting story of her own, you're pretty quick to jump to conclusions on someone else's, Quinn. The Shepherdson family went through hell these last few years. James Senior and his daughter were killed in a car crash almost five years ago. Old Willie had a stroke the night it happened because he couldn't cope, and then died less than six months later. The whole family empire landed square in his grandson's lap, and there's a whole hell of lot more to it than just enjoying the fortunes it comes with." Nate lowers his head, shaking it slowly, and I wonder how much more he knows that he's not telling. I get the feeling he knows this James guy personally. Like maybe they were friends in the past. "I'm guessing that's why his wife took off. Took all three kids with her. After that, James Shepherdson just kind of dropped off the face of the earth. Business is still running, though. Ranch is still standing. So he's a far cry from stupid if you ask me. Unmotivated, maybe. But not stupid."

"Fair enough." I suddenly feel like I need to play a one-upping game of personal tragedies with this guy. It's stupid. I don't even know him. And, in all fairness, he'd probably win. I'm pretty sure I'd have to disqualify myself anyway, since tragedies typically aren't self-inflicted. Besides, really, I just feel like an ass for being so judgmental and then being called out for it, by Nate of all people.

"Why are you asking about the Shepherdson place anyway?" Kirsten's otherwise perfect face is still showing a distinct line of disapproval straight across her forehead.

"Wasn't really asking. Merely pointing out that there's a castle bigger than your majesty's sitting smack in the middle of your kingdom."

This time Nate's not as successful at hiding his amusement, and Kirsten swats him with a dishtowel. "God! You two are ridiculous. Why would I care if there's another house bigger than mine? Ours." Her little slip is reason enough to drop the topic altogether and move onto something else. "Meanwhile, C.J. invited all of us over to their place today. Rick is cooking out on the grill and she's invited over a few other families as well. The girls can all play in the pool. It'll be fun." She's nodding at me with an extra dose of enthusiasm, probably hoping some of it will spill over and land in my oatmeal or something.

I push away my bowl. Just in case. "Sounds like you guys are going to have a great time."

"And?" The only thing raised higher than her brows right now are her expectations of me.

"And I'll be there suffering in silence." Only, even as I say it, I realize I'm not actually bothered by the prospect of spending the day with Kirsten's friends. I wait a moment to see if the panic attack is merely delayed today, but nothing happens. I feel . . . nothing. Not happy. But I'm not visualizing myself crawling up the walls using my teeth and fingernails either, so that's bound to mean something.

Apparently, Kirsten's noticed as well. "What's going on?"

I do my best to look innocent, but I feel a smirk spreading on my face, so I reach for my glass of juice to try and hide it. "Whaddayamean?"

"You. There's something different. You didn't even try to get out of coming with us. What happened between yesterday evening and this morning to take you from the terrified of happy people recluse to this casual 'sure why not, parties are no big deal for me' person sitting in front of me?"

Cowboy and his five orgasms happened. But I can't tell her that. She'll freak. Provided she even believes me. Actually, she probably won't. I set my glass down and look her straight in the eyes. "I got laid."

Without saying anything to either of us, Nate gets up from his seat and scoops Sophie up in his arms. "Come on, sweetie. We're going to let the big girls sort this one out without us."

Kirsten waits for her husband and daughter to turn the corner and disappear down the hall. "You going to tell me what's really going on now, or what?"

I want to. I really do. I want nothing more in this world than to tell my sister everything. But I've tried. So many times. We never agree. Neither of us ever understands the other. In the end, I'm never able to live up to her standards. I understand why she sets them so high. I really do. But I can't stand letting her down anymore. I don't want to see her disappointment, or the disapproval she's bound to express if I tell her what really happened. *Who* really changed me. So I don't. I lie.

"Honestly? I went for a run just like I said I was going to. I just went for a longer run than I've ever gone before. After our talk in the car . . . and being out with the horses again . . . I felt like everything was closing in on me and I just needed to . . . blow off some steam." I shrug. "So I did. And I didn't come home until all of that pent-up anxiety and anger and fear mellowed out a bit. Don't get me wrong, I'm still all broody and cranky just like before." I grin to ease the tension. "But going out last night definitely took the edge off."

Kirsten scans me with her mommy vision, and I'm really hoping it won't work on me since I'm her sister. "Well, if running is really all it takes, may I suggest you start upping your mileage? Maybe even start going twice a day?" She breaks into a small smile as well. "Because this is nice. Seeing you less tense. It's almost like some old part of you is clawing its way back to the surface."

I do my best to smile back. "Yeah. Maybe." I don't have the heart to tell her that's not possible.

As per Kirsten's suggestions, I do start running twice a day. However, it's not really having the same effect since I'm purposely running my old route. The one that takes me away from Cowboy and not to him.

I mean, I got the feeling I was welcome back when I left, but it wasn't exactly discussed. Nothing was really discussed. That was a big part of what I liked about our encounter. The absence of talking. The lack of questions. The just being. No past. And sure as hell no future. And with that in mind, I keep running. As far away from his place as possible.

Until now. It's five a.m. and I'm on the sand. Alone. Running for my life. Running toward his house. I had a dream. *The* dream. Only this time I couldn't wake up in time. When I finally broke free from the iron grip of my own sleep, I was drenched in sweat and screaming. Thank God for the extra soundproofing they did when they turned the downstairs into the gaming slash movie room, or Kirsten would have been standing over me with a kitchen knife in hand and the cops on their way, ready to fight off whatever was coming for me. Only it's too late for that. She can't stop something that already happened. Neither can I. But with Cowboy's help, I can forget.

It's not until I'm standing in front of his door in the dark about to knock that I realize how insane this is. He doesn't know me. I don't know him. One random hookup does not give me permission to stand on his doorstep in the early morning hours expecting another one. On the other hand, I've never met a guy who turned down sex.

I need to have sex. With him. Right now.

I'm still pacing back and forth in front of his door, trying to decide what to do, when it opens and his broad frame fills the entire doorway.

Looking half-asleep, he rubs his eyes with the back of his hand. "Is it working?"

I stop dead in my tracks and stare back at him. "Is what working?"

He loosely points in my direction. "Whatever that was you were doing out here before I interrupted you."

I bite my lip. Offering sex to a perfect stranger is only sexy when you don't look like a jackass while offering. "I didn't know you were up."

Much to my frustration, the left corner of his mouth creeps up into the hottest-looking half grin I've ever seen in my life. I'm having flashes of what it felt like to have his lips pressed to mine, and my calves tighten as my body instinctively preps to pounce on him. Then he speaks.

"So is this like a frequent thing you do now? Pace back and forth outside my apartment at night while I sleep? Call me crazy, but that seems like a misuse of your time and energy considering what we could be doing with it if you brought it inside. Not to mention, the wrong guy might find it to be a little on the psycho-stalker side."

I want to be pissed. Offended. Turn around and stomp off with a haughty huff. But instead I practically tackle him, flinging my arms over his neck and jumping up to wrap both legs around his waist while he catches me like this is neatly timed choreography we've practiced many times over.

My lips move with an almost frantic need, seeking out his mouth and waiting for his kiss to take me in. Somewhere in the distance the door slam shut, and I know we're inside. Safe. He's got me securely in his arms, moving across the small apartment until we're in the bathroom.

"What are we doing in here?" I ask, catching my own reflection in the mirror as he sets me down. I flinch. This isn't going to work. I can't escape myself while I'm watching the whole thing.

"Multitasking. I've got to be at work in less than an hour." He reaches past me and into the shower. Half a second later the water come on.

"Oh." Shower. Steam. The mirror will be fogged up in no time. "Um, thanks for squeezing me in."

His hand slides down to my ass and pinches it hard. "No problem. Tomorrow don't waste so much time strolling around on my front porch before you come inside."

Tomorrow. "I won't." I barely get the words out before his lips seal themselves to mine again. *God, this man can kiss.* And speaking of multitasking, my clothes are already lying on the floor somewhere, mixed in with the sweats he was wearing when he answered the door.

Using one arm to open the shower curtain, he keeps the other snaked tight around my waist as he backs both of us into the hot stream of water. Giving me the prime spot, he briefly breaks away, taking a step back to watch as the water runs over my naked body. It's weird because I despise being watched. Maybe because I've spent years attempting to be invisible. My survival was kind of dependent on it. But now, with him, it's different. He's not studying me in search of flaws. He's not seeking out my weaknesses. He's simply enjoying the sight of me. And I'm enjoying being seen.

A mischievous smirk trails his lips as he reaches for a bar of soap and begins to lather it up under the water. Next, he turns me around and begins to move the suds over my shoulders, slowly working his way down. It's the most sensual thing I've ever experienced. Combined with the bubbles and water, his otherwise callous hands are softly moving over my now silky-smooth skin.

His hands continue to move around to my front, gently caressing my chest and stomach. One arm wraps over my breasts, holding me to him, while the other reaches down, still moving in soft circles over my skin and washing my hip and top of my thigh. Dropping my head back to his chest, I close my eyes and let myself get swept away in the moment as his hand slides between my legs.

Behind me, I can feel him. He's hard and ready, pressing against me, and I curl my arm around my back, then wrap my hand around his large shaft.

He moans into the curve of my neck, and the sound mixed in with the sensation of his hot breath against my skin turn me on even more. I tilt my head back to kiss him just as his mouth is coming for mine. I turn around to face him, then, moving together, our hands mimic the rhythm of our bodies. It doesn't take long before my back is arched against the cold wet tiles of his shower and I'm gasping for his kiss, and air, and a functioning brain cell, because all that's left of me is turning to putty in his hands as the sensation climbs until it spreads into every last inch of my being.

"Oh my God, Cowboy," I whisper as he brings me to him, letting the now cold water run over both of us.

"That's not my name," he rumbles into my ear as he begins to wash my hair.

"I don't care." I move my hands over his chest, rinsing what's left of the suds from his skin.

He stops what he's doing and lifts my chin toward him. "You don't know my name, do you?"

I want to turn my head away from the intensity of his gaze, but his thumb and finger have a firm hold of my jaw and I'd have to force it to move. I'm not doing that. The last thing I want to do is make a big issue out of this. It's not.

"I don't need to know your name."

He lets go of my face and shakes his head. "What? Afraid things will get too serious if you actually know who I am? Trust me. They won't. They can't. This? It can't be more than what it is right now. Ever."

I laugh. Maybe because this conversation is making me uncomfortable. Maybe because it's annoying me that he's trying to turn the tables on me, like I'm the one who's trying to turn this into something deeper than two strangers fucking for the sheer fun of it. "Oh, believe me. I know that. There's no way I'm falling for another asshole who doesn't have his shit together."

Fully expecting him to have his little male ego bruised by my comment, I spin around and turn the knob, bringing our shower to an instant ending.

This conversation is a total buzzkill, and it's ruining the phenomenal orgasm I had less than five minutes ago, which truth be told is pissing me off, considering it's what I hauled my ass over here for this morning.

"Quinn," he says my name. Calmly. I don't know if he's making a point about knowing it, or just wants me to stop huffing and puffing around his bathroom like an angry five-year-old. Either way, it works, and I stop moving long enough to let him wrap a large towel around my soaking wet body.

"You know, just because we're not going to have an emotional relationship, doesn't mean our physical one wouldn't benefit from a certain degree of communication," he says quietly as he rubs the excess moisture from my hair with a smaller towel he pulled from the hook by the sink. I can't help but notice how good he is at this. This nurturing thing. And how easy it is for me to let him. And then I quickly try to forget.

"I'm not good at that." Not with people anyway. It's one of the main reasons I've always been drawn to animals. They're less complicated. And for some reason, they make *me* less complicated. And then I realize that's why I like being around Cowboy. He makes me feel the same way.

He unravels the towel from my body and uses it on himself before he tosses it into the hamper next to the door. "We'll stick to the basics. For starters, when you talk to me, you call me Riker. Because that's my name. And I hate goddamn nicknames." He leans in and kisses the top of my head. "And when you want to come over, you knock on the door and let yourself in. You don't pace back and forth outside and make me guess if you're coming or going."

I suck in my bottom lip. I'd rather chew it off right now than let him see me smile. "I can probably manage that."

He gives me a sideways glance.

So I add, "Riker."

He nods, satisfied.

Releasing my lip from my teeth, I turn around and bend over to retrieve my clothes from the floor.

"Whoa. What do you think you're doing?" His arm slides under my chest, bringing me back into an upright position.

"Getting my clothes so I can get out of here."

He turns me toward him, a telltale smirk on his face. "What makes you think it's time to go already?"

Confused, I search the bathroom for anything that functions as a clock. "I thought you said you had to get ready to go to work, so I figured I better get out of here and let you do what you've gotta do."

Riker grins like I said something funny, and I recognize the look in his eyes. It's the one he gets right before he kisses me. "You're not getting *out* of here until after I get *inside* of you."

I suck in a ragged breath just as his lips come crashing down on mine again. Next thing I know, his hands are reaching down to the back of my thighs and he's lifting me up and setting me down on his bathroom counter. He can't possibly be ready again. Although, truth be told, I am. Holy shit, I'm not just ready, I'm already desperate.

The intensity of his embrace ebbs as he pulls back, and through half-closed lids I watch him watch me in the aftermath of his kiss. His thumb gently brushes over my lips, and I flick my tongue out to catch it. He slides it into my mouth, and I softly suck the tip of it, imagining what it would be like to give him a blowjob and wondering why in the hell I haven't done it yet.

He clears his throat like he's trying to gain control of himself, and I open my eyes again. He cups my face in both of his hands, then rests his forehead against mine as he groans. "Jesus Christ, Quinn." After a moment, he stands up tall again and flips open the door to the medicine cabinet. He wasn't kidding the other day. It really is overflowing with condoms and toothbrushes. Not that I'm surprised. A guy doesn't get this good at what he's doing without practice.

He grabs a condom from the only open box, slides it between his teeth, and flips the door shut again. Then he grips my ass in both his hands and carries me into the bedroom where he drops me, rather unceremoniously, onto his mattress.

"Hey!" I try to sound indignant, but I'm giggling.

"What? I figured a hard-ass like you could handle it." He's doing the annoyingly sexy half-grin thing that makes me want to launch myself across the room and attach myself to his mouth. But I don't. I just watch as he pulls up his jeans, covering up the nicest ass I've ever seen on a man. Rummaging through the pile of clothes on his recliner, he finally finds what he's looking for and throws it my direction.

I catch it. It's a t-shirt. "What's this for?"

"Easy access." He wiggles his eyebrows, dropping his gaze below my belly button.

"Pervert," I mumble, but I'm putting the shirt on, so I clearly don't have a problem with it.

Meanwhile, he's still shirtless as he makes his way into the small kitchen. I follow him and find him bent over with his head inside his nearly empty fridge.

"Water?" He offers me a bottle and I take it. It's ice cold and delicious.

"So what's for breakfast?" Judging by the takeout boxes in front of him, it's a choice between cold pizza and cold egg rolls.

But he closes the fridge without taking out either one. "You are."

"Excuse me?"

He just nods, slowly backing me into his kitchen table where he lays me out flat before he spreads my legs and does that thing he does where he just takes in the view. Like I'm some sort of a natural phenomenon he can't quite believe he's witnessing with his own eyes.

Riker takes the water bottle I now have in an iron grip from the anticipation of what's about to happen and moves my hands to the top of my head at the edge of the table.

"Don't move those," he warns softly. Then he takes a long sip of the ice-cold water before he lowers himself between my thighs.

The second his tongue touches me I want to jump out of my own body from the sensation. The chill of the water and the heat of his breath are coming together on the most sensitive part of me, and I can't help but writhe under his touch. Then the palm of his hand comes to rest heavily on my stomach, holding me in place while he continues to inflict the most euphoric torture on me I've ever endured.

"Riker. Oh, God. Riker!" I want to say his name over and over again, because I want him to keep doing what he's doing, over and over again. But his idea of pleasuring me is a lot like watching the waves on the sand. They come closer and closer and then, just as you think you're about to get soaking wet, they retract and return to the sea. And I love it. But I hate it too. Because I want to feel it all. And I want to feel it now. And mostly, I'm terrified of how much control he has over me in these moments. How he can manipulate my body into doing and feeling exactly what he wants. But I let him because it feels too damn good not to.

I'm clawing the edge of the table and I swear I'm on the brink of coming when I feel him moving away and force myself to open my eyes again just in time to see him slide the condom over his perfectly erect penis.

Grabbing my hips, he tugs me to him, and I sit up to watch him move inside me. It fascinates me. And it turns me on beyond reason.

Riker moves his palm up under my shirt and gently presses down on my chest, making me lie back down. "I thought I told you not to move," his deep voice growls quietly.

As soon as I'm spread out on his table again, he begins to thrust inside me, pulling nearly all the way out before sliding back in until he fills me completely. He does this several times before gripping me harder with both hands and building the intensity of his motions until I'm screaming his name from the waves of pleasure washing over me, this time taking me from head to toe and pulling me under to the place I've been yearning to go ever since I ran out of my sister's house this morning.

CHAPTER FIVE

RIKER

"Is it me or are you in an unusually good mood this morning?" Sid's leaning over the side of the round pen watching me work Nox.

"I'm here at the crack of dawn taking care of this damn horse like I am every morning. I don't really see what part of that is supposed to put me in a good mood." Nox snorts. I swear that son of bitch understands every word I say.

"Don't give me that shit. I know you don't hate him nearly as much as you'd like him to believe you do." She swings her leg over the top board and jumps inside. Waiting until he passes her, she continues toward the center where I'm standing listlessly swaying an old lead rope back and forth to keep him moving. It's habit, really. Nox is trained on voice commands, so I'm really just holding the rope for my own sake, not his.

"What? You don't have enough shit to do this morning, you gotta come here and give me a hard time too?"

She laughs. "Oh, I've got plenty to do. You know that. Running this place keeps me busy every second of every day. But that doesn't mean I won't squeeze in a little time here and there to check in with you. Especially since I know how much you hate it." She nudges me in the side with her elbow. "Now spill it. You've been acting weird since last Sunday. And this morning when you pulled up, I heard you singing along with the radio. So think twice before you try to feed me some line we both know is total bullshit."

Sometimes I forget how well she knows me. "Let's just say your little drugstore run actually went to good use."

Her eyes look like they're about to pop out of her head, and her jaw is dangling somewhere near her belly button. "Are you shittin' me? You got laid?"

"Damn, Sid. You could at least act like you thought it was a possibility." I drop the rope. Nox notices instantly, slows down, and walks toward me. "What the hell did you buy me all those condoms for if you didn't really think I'd ever get around to using them?"

She shrugs and brings her jaw back up to where it belongs. "I figured if it at least got you to reenter society with some miniscule hope of maybe meeting someone again, it was worth the investment."

I pat the black stallion on his neck, running my hand under his long thick mane. If he didn't drive me absolutely insane, I'd have to admit that I understand exactly what my grandfather saw in him. He's smart. And kind. And probably the most beautiful horse I've ever stood shoulder to shoulder with.

"Well, joke's on you, because I didn't go anywhere near society. She just showed up at my house. And as far as the second part—"

"The wanting to meet someone again?" she finishes, a small hopeful smile on her face. It's small because she knows. I'm not someone anyone ought to be wasting a lot of hope on.

"Yeah. That. Let it go, Sid." Nox's halter in hand, I start for the gate. "I have."

"But what about this mysterious woman who just showed up on your doorstep? I mean, that sounds like it has fate written all over it!" Sid isn't ever going to accept it. I get that. She needs me to find happiness again. Because somehow that will give her reason to believe that she'll find it as well someday. But I can't be the one who keeps us both from disappearing in this purgatory we've both been stuck in for the last few years.

"It's not fate, Sid. It's just sex. It's amazing sex. But it means nothing. Not to me. Not to her." I close the gate behind us. "So it definitely shouldn't mean anything to you."

• • • •

QUINN

"Where are we going?" The trees outside my window get denser the longer we drive. The last time we were this far inland we were headed to the Shepherdson Ranch for Sophie's birthday party. And I don't really remember seeing much else that would interest Kirsten. But then, I'm still new here, so there are plenty of places I haven't seen.

"Sophie has her first riding lesson today." Kirsten winks at her daughter in the rearview mirror, and she giggles in return.

"Riding lessons? I didn't know you signed her up for those." I shift in my seat, suddenly fighting the urge to vomit all over her pretty BMW. I really hadn't considered running into Riker anywhere other than his apartment. And even though we established that we wouldn't be pursuing a relationship, I didn't get around to mentioning the importance of keeping our little arrangement from my sister.

"Well, if you hadn't been so busy flirting with the scuzzy barn hand, you would have been around to hear me talking to Miss Sidney about getting Sophie into lessons with her." Her perfect little nose is scrunched up, and I know she's totally disgusted with me right now. And she doesn't even know about the stuff I did with the scuzzy barn hand after we left. Although, honestly, he's so the opposite of scuzzy. I don't know why she's being such a bitch about it.

"Kirsten, I wasn't flirting with him. And even if I was, so what? I'm twenty-two. I may not be a ten like you, but I can still walk out in public without wearing a paper bag over my head to cover the ugliness, so, you know, on occasion, men *may* find me attractive."

The car stops and I realize we're here. "First of all, you are gorgeous. Second, I'm not a ten. A nine, maybe, but that's not important right now. And third, I want men to find you attractive. In fact, I would love nothing more than for you to meet a wonderful guy and fall in love and have the kind of life I have with Nate. What I don't want is to have to worry about you. And when I see you falling right back into your old life, that's all I can do."

I want to get out of the car so badly right now, just so I have a door to slam in her face, but I don't. And for Sophie's sake, I clench my jaw and grit my teeth to keep from shouting. "How can you even say that to me, Kirsten? I'm not the one who keeps dragging us out here. You are. I've done nothing to start up old habits. Nothing."

She shakes her head. "You honestly don't see it."

"See what?" I can see me losing my freaking mind if she keeps this up, but that's about all.

"He's Jackson," she whispers so Sophie won't hear.

The sound of his name is enough to send chills down my spine, and a brick lands in the pit of my stomach. I can't even answer her.

"That guy. He's totally Jackson—the way he dresses in those jeans and long-sleeve work shirts. The whole unshaven thing and the horses. It's so obvious, Quinn. And in the months you've been here, he's the first guy you've been interested in. Why do you suppose that is?"

I close my eyes as if that will somehow take away the sound of her voice and the words she's saying, but all it does is make me see the thing that makes me scream in the dead of night and sends me running for comfort from the only person who's ever been able to give it.

"You're wrong, Kirsten." My voice is eerily calm. "About him. And me."

"Quinn, you don't even know him—"

"I knew Jackson. And the things that attracted me to him had nothing to do with the way he dressed or that he was too lazy to use a razor more than once every two weeks. The horse thing, fine, that played a role. But all the other stuff, the stuff that sucked me in and held me captive, all that stuff you never saw. But I did. I know what it looks like, and I'm telling you that if I ever see it again, I won't be flirting, I'll be throwing punches and a swift kick straight to the balls."

This time I do get out of the car, although I miraculously manage to refrain from throwing the door back into place. Wouldn't have mattered either way, because Kirsten is already out as well and headed for the back seat to get out Sophie.

Her lips are pressed into a thin line. For once, I don't think it's because she's mad at me. Mostly, I think she's not convinced she doesn't have a good reason to worry. Hell. Maybe she does. I am sleeping with a man I hardly know and have no intention of getting to know any better. Although, from where I'm standing, it's the smartest thing I've ever done when it comes to men. Maybe that's because it's the first time I can honestly say my heart isn't in it and my brain is making all of the decisions.

For the time being, Kirsten seems to be done scolding me, though, so I put on my semi-polite public face and follow her toward the main barn. A woman in her early thirties with black hair cut in one of those cute short pixies is walking out to greet us. She's pretty, and for some stupid reason I feel like I know her. I probably saw her during Sophie's party, although I honestly have no recollection of her. But I was in a pretty foul mood for the most part that day, so who's to say what I did or didn't see.

"Well, hello there, Miss Sophie," she greets. "Are you ready to get some serious one-on-one horse time with our Sassy girl today?"

Sophie starts jumping up and down, squealing a loud yes. I'm thinking she's ready.

"Hi, Kirsten." She shakes hands with my sister before turning toward me. "And you must be the famous Aunt Quinn. I'm Sidney. Sophie was telling me all about you and your barrel racing days last time she was here."

I nod uncomfortably. Barrel racing seems like a lifetime ago now. "Yep, that's me. Although I'm pretty sure I'm not nearly as famous as Sophie made me out to be." At least not for the years I spent in the rodeo circuit.

"Well, we've always got plenty of horses in need of exercising if you ever want to come out and ride. Experienced riders are hard to come by around here." It's a really nice offer, but I know I can't accept it.

"Thanks, but I haven't ridden in years." I glance over at Kirsten, surprised she hasn't chimed in yet. Then we both see Riker at the same time, and her mouth opens instantly.

"Horses were really more of a childhood phase for her. Unfortunately, I do believe she's grown out of them." She gives me a look I don't have to struggle to interpret. She's reminding me of our little conversation about Jackson. As if I need reminding. It was less than five minutes ago.

"Well, that's too bad. But if you ever change your mind, our barn doors are always open." Sidney smiles warmly. Then she notices Riker as well. Kirsten's face looks like it might explode when Sidney actually waves him over. "Hey. You got a sec?"

He rolls his eyes, clearly wishing he was too busy to agree to her request. I'm a little offended since he's definitely seen me at this point.

"What's up?" He completely ignores the rest of us, instead busying himself with readjusting the baseball cap he's wearing today as if it's a really big, really important job. On the plus side, I'm assuming the talk about keeping our hookups a secret won't be necessary.

"Sophie's here for her first lesson, but I haven't had a chance to bring Sassy in yet. Do you mind? I'm going to go take her down to the tack room and start there."

He nods. "You got it, boss."

She laughs. "Yeah, okay." She shoves him playfully. "Just go get the horse, would ya?"

He doesn't smile, or even do the half-grin thing, but I can tell he likes giving her a hard time. He likes her. And suddenly ignoring me makes all the sense in the world. It also totally pisses me off. I don't mind being used since I'm using him too. But the whole point of what we're doing is for no one to get hurt. If he's got a thing going with Sidney, that sort of negates the whole premise right there.

I watch as he takes off toward the pasture behind the main barn.

"Right this way, ladies." Sidney begins leading us all inside.

I tug at Kirsten's sleeve to get her attention. "Hey, give me your keys. I forgot something in the car."

She frowns but hands them over anyway. "Don't get lost."

"It's a straight shot between the barn and the parking lot. I think I can manage," I say as she turns to catch up with Sophie who's already inside. As soon as Kirsten is out of sight, I follow the same path Riker disappeared down.

When I find him, he's standing at a gate sorting through a collection of halters.

"Are you and Sidney together?"

He spins around, startled by my outburst. I don't blame him. I kinda scared myself a little.

"What, you following me now?" That sly grin begins to creep in.

"No, jackass. I was duped into coming here, as usual." I walk up beside him. Next thing I know he's dumped the whole load of halters into my arms, making it easier for him to untangle them. "I notice you conveniently avoided answering my question."

He doesn't break his focus from his task for even a second. "Why do you care? I'm not with *you*."

I forcefully cram the load of halters back against his chest. "I don't care. About me. Or you. I do care if you're cheating on some innocent bystander. I don't want any part of that."

His jaw grinds back and forth for a moment. Apparently, he needs to contemplate his answer. Which probably isn't a good sign.

"I'm not cheating on anyone. And not that it's any of your business, but you're the only one I'm sleeping with." He untangles the halter he was looking for and places the rest back over the fence post.

"Oh." I'm not really sure what to say now. "Well, good. Because I'm not sleeping with anyone else either."

He grins again. "Yeah. I kinda already knew that."

I feel my face flush and hate him for it. "Keep it up and I won't be sleeping with you either."

Riker's deep-blue eyes go dark as he lowers his head to be level with mine. He's not grinning anymore, but he's got the look in his eye. The look that turns my knees to mush and sends a sea of butterflies ripping through my stomach because I know what's coming. And the anticipation is already killing me.

"You know, you really shouldn't make threats you can't deliver on." The throaty rasp in his voice is enough to give me chills.

"You don't know the first thing about what I can and can't deliver." My stubborn side is showing again, but the way I nearly stuttered while muttering my lame comeback, it's probably not all that convincing.

Riker takes another step closer, his tall body towering over me, his face barely an inch from mine. "Quinn?"

"Yeah?" I can't even swallow. I've forgotten how to freaking swallow.

"Don't make me prove you wrong right out here in the open for the whole damn world to see." His lips brush over mine as he speaks, taunting me.

I have to avert my eyes to even string together a coherent sentence. "I wouldn't try if I were you. I'd only embarrass you." The words have barely passed the tip of my tongue when his mouth comes crashing down on mine and I lose all sense of reason and responsibility.

By the time I become aware of my surroundings again, I'm straddling Riker, who's sitting on a stack of hay bales near the fence line. His hands are in highly inappropriate places, as are mine, and I have to double-check to make sure I'm not completely naked. Because let's face it, based on my previous experiences with the man, my clothes do tend to magically wind up on the ground without my knowledge of how or when.

"Fuck," I gasp, breaking away from his kiss while simultaneously jumping out of his lap.

He smirks. "Later." Then he stands up, brushing the hay from his jeans. He loops the halter around my back and brings me toward him, then bites my lower lip before sliding his tongue inside my mouth again. I'm about to melt into his embrace when he smacks me hard on the ass, slapping me back into reality. "Now stop being so damn difficult. There's no need to complicate a good time." He kisses the tip of my nose before he releases me and returns to the gate.

"You know, you're pretty cocky for a thirty-something-year-old man who lives in a one-bedroom garage apartment and can't seem to accomplish even the small tasks of adulthood like grocery shopping and the occasional load of laundry." I have no reason to still be standing here hurling insults in his direction other than I'm not ready to walk away yet.

Leading a solid-looking red roan, he comes through the gate. "And yet you still can't seem to get enough of me." He keeps walking with the mare, leaving me standing here unable to even muster a solid response, desperate to fall into step behind him and follow him wherever he's going next.

It's like he's got some sort of mysterious magnetic force pulling me toward him. Except it's really not all that mysterious. It's lust. Love's ugly stepsister. That manipulative bitch is always doing whatever it takes to get her way, because she's selfish and has a one-track mind that's unable to formulate any thoughts other than, "What will it take to get laid again?" Stupid, stupid lust. I always thought I liked her better than love. I was wrong. Really wrong.

I take another thirty seconds or so to shake off the lingering effects of my new drug of choice before I sneak back up around the barn and do my best to fake a trip in from the parking lot.

"So much for not getting lost," Kirsten says the second she sees me. "What on earth took you so long? And it better not be wearing dirty jeans and a backward baseball cap."

Out of the corner of my eye, I catch Sidney's expression perk up, but I try not to react to either one of them or their assumptions.

"Mom called while I was at the car, and you know how that goes." My mother's a worrier. Anytime I go longer than forty-eight hours without checking in with her, I'm setting myself up for a lengthy conversation complete with tears and a guilt trip. As it is, I've been due for one since yesterday, but I've managed to dodge her calls thus far, and will have to keep doing so at least until we get back home and I get some privacy, at which point I'll have to hurry up and get it over with before she speaks to Kirsten and blows my little lie here to shit.

"You really shouldn't go so long without calling her." Holding Sophie's hand, she starts walking to the opposite end of the barn where Riker has turned up with Sassy.

"I hardly think three days is a long time. Besides, what do I have to talk about? I don't do anything different from one day to the next," I grumble as I follow behind everyone else. I have to keep my head down to avoid accidentally exchanging some sort of a loaded glance with Riker. With Kirsten's eagle eyes watching my every move, there's no way even a hint at a flirtatious smile would go unobserved.

"Sassy give you a hard time?" Sidney asks when we reach the crossties.

He takes a step away from the mare, letting Sidney take over to start her lesson. "Wasn't Sassy's fault. Someone else was feeling a little feisty and caused a bit of a distraction. But it's all good. I straightened her out." He looks and sounds completely serious, so the fact that I'm turning a thousand different degrees of red right now is entirely unfounded and, thankfully, goes unnoticed by my sister. She's only all too happy to get back to her daughter's riding lesson so she can get this part of her day done and over with.

With everyone else once again occupied, Riker takes off to do whatever it is he does around here. I have every intention of ignoring him as he passes me by, but lust, the traitorous bitch, ignores me and lifts my eyes to lock with his. He doesn't smile or even smirk. He just winks, and I swear my panties evaporate into thin air.

CHAPTER SIX

RIKER

It's nearly three in the morning already. I should really be sleeping. But Quinn showed up sometime before midnight and hasn't left since. I'm not complaining. On the contrary. I'd rather spend all night not sleeping with her than spend all day tomorrow thinking about how well rested I am.

She's been on my mind more than usual today. That's a lie. She's been on my mind nonstop ever since I saw her at her niece's birthday party more than three weeks ago. Today was different, though. It wasn't just about missing the feel of her skin on mine or wanting to press my lips to her perfect mouth, or the million and one other horny thoughts I have about her every three seconds or so. It was about her. Little things have been collecting in the back of my mind. Like the way she is with Harley, protective and almost possessive, but in the most tender way possible. She loves that dog. Sometimes I think she doesn't know how to love, but then I see her with Harley and I know she's capable of depths some of us will never reach. Same when she thought I was cheating on Sid. How she said she didn't care about me or her but that she wouldn't hurt someone else.

I already knew I wasn't part of the equation. I'm good with that. I shouldn't be someone she cares about because I'll never be able to return those feelings. But she should care about herself. Being here with me should be about both of us getting what we need and walking away content. Or, at least, not any worse off than we were before our paths crossed. I may not be the guy to make her dreams come true, but I don't want to be the piece of shit who adds to the nightmares either. And I need to be sure she won't let that happen. I need her to care about *her*. Because I won't.

She's lying next to me, quietly staring at the ceiling. Our heads are on opposite ends of the bed as a result of our most recent entanglement. I don't think I've sixty-nined anyone since high school, but then that's kind of right in line with everything we're doing right now. Just fucking our way through the encyclopedia of sex one position after the other.

I run my hand over her smooth calves. They're toned and tight from running just like the rest of her body. Moving down toward her feet, I take one of her soles into my hands and start rubbing it, pressing into it with my thumbs.

"Oh, that feels good," she moans from the other end of the mattress. I like the sounds she makes when she's enjoying herself. I like how expressive she is in everything she's thinking and feeling. There's never any guessing with Quinn. At least not in the present. Her past is another story entirely.

"Quinn?"

"Uh-huh?" She barely even moves. Just lies there, still staring dreamily at the ceiling. I know that expression. She's in between. Disconnected from the world and whatever haunts her here, but still hovering too close to truly escape it. It's where I go, too, when I'm with her.

I lift myself up onto my elbows to get a better view of her face. "How old are you?"

Her brows furrow, and I know I've brought her back. I feel an instant sense of guilt because I know how hard it is to leave and how precious the time spent in between is.

"Twenty-two."

Twenty-two. She doesn't seem like twenty-two. Shit, one look into her eyes and anyone'd think she's older than I am. This girl has seen things. Life-altering things. Things no twenty-two-year-old is meant to see. And now more than before I want to know what they are. But I won't ask. I shouldn't. I can't.

"What the hell is a twenty-two-year-old doing screwing an old guy like me?" It's all I can think to say to lighten the mood.

She sits up, grinning from ear to ear. "Benefitting from all your years of experience, one orgasm at a time." I know before she's even lying on top of me that I'm not getting even a minute of shut-eye tonight. And I don't give a damn.

• • • •

QUINN

It's been nearly a month now. A month of running at least once, sometimes twice, a day and winding up at Riker's place. If he has a life outside of work and fucking me, I don't know when he has time for it. I don't have one. So it's not interfering with anything other than time spent listening to Kirsten tell me all the ways I should be living my life right now, and I'm always happy to take a break from that merry-go-round.

She has a point, of course. I can't spend the rest of my life living in her game room. Nor do I want to. But things are . . . complicated.

The sun is starting to set later, now that we're moving into summer, and I have to keep reminding myself that Riker won't be home from work for another hour because feeding time has been pushed out as well. I'm antsy and tempted to go for an actual run, when the phone rings and my heart stops. Only two people ever call me. And I spoke to my mother this morning, so I know it's not her.

"Hello?"

"Quinn. Got a minute?" It's Devyn. My lawyer.

I sink down onto my bed. "There's news." It's not a question. She wouldn't be calling me if there wasn't. She knows how much I hate the phone.

"I'm sorry, babe," She sighs on the other end of the line. "Looks like we're going to trial again."

I bite my lip hard. Not because I'm about to cry, but because I want to feel the pain of piercing a hole into my own flesh with my teeth. Pain and pleasure seem to be the only two sensations still connecting me to this body, and I need to know I'm still in it right now.

"When?" I don't know what I want her to say. Next week? So I can face it and get it over with? Two years from now so I can pretend until then that my life has the capacity to be normal? That it's worth getting up every day. Worth planning for a future I may never really have.

"Three months. Trial is set to start August 19th. You'll need to come back before then so we can discuss how we want to proceed. It'll be different this time. It's a civil trial, not criminal court. The stakes aren't nearly as high, and I think it's important that you know one verdict doesn't guarantee another one. It's a new trial. New judge. And a new opportunity to prove your innocence."

I let out a harsh laugh. I don't mean to. Devyn has been nothing but good to me. She's seen me through everything and been there defending me every step of the way. Even when I was ready to give up and told her I didn't need her to do so anymore.

"I'm sorry, babe. I really am." And I know she means it. Even though she doesn't have a damn thing to apologize for.

"Don't be. Seriously. This is not your doing. It's mine. I'm the reason for all of it. So now I need to figure out a way to face the next round of consequences." I run my hand over my face and through my hair. I should really brush it. I don't think I've done anything with it since I left Riker's place early this morning after another one of our joint showers.

"Are you at least liking it out there? Are you getting out? Meeting people?" Devyn's not much older than Kirsten, but she's been like a second mother to me since the day I met her. Only one I actually feel like I can talk to. Probably because of that legally binding confidentiality agreement we have.

"I'm not getting out exactly . . . but I'm working a lot and I've got a little project I'm trying to grow into something bigger. Something that could maybe someday make a difference and would make me feel like I had more purpose in my life. Of course now I'm not sure there's much point in pursuing it." I flop backward onto my mattress and reach over to pet Harley, who's lying curled up by my pillow.

"Don't say that. Of course there's a point in pursuing things. This trial is just a minor hiccup. The worst is already over, you'll see." She's trying too hard to sound optimistic. Apparently, she doesn't even believe herself. "I hate this. Please tell me you're at least getting closer to your sister so that I don't have to picture you there all alone, wallowing in self-hatred and despair until someone finds your stinky, decaying body."

I roll my eyes at the ceiling. I suppose we don't have the most conventional attorney-client relationship. "Kirsten is trying. I'm just not cooperating as well as she would like." I pause for a moment, then decide she's legally obligated to keep my secrets, so there's no harm in telling her. "But you can rest easy knowing I will not be alone tonight and my body will live to be decay free another day."

Her office chair squeaks, and I picture her leaning in. "Do tell."

"His name is Riker. He lives a mile up the beach, and he is hot as hell. Also, he's been fucking my brains out for the last month or so and it has done wonders for my mood swings."

"Abigail Quincy, you watch your language." Devyn tries to muffle her laughter, but I can still hear it. "But seriously, good for you, babe. You deserve it."

"I don't know what I deserve, but I know I'm taking it anyway. At least until August." I squeeze my eyes shut as if that will somehow erase the new knowledge I've gained regarding my looming fate.

"Why does it have to stop in August? Wait. You haven't told him, have you?" Her tone is quiet and almost sullen. Funny how I do that people. Take them from perfectly happy to perfectly miserable in no time at all.

"I haven't. And I don't plan to. That's not what being with Riker is about. I was being very specific when I said I've been sleeping with him. That's literally all we do. It's not a relationship. And it's not going to become one. And if you tell Kirsten any of this, I will have you disbarred."

"You can't have me disbarred for that, you psycho. Telling me about your little booty call hardly applies to your legal case or my job as your attorney. That was all girl talk, my friend. And I won't tell. But because I'm not a gossip, not because you threatened me." She's laughing again, but it's different. It's dry and bittersweet, like it's taking a great deal of effort.

"Thank you." I force myself back into an upright position. I know this conversation is coming to an end, and if I wait too long I'll just end up lying here all night curled up in a ball caught in some time warp where I'm still the old me, too scared and weak to get up.

"Well, I'm going to let you go in a sec so I can finish up here at the office and get the hell home . . . where there is no hot guy waiting to screw my brains out, I might add bitterly." She chuckles, and I mimic her automatically. "But before I go, I'm going to impart one last little piece of wisdom on you, one single girl to another. You can only be intimate with a man for so long before you become *intimate*. Maybe you think your head is running this show, but I'm telling you, your heart isn't far behind. So, you know, you should probably try talking to him in between your sexcapades."

"Yeah, I'm starting to think I shouldn't try talking to *you*." It's not like I didn't know she would say it. Of course she would insist on seeing the romantic side of life. It's the fun side. The fairy tale side. Who wouldn't prefer to live there?

"Yeah, okay. Bye, Quinn."

"Bye, Devyn. And thank you." Gratitude. That I still feel. Because that one comes from the soul.

"Always, babe. I've got your back. You know that." There's a brief moment of silence between us before the line breaks and she's gone.

I glance at the time. Riker's still not home.

"Wanna go for a run, boy?" Harley's head perks up. Although, even he thinks going for a run means going to Riker's now. Not that he minds. There's been a steady stream of leftover peperoni pizza coming his way ever since it became a regular thing. Riker even started leaving an old quilt piled in the corner of the room for Harley to lay on. He made it look like it was just dumped there, awaiting some sort of fate that would eventually land it in the garbage can out front, but I know he did it so Harley would have somewhere comfy to hang out when we come over.

I'm on my feet again and making my way to the fridge to grab a bottle of water, since I'm actually going to do the running thing, when there's a surprise knock on my door and Kirsten's head pops in, followed by the rest of her.

"Damn, girl, don't you ever get tired?" She's eyeing me in my shorts and sports bra. Thankfully, I'm still getting a workout either way, so my body still mostly reflects one of a runner's.

"Just helps clear my head. You know that." I try to smile. If I don't smile, she'll know something's up. Not that I smile a lot. But I can feel my face doing the scowly thing, and it hasn't done that in weeks.

"You know what else might help clear your head?" She says this in the most enticing way possible, and I already know I want to say no to whatever she has in mind.

"What's that?" I'm cringing. That part I don't need to hide. That she's expecting.

"A fun night out!" She claps her hands in excitement, probably hoping it will rub off on me if she exudes enough of it.

"You and C.J. planning a girls' night or something?" Because I would possibly consider going to one of those. I could go for a round of C.J.'s stories right about now. They'd sure as hell be more entertaining than my own.

"Better! Nate's friend Carson just broke up with his girlfriend and he's dying to meet you."

I almost choke on her choice of words. It's all I can do not to make a snide comment about the way men tend to do that with me. "Why on earth would he want to meet me? What have you guys told him?"

She shrugs innocently. "Nothing, really. Same thing we tell everyone."

"The missionary work thing?" I curl my lip in disgust. Not because I find missionary work so appalling. It's more so that what I was actually doing could easily be considered the exact opposite.

"I think. I don't know for sure. Nate talked to him, mostly. But that's not what triggered his interest." Her eyes light up as they attempt to burst out of their sockets. "He saw your picture. Nate was showing off pics from Sophie's birthday party and you were in a lot of them. The second Carson saw you, he started asking questions. Nate thinks he really likes you."

I roll my eyes into my skull. Maybe staying in bed wallowing would have been the better option after all. I could be sleeping right now. Then Kirsten would be talking to herself about this Carson person.

"Kirsten, he doesn't even know me. He couldn't possibly feel one way or another."

But she's not giving up. My sister is nothing if not determined. "So let him get to know you. Tomorrow night. He wants to take you to dinner at La Sirene. And trust me, you want to go have dinner at La Sirene. The food is amazing."

"Do I have any hope at all of getting out of this?"

She shakes her head. "Nope."

"Why is this so important to you, Kirsten?" Maybe if I understand, maybe if I get where she's coming from, I'll feel better about giving in.

"Because I want you to have the kind of life you were always supposed to have. The life you wanted before . . . before everything happened that took it away. And I know you don't think you can have it again, but I'm going to prove you wrong. I'm good at this, Quinn. Look at me. I found a wonderful husband who loves me and treats me well. We have a perfect little girl, and our lives are complete. Let me find your happily ever after for you. Please."

I take a deep breath in and exhale it loudly through my mouth. "Carson what?"

"Winn. Why?"

I hold up my phone. "Because I'm going to google his ass, that's why. If I'm going to spend an evening with him, I at least want to know as much about him as he does about me."

She grins. Because she won. "Fair enough. Alright. You go run and we'll go shopping in the morning. We've got to find you something a little more feminine to wear for your first big date."

"Yeah, okay, crazy lady." I follow her to the door and shove it closed behind her, just to make sure she doesn't change her mind and try to come back in. My eyes dart back for the clock. Finally. He's home.

CHAPTER SEVEN

RIKER

I check the table one more time. Everything's there, and if she shows up soon it'll even still be hot. It's not fancy, just takeout from Joe's. But I was starving and figured I might as well get enough for two.

Now that I'm looking at the food sitting there, I'm rethinking the whole thing. Sharing a meal sort of implies a date. And a date would imply an interest in developing other aspects of our relationship. Which I don't have.

On the other hand, it's just fucking food and we've both been very clear about the fact that neither of us is looking for more.

So why am I overthinking this?

• • • •

QUINN

The sun's setting by the time I walk onto his deck with Harley in tow. It's beautiful out, in spite of the unexpected chill in the air. It didn't bother me on the run over here, but now that I've slowed down again it's getting cold fast.

My heart sinks when I spot the note taped to his front door. I peel it from the wood only to find it marked with an arrow. No words. Just an arrow pointing straight up.

"What the . . . ?" I take a step back and glance upward. There's a rooftop deck three stories up that I never noticed before. Now that I have, I'm not any closer to reaching it. I'm tempted to shout his name, but it's Riker. He wouldn't leave me standing down here, with a note suggesting I go up with no way of getting there.

I twist my mouth back and forth while I contemplate my next move. There's a second door just three feet down from Riker's. I always assumed it went to the main part of the house. Maybe I was wrong.

With limited options, I reach for the handle. It's unlocked and the door opens, revealing a dimly lit spiral staircase leading straight to the top.

"Well, bud, I think you're going to have to sit this one out." I walk back over to Riker's place and try his door. It gives way instantly, and Harley runs inside and goes right to his blanket. "See you in a bit." I close the door again and head back to the staircase.

Taking two steps at a time, I hurry upstairs.

Because I'm eager to see the view from up there.

Not because I want to see him.

I do want to see him.

Damn you, lust, you horny bitch.

As I pass the second floor, I notice the door to the main living area is cracked open. Curiosity gets the better of me, and even though I know I shouldn't, I detour onto the small landing leading up to it. There's barely any light, but my eyes have adjusted enough to the dark for me to make out some very noticeable basics. For starters, the place is completely trashed. There's broken frames lying scattered in the foyer, and from what I can tell there's no furniture. My first instinct is to run upstairs and tell Riker the Shepherdsons have been robbed. Then I realize how ridiculous that is. I mean, he lives right downstairs. He walked by here same as I did. He would have to know.

Which brings me to my second realization. I haven't seen a single renter since I've been coming here. Whoever this James Shepherdson is that's running the family business, he sure seems to be doing a shit job of it. Or, as Nate so kindly put it, he's definitely unmotivated.

But then, who am I to judge? The only thing motivating me these days is the prospect of getting naked with Riker. That's not exactly what I'd deem an admirable ambition in life.

Properly grossed out with myself, I return to the stairs and this time don't get distracted until I reach the top.

"I was starting to think I didn't leave you with good enough instructions." He's standing near the railing, smirking and wearing entirely too many clothes for my liking. Then I notice the table. And the takeout boxes.

"What's all this?" I can hear myself. I sound . . . pleased. Happy, even.

"Just burgers. Fries." He picks up one of the Styrofoam boxes and hands it to me before taking one for himself. "I didn't have a chance to eat before, and I knew you'd be coming over, so . . ." He shrugs. Like it's no big deal. Except we both know it is.

"You know, you don't have to be nice to me. I'm going to sleep with you anyway because you're so *nice looking*." I stack my box on top of his to free my hands so I can take ahold of his face and pull him toward me. Usually, I let him do the initiating. I don't know why. Maybe he just always beats me to it. Today, it's my turn to kiss him. And I do. Long and fervidly, until every other part of my day disappears and he's the only thing left.

"I missed you today." His words rumble quietly into my mouth as he slowly breaks away.

"You saw me this morning." I want to sound stern. I don't. But I want to.

"I know." He grins wickedly, and I know we're about to go from sweet to dirty. "But then when you were leaving, I saw you stop and bend over to fix your shoelace, and I've been thinking about getting you back into that exact position all damn day."

Simultaneously, our eyes travel toward the railing, and I suddenly have a pretty good idea why we're up here tonight. "Sex with a view. I like it."

He chuckles, and my stomach flips back and forth at the deep sound. "But first, we eat." Still holding both of our boxes, he takes a seat in the chaise lounge, gesturing for me to come and sit with him. Straddling the back end of it to face him, I slide both legs over his knees, leaving just enough room for our food between us.

"Saw you running over from up here," he says, about to take his first bite.

I've already had mine, and I hurry and swallow to answer him. "Oh yeah?"

He nods. "You were talking to yourself. You looked pissed."

I was. And I wasn't so much talking to myself as I was making all the arguments I should have made to Kirsten against going on this stupid date tomorrow night. "Just finishing up a chat I had with my sister before I left. Unfortunately, I'm one of those people who always thinks of the perfect thing to say ten minutes after the conversation is already over."

He's chewing. And thinking. "What was the conversation about?"

"Oh, you know. The usual. She wants to run my life for me. And that apparently now includes finding me the perfect man." I squirt the contents of a ketchup packet into the corner of my box. "So, naturally, I have a date tomorrow night."

I purposely pretend to be extra focused on the french fry I'm swirling around in my ketchup, but I can feel his legs tense up under mine. He's surprised by the news.

"A date? With whom?" He sounds casual. Like we're just making small talk.

"Some guy Nate works with. Carson Winn." I shrug. I haven't had a chance to google yet, so that's all I know.

Riker stops mid bite and does a weird thing with his jaw like he wants to say something, but then he changes his mind and just keeps chewing.

"What? You know him?"

He leans over his box to keep from dripping burger grease onto his pants. "Sort of. Went to school with his older brother, Derek."

Clearly, there's more. "And?"

"And . . . I don't know. Derek was one of those popular kids. You know, like high school was his shining moment in life. Prom king. Football player. Dated all the pretty cheerleaders and still had time to make the honor roll." He laughs, though he's obviously not amused. I guess those things wouldn't mean much to a guy like Riker. "Anyway, Carson seemed to always have a chip on his shoulder. Not that I blame him. Sucks being stuck under someone else's shadow everywhere you go."

I drop a fry back into the Styrofoam container. "Damn. And here I was hoping Kirsten was onto something with this find me a man business." I bite back a smile because it would ruin my faux disappointment.

Riker eyes me skeptically as he wipes the corner of his mouth with his thumb. Why does that make me want to jump out of my own skin and into his? His perfect lips thin out when he presses them together, and I'm tempted to lean in and kiss them just to see them fill out again.

"Since when are you in the market for a man? I thought you were all anti-relationships and feelings and shit."

I nod. "Oh, I am, but I know Kirsten. Once she locks in on a target, there's no avoiding that missile. And right now, she's aiming that shit directly at me and my lacking love life, so, you know, I'm thinking I could make this work for me." I brush my hands off and put them behind me to lean into them. "Obviously, getting seriously involved with someone is out of the question, but in lieu of one man with expectations and demands I have no desire to meet, maybe I could use several. You know, play a little game of build-a-man using only the parts I want and leaving out all the parts I don't."

Riker lies back against the chaise and runs his hands over his face several times. "What now?"

"Well"—I lift my leg and rub it over his thigh—"I mean, I've already got a good thing going here with you. But I wouldn't mind eating something every once in a while that didn't come out of a to-go box or Kirsten's kitchen. Maybe finding a guy to provide an occasional grown-up dinner and entertaining conversation wouldn't be a bad thing. And after that, I'll have my sister keep an eye out for someone with a spare credit card and the inexplicable need to spoil me with lavish gifts from time to time." I add that last bit just in case he hasn't figured out yet that I'm screwing with him.

He takes both boxes and moves them down to the ground, eliminating the Styrofoam barrier between us. "You know, if meals are so important to you, I'm sure I could arrange for something other than takeout from time to time. I'm not about to promise any kind of conversation, but I could probably come up with some alternative ways to entertain you . . . other than the way I *already* entertain you. Maybe a movie or something along those lines? I mean, if that would help slim down the list of men you need to acquire."

I crinkle my brow. I'm not sure I like where this is going. "Why would you do that?"

He comes toward me until our lips are touching. "Well, for personal reasons, I'd prefer you didn't start a collection."

Without moving away even the slightest little bit, I whisper back, "You're not supposed to have those."

He's still not kissing me, just sweeping his mouth over mine while he continues to explain in his steady, deep voice, "They're very selfish personal reasons. I like having you. All to myself. All the time." His hands come up and reach around the back of my neck and head, tenderly massaging me and somehow managing to bring me even closer to him without fully connecting us. "But if you think you'll have more fun with some suit-wearing douchebag like Carson, eating pretentious food from porcelain plates and using actual silverware while he drones on and on about his exciting life as a junior accountant, than you do here with me, where we wear nothing but skin and devour only each other while uttering words so filthy I bet you can't say one right now without blushing, then by all means, go out with him and any other man you think can be of some use to you. I don't want to get in the way of your needs being met."

My hands reach for his belt buckle as I bite down on his bottom lip and briefly suck on it. "You make a very compelling argument. Now shut the fuck up and take off your clothes. I'm ready to be entertained." I move in to kiss him, then stop. "And make it good. I have a boring dinner to suffer through tomorrow."

There's a flash of his wicked smile right before his mouth comes for mine. And I know this kiss is different. It's like I've awakened a primal need within him to stake his claim on me. It's intense and wild and passionate. And unwavering. And for the first time in a long time, I wish I wasn't too dead inside to feel what it would mean to be his.

• • • •

BY THE TIME I GET BACK to Kirsten's the next morning, she's sitting on my bed, waiting. Impatiently, I might add.

"The sun is barely even up. What time did you leave?" She gets up and tosses me the water bottle she's been cradling in her lap. It's still cold, so she hasn't been down here too long.

"I took off around seven thirty." It's sort of true. That's what time I left Riker's place. "I'm sorry. Did we have some sort of appointment?" I chug my water, careful to hide my smirk.

"Don't be a jackass. I came down here to tell you Nate and Sophie went to get cinnamon rolls from the Eat Three Bakery. I don't think you've had those yet. They're amazing." She heads back toward the stairs. "Anyway, I notice you're wearing the same running gear I saw you in yesterday evening. And your bed is perfectly made. Almost like you didn't even sleep in it."

I shrug, purposely gulping more water to pass the time. "Making the bed's a nice little habit I picked up while I was gone. I do it without even thinking about it now. And there's no point in washing my running gear after each run. It just gets gross and sweaty again."

She scrunches up her nose as if she can smell me from across the room. Which is doubtful. I took a shower before I left this morning. We took a shower. Whatever. I'm clean. If anything, I smell like Riker's standard mix of soap, sea, and sex, and that shit pretty much makes you wish your clothes could vanish into nothingness the second you get a whiff of it. It doesn't make you contort your face into a pig's snout.

"Something is up with you. And I'm going to figure out what it is." She nods, but I'm pretty sure it's more for herself than my sake. Then she leaves, closing the door behind her.

I turn toward Harley. "Well, that was close." I'd planned on crawling into bed as soon as I got home to catch up on the sleep I missed last night. Kinda felt like I probably need to be well rested for the shopping spree Kirsten threatened me with yesterday. But now that I know cinnamon rolls are headed my way, I might as well go with the promise of a sugar high to get me through the day.

Since Kirsten expects me to be disgusting, I step into the bathroom and turn on the shower. I let the water run for a few minutes while I change clothes. I didn't even break a sweat coming home this morning. Just walked down the beach, enjoying the peace and quiet. This time of year the tourists are out of control most of the time, but I still have the place nearly all to myself in the early morning hours.

When I venture up to the main living space, the whole family is already spread out around the kitchen island, digging into the hot and gooey rolls of sugar.

"You want one?" Kirsten reaches for a plate as soon as she sees me.

"Nah, that's cool. I'll just have the half Sophie's wearing on her face here." I dip my finger into a glob of cream cheese frosting and then tap her nose. She giggles, then unsuccessfully tries to reach her nose with her tongue.

Nate observes me over his coffee cup. "You're in a good mood."

I take the plate Kirsten made me anyway. "I really like cinnamon rolls."

He puts down his mug, smiling like he knows something. "Oh. I thought maybe you were looking forward to your date with Carson this evening." He knows nothing.

"Nope. It's the cinnamon rolls." With my plate in hand, I move over to the kitchen table and have a seat by myself. Until Kirsten takes the chair beside me.

"Listen. What are the odds of getting you into a dress tonight?"

I smile back at her. "I don't know. About the same as getting you into a pair of overalls made entirely of burlap."

She rolls her eyes. "Be serious, Quinn."

"Back at ya." I take a massive bite and practically rip it out of my cinnamon roll like an uncivilized animal. I don't know why she always brings out my inner four-year-old. Maybe because she treats me like one.

Judging by her expression—and the smear of frosting on my cheek—I'm pretty grotesque to behold right now.

I swallow hard to get it all down, then surrender. "Fine. I'll wear a dress. Whatever. But be warned that putting me in heels could prove potentially dangerous for myself as well as anyone within a ten-foot radius."

She flicks her wrist, instantly dismissing my concerns. "It's early. You have all day to practice walking in them."

And I want to cry, because I know she's not kidding.

From there, the day doesn't get much better. After breakfast, Kirsten and I pile into her car, while Nate takes Sophie over to C.J.'s house for a play date with her husband and daughter, since C.J. winds up joining us on our shopping spree.

Four hours and three potential outfits later, we wind up back at the house, where Kirsten really does make me practice walking in the four-inch stilettos she purchased for me, insisting they were the only viable shoes for an evening out with a guy like Carson Winn, which instantly made me think of Riker and his considerably simpler dress code.

For some reason, almost everything that happens after I'm doomed to suffer for Carson's sake triggers some thought of Riker in one form or another. Reminding me of something he said, something he did. A look he gave me. Anything and everything from the last month crosses my mind, suddenly making my afternoon a thousand times more bearable.

Until it's time. Time for my date. Time for Carson Winn.

CHAPTER EIGHT

RIKER

"Hey. You wanna go out and grab a beer with me?"

I picture Sid doing a double take, staring at her phone in disbelief. "What? You want to go out? Like, in public? What if people see you, Riker? They might realize you're not dead after all."

She thinks she's so fucking funny.

"Nobody thinks I'm dead, Sid. Crazy, sure. And missing. Isn't that a thing too? Whatever. I want to get out of the house. And drinking alone will only fuel the rumor mill, so are you in or what?"

She laughs. "Yes, of course I'm in. Where do you want to go?"

I stare at the fridge blankly. I don't know what the hell I'm doing anymore. "I don't care. Somewhere on the main drag? Near the water?"

I hear a horse snort in the background. She's still at the ranch.

"Sounds good. Give me an hour and I'll swing by and pick you up."

My eyes automatically travel to my mattress. "Nah, that's fine. I can just meet you." I know it's stupid, but I don't want to risk being stranded if there's any chance at all of seeing Quinn tonight.

"That works too. See you in a bit." She hangs up and I'm back to standing in my kitchen, aimless and annoyingly unsure of what to do with myself. What the fuck did I do with my time before Quinn filled every waking second of it?

• • • •

QUINN

I'm sitting here staring at Carson Winn and wondering who in the hell thought this would be a good idea. It's not that he's unattractive. I mean, I think he's probably attractive. I'm not attracted *to* him, but I would be happy to believe other women are.

As expected, he showed up wearing a suit. No tie, but still. Very proper. I was almost relieved I gave in to Kirsten and wore the dress.

Aside from the nearly formal wear, Carson is completely clean shaven with short black hair and brown eyes. He's tall and definitely hits the gym. He's got the gym body. Not like Riker who has the hard work body. And yeah. There's a difference. Personally, I prefer the latter. But this isn't a competition. There's no comparing the two, and I knew long before I ever even met Carson that I'd rather be spending the evening with Riker.

Nevertheless, here we are and I'm doing my best not to embarrass Kirsten. I'm listening politely and nodding every time I count to ten while Carson tells me all about his work and golf, the real passion of his life. Apparently, he's really good. I'm assuming. He could be speaking another language for as much as I'm understanding.

He interrupts his story to point at my nearly untouched dinner. "Are you enjoying your beef bourguignon?"

"Oh. Yes." I hastily reach for my fork and enthusiastically stab a slice of meat with it. "I've just been so engrossed in your stories I guess I forgot to eat."

His head practically expands as my little lie goes straight to his inflated ego.

"You know, you're not the first person to tell me that." He smiles. Not a nice smile. It's an icky smile that makes my insides churn. Then his eyes travel below my collar bone while his finger rounds the rim of his scotch glass, and I'm certain I can't force down another bite of my food without throwing it up.

I do my best to smile back. "I can only imagine how many people have missed a meal because of you."

As expected, he mistakes my insult for charm. "Yes, well, I'll be sure to make up for it when the time comes for dessert."

Seeing an easy out, I place my fork down in a hurry. "Oh, to be honest, I don't think I could eat another bite."

Carson's menacing grin widens as he covers my hand with his, then leans over the table. "Who said anything about eating?"

I'm too stunned to even speak. And that never happens. *What the fuck?* Clearly, Nate doesn't know this asshole as well as he thinks. Or else Kirsten doesn't know Nate. Because there's no way in hell my sister would have purposely set me up with pervy creeper over here, no matter how respectable his job and family are.

Clearly mistaking my silence for some sort of a yes, Carson flags down our server and pays our tab. Before I know it, we're out in the parking lot walking toward his Chrysler 300. As if the drive here wasn't bad enough, the drive home is going to be that much more awkward when he finds out I intend to go straight back to Kirsten's place.

I'm standing beside the car waiting for him to open the door when I feel his hand on my back, then quickly move down over the curve of my ass.

"Excuse me. What do you think you're doing?" I take a step forward to get out of his grasp, a mistake I realize too late, because it only places me deeper into the darkness between his car and the Suburban parked beside him. My heart begins to race, and it takes every ounce of effort I have to keep reminding myself that I'm here. In the present. I'm safe. I'm with a gross guy. But I'm safe. *I'm safe.*

"Come on, Quinn. There's no reason to play coy with me." Carson takes another step to close the distance I just placed between us. His hands are already touching me again. This time they start at my waist. But they're roaming, so there's no telling where they're headed next.

"What the hell do you think you're doing? Get your fucking hands off me." I shove him hard in the chest, and he stumbles. He didn't see it coming this time, but I won't have that same advantage again.

"Would you chill the fuck out? Nate already told me all about you, sweetheart. So there's really no reason to keep up this little act of yours. Just relax and we'll both have a good time. I promise." He leers at me, and my skin crawls.

"What exactly did Nate tell you?" I fight the urge to back up any farther. There's nothing behind me except a brick wall I can't get over or around.

Carson chuckles. It sounds downright evil, and it makes me feel dirty just having heard it. "He just explained why you came here. How you had to leave your hometown because of your reputation there and that Kirsten insisted you move in with her and Nate to get a fresh start." He grips my chin with his thumb and finger. "It's cool. I won't tell anyone your little secret. They don't even have to know about us hooking up. Although, truth be told, that would probably go a long way in fixing your bad rep."

I close my eyes, certain he's about to kiss me. I don't want to see it. Don't want to know what he looks like as he closes in on my lips with his. His disgusting lips. And his disgusting hands as they move up my waist and under my rib cage.

Shock is setting in, leaving me completely frozen and at his mercy. I have no choice but to simply zone out. I can do this. I can let go long enough to survive this. I've survived worse, so I know it won't kill me. It won't even hurt. Because I won't fight. I'll just disappear. He can do whatever he wants with my body. I won't be in it. *Damn it. I don't want to be in it.*

But I am. Because I can feel him. Can feel his mouth moving over the skin on my neck. He's sloppy, leaving a wet trail behind, which runs cool as the evening breeze catches it the same way it does on my damp cheeks. Tears. Silent sobs ripple my chest as he continues to touch and caress me in ways that make me ache at the core of my being.

"Quinn?"

The sound of his familiar voice rips me out of my trance. My eyes open and search for his, locking on them instantly.

But I'm not the only one who takes notice of him.

"Do you mind, asshole?" Carson barks. "How about some fucking privacy?"

Riker's still staring at me. Then, slowly, his gaze moves to Carson, turning hard. And terrifying. I've never seen him like this. He barrels straight for Carson, gripping fistfuls of his shirt as he practically carries him to the edge of the lot, then slams him into the brick wall.

"I'm going to kill you! You hear me? I'm going to fucking kill you!" He shakes Carson, repeatedly ramming the back of his head into the stone.

"Get your fucking hands off of me!" Carson tries to fight back, but it's pointless. He may be taller than Riker, but height is nothing compared to brute strength fueled by emotions so deep and dark I know Carson doesn't even have the capacity to feel.

Riker ignores his request to be let go and looks over his shoulder at me, still keeping Carson pinned in place. "Call the police. Right now."

His tone is completely different from ten seconds ago. Even the ferocious glare in his eyes is gone. There's something else there now. Sadness. Worry. Pain. It's even more terrifying than his anger.

"I can't." I shake my head. It's the first time I've been able to move since Carson first assaulted me.

"Yes, you can," Riker reassures me calmly.

But he's wrong. The tears continue to stream down my face because now I'm not the only one being hurt by this. Riker's in it too. He won't walk away untouched by this, and that knowledge is enough to make me want to dissolve into a puddle on the cold, hard pavement. "I can't call the police. I'm sorry. I can't. I can't." I don't know what else to say.

He doesn't understand. "Why not? Quinn. I saw what he was doing. I saw it!" He nearly chokes on the words, forcing them out through clenched teeth.

"Please," I beg. "Just let him go. And take me home." I timidly place my hand on his shoulder. "Please."

Carson hasn't said a word since realizing Riker has the upper hand between them.

Still holding him by his shirt, Riker begins to move him into a more natural position again, letting him put weight evenly on his feet.

"You listen to me, you piece of shit. You never, *never* touch her again. I ever see you so much as walking in her general vicinity, I will come after you. And I promise you, Quinn won't be able to save your sorry ass a second time." He doesn't wait for Carson to answer. Just releases his grip on the now-ripped dress shirt and then turns away.

Riker's barely reached my side when Carson comes at him from behind. All I see is Riker's fist swinging past my face and making impact with Carson's jaw. Two more punches and he hits the pavement, giving no indication that he'll be able to get to his feet again anytime soon.

"Quinn. Quinn!" Riker's hands are firmly on my shoulders, holding me in place. "Quinn. You need to take a breath for me. Okay? Deep breath. Come on. You can do it." His deep voice is calm in spite of everything else around us.

I try to do what he says, but my whole body is shaking so hard I think I might be having convulsions. Unable to do anything but nod, I close my eyes and try to retreat to somewhere within. Somewhere far, far away from here.

I'm already drifting off into the black abyss that is my soul when I vaguely take note of being carried. I can smell him. Feel his skin on mine. The stubble on his jaw brushing against my forehead. And I start to come back. Because there's nowhere safer than here. With him.

Next thing I know, I'm sitting in his old Ford pickup and listening to the sound of his voice. He's talking to someone. It's not me. He's on the phone.

"Sorry, Sid. I know it was my idea. I feel like an ass, believe me, but I can't make it. Not tonight." Out of the corner of my eye I watch him push the phone across his dash. It slides until it gets stuck right below the windshield.

"I ruined your plans," I croak.

His hand reaches out to rest on my leg, squeezing it lightly. "You didn't ruin anything. Besides, you know damn well I'd rather spend the night in with you than be out with anyone else." He smiles, but it's not the same as before. *He's* not the same as before. Because of what he saw. He'll never be able to unsee it. And he'll never be able to look at me the same because of it.

"Thank you." The words seem hollow in comparison to what he did. But they need to be said, so I say them.

He just shakes his head. "No. Don't thank me for doing the only acceptable thing." The hand he has on the steering wheel curls into a fist before it flattens out again, slamming into the rim. "Fucking

Carson Winn! Motherfucking piece of shit!" Then out of nowhere, he turns toward me, anguish in his eyes. "I swear if I had known he would do something like this . . . that he was capable, Quinn, I never would have let it get this far."

"What are you talking about?" My throat clenches up mid-sentence as another tsunami of emotions threatens to take me down. "This was not your fault. If anything, it was mine."

Riker doesn't say anything. He just yanks the steering wheel to the side and then slams on his brakes, parking on the shoulder. He pulls me into his lap, cupping my face in his hands, and leaves a trail of kisses from my temple down to my chin, until he finds my lips and covers them whole with his.

"Nothing about what happened tonight was your fault, Quinn," he whispers. "Nothing."

I suck in a ragged breath and squeeze my eyelids shut. He kisses them too.

"I want you to hold me."

His arms are wrapped around me tightly. "I am holding you."

I open my eyes again and meet his gaze. "No. Not like this. I want to feel you. The weight of your body on mine. The warmth of your skin. I want it all. I need it. Please."

Riker doesn't say anything. He just turns the key in the ignition and shifts into drive, pulling the truck back onto the road while I stay where I am, my head resting on his chest, listening to the calming beat of his heart all the way back to his place.

Once inside, neither of us says anything as he unzips my dress and lets it fall to the ground, where I step out of it on my way to his bed. I lie back onto the mattress while he takes off my shoes and removes his own clothes.

It's the first time we've ever undressed without any sense of urgency. Without a basic need for one another. Now the need is one sided. I need him. And he pities me. That maybe hurts worse than anything else that happened tonight. Even if Carson didn't get what he wanted, he still succeeded in taking something from me.

Before tonight, Riker didn't know. He was the one person in my godforsaken life who didn't look at me and see someone weak and broken. Damaged. I needed that. I needed him to just accept me at face value, never questioning my past. Never expecting a future. Now that's gone. I can see it in his eyes. Feel it in his touch.

He cares. Maybe more than he should. More than I want him to. But things have shifted. We're not equals in this anymore. He's become the caregiver. I've become the victim. I hate being the victim. And as absurd as it sounds, I'd so much rather he was using me for sex right now, instead of caring so much that he'll never want to touch me again out of fear he might hurt me too.

I tilt my head up from where it's nestled to his chest. "Thank you."

His fingers gently dance over my shoulder. "I already told you not to tell me that."

It's the opening I was hoping for. I lift myself up and move my leg over his hips to straddle him. "Then let me show you instead."

He looks confused. "What are you doing?"

I bend down to kiss him. "What we always do."

But he turns his head. "No, Quinn. Not tonight. Not after what happened." He lifts me by my waist and sets me back down on the mattress beside him.

"But nothing happened. You stopped him." I'm lying of course. Something happened. A lot happened. So much more than he could possibly even know happened. But I want to erase it from my mind. His mind. I want to erase it right out of existence, and there's only one way I know how to do that. "I'm fine. I swear." I can feel the lump in my throat growing as it climbs. The last thing I want to do is cry in front of him again.

"No. You're not." He scoots himself up against the wall, not quite sitting upright, but enough to face me full on. "And who would be, Quinn?"

I want to punch him. I want to scream. Why is he making this so much more difficult than it already is? "Stop it! No one asked you to worry about me. The only thing I come here for is sex. So if you're not going to fucking screw me right now, I might as well put my fucking clothes back on and get out of here!" I have every intention of getting up in a huff and stomping out of his apartment, but he's already got a hold on me and he's not letting me go.

"I'm not worried about you." He flips me onto my back and moves over me, encasing me with his entire body like a cocoon. "I'm merely doing what you asked me to do earlier. Holding you." The whole time he speaks, his tone never reflects even an ounce of emotion. Maybe I was wrong. Maybe I'm the one whose feelings are running amok and fucking everything up. But I can't stop them. And I'm too desperate to care that I'm begging him to sleep with me now.

"Please." With his weight on me, I can't even move my arms, so my hands are pressed to my chest. My heart's pounding so hard and fast I think it's trying to escape. And I can appreciate the sentiment. That's all I want too. "Please, Riker. I just . . . I need you to still want me. If you stop, if you can't see me as anything but this fragile, wounded woman, then that's what I'll become. I don't want to be her. I want to be the girl who struts in here owning the room because of the way you look at me. Please. I can't lose that. You can't let Carson take that. It'll be worse than anything else he could have done to me tonight." I'm gasping for air, trying to stop the tears. I have no choice but to look at him looking back at me, because we're so close there's nowhere else to aim my eyes. So I close them. And he kisses me.

Hard. With a need so overwhelming it's almost desperate, and I feed it with my own frantic urgency.

"Feel that?" His raspy growl is strained and breathless as his mouth hovers right above mine. "I know you do. That is me wanting you with every fiber of my being. But I'm not going to have you. Not tonight. Tonight, I'm just going lie here, holding you in my arms. Feeling your vulnerable and exposed body against my bare skin. Wanting you more and more with each passing second because you're the sexiest goddamn woman I've ever laid eyes on." And the hunger in his eyes flares wildly as he says it. "But I'm not going to have you. Because I need you to know that a *real* man can respect your boundaries. A *real* man knows that your body is sacred, and his physical needs are not. And because consensual sex is never about exerting control over someone else to get what you want. It's about being in control of yourself. So yes, believe me, I still want you. I want you like I've never wanted another woman in my entire life. But I want you to want me for the right reasons. In the right way. Because there's no way in hell I'm going to connect what we have when we're together to what happened in that parking lot tonight."

His lips taste salty when he brushes over mine, and I know I've been crying again. I don't care anymore. Nor do I care that I know that from here on out we'll be lying every time we claim we mean nothing to each other. It won't keep us from lying any more than it will keep me from knowing the truth.

CHAPTER NINE

RIKER

I wake up to find her still lying in my arms. This hasn't happened before. All the nights she's spent here with me, we've never both fallen asleep. Together. Until last night. But then, a lot of things never happened before last night. Things that can't be undone. Things I'm not sure I'm ready for, and I know she sure as hell isn't.

Her muscles tighten against me, and for a moment I think she's waking up. Then I see her face twist in pain with her eyes still sealed shut and I know she's dreaming, face-to-face with whatever nightmares haunt her day in and day out. I know she thinks I can't tell. Maybe she thinks I don't care enough to notice anything beyond her beautiful face and amazing body, but that's because it's all I pay attention to when she's watching. Because that's all she wants me to see of her. But it's not all I see. It's never been. There's always been more. And it's the things she wants to hide from me the most that make me want to see her more.

"Quinn." I whisper her name. I don't want to startle her, but I can't leave her trapped in her own subconscious hell. "Wake up."

Her eyes flutter and immediately dart around the room as if she's forgotten where she is. She takes a deep breath in as her chest moves against mine.

"Well, this is different." I knew she'd do that. Make a joke to deflect from the possibility that we might have actually experienced some sort of emotional intimacy.

"You could say that." I go along with her. I let her set the tone. Always have. Because she's the wind and I'm the sail.

"I don't suppose you know where my phone is?" She lifts her head to scan the room, but little else moves with it.

"I plugged it in last night to charge it." I reach across her to the turned-over milk crate I use as a nightstand. "Here."

"Thanks." She unlocks the screen and lets out a whistle. "Holy hell, Kirsten. She called seventeen times." She drops the phone to my chest and lays her head down beside it.

"She's probably worried. You should call her." Kirsten's never called while Quinn was here. At least not that I know of. I'm not sure she's ever checked her phone before.

"No way. I'm not calling her now. You don't know my sister. This will not be settled in one little phone call." She's not even done saying it when her phone vibrates on my chest and the screen lights up. Her finger moves up to swipe the screen, but it's not to answer, it's to ignore the call. Then, to make it easier to forget, she moves the phone back over to my makeshift nightstand, keeping Kirsten and her concerns out of sight until she's ready to deal with them.

I don't argue with her. Not about this. I just lie back silently and watch as her mind continues to wake up, becoming more alert and slowly beginning to digest everything all over again. It doesn't take long for her to zone out. She does this a lot, but today I have a feeling I know where she's gone. And if I'm right, I honestly don't know how I'll handle it.

So, keeping my voice as low and as calm as I can, I ask her, "Who hits you, Quinn?"

Her head shoots up to turn in my direction, and I know before she even lies to me that I'm right. "No one hits me. Why would you even ask something like that?"

My jaw locks, and the tension builds within me. But I can't let her see it. So I take a silent breath in before I answer her. "Yesterday, when I found you . . . you didn't fight back against Carson. It was like some sort of deeply ingrained instinct kicked in. Like you were prey to some wild animal, and you knew your best chance of survival was just to play dead."

I expect her to counter with some bullshit reason, but she doesn't. She just stares at me blankly.

"And then when Carson came at me and I swung at him, you flinched. Like you thought you were the one I was aiming at. Your face froze up with fear, and then you just started shaking. For a moment I thought your entire system was shutting down on me." It scared me. Really fucking scared me.

She still doesn't answer me. Just lies her head back down on my chest and absentmindedly begins to drum her fingers on my palm.

"Remember when you asked me how Harley lost his leg?"

I remember, but she doesn't really need me to confirm that.

"I was barely nineteen. And this guy . . . he attacked me. Harley was there. He tried to protect me, but the guy was big . . . and strong. He threw Harley across the room like it was nothing. I was on the ground and there were too many things blocking my view to see it happen, but I heard this god-awful thud as Harley hit the wall, and then a heartbreaking yelp. The impact broke his back. He had to relearn how to walk. And the front leg, it just never recovered. For weeks, he just sort of dragged it along, like dead weight. Finally, the vet said it would be best to just take it. So that's what they did."

Her tone is eerily empty. Like she's told the story before. Many times.

All I want to do is pull her close. Protect her. Create a world for her in which the monsters in her mind can't reach her. But I can't even do that for myself. So how could I possibly give it to her?

"What happened to the man who attacked you?"

She doesn't even blink. "I killed him." Then, before I can ask her again, she gets up onto her side. "Or maybe he got swallowed whole by the devil for attacking a defenseless girl and her puppy. Who can recall? He'd certainly deserve it."

She's making jokes. About things that aren't funny. She's done sharing. Probably already regretting having opened up to me this much. So I let it go. For now.

"Hey, let me see your phone." I stretch out my arm, but she's got her weight on it, so I can't reach it on my own.

"Why? Are you going to call my sister? Because that could be interesting." She hands it over skeptically.

"No, I'm not getting in the middle of that. I'll beat up other guys for you, but I'm not taking on your sister. She scares me." I unlock her screen by tapping the number five four times. I saw her do it earlier. It's not much of a security code, and I make a mental note to mock her for it later.

"Then what are you doing?" She leans in so far that she blocks my view of the phone.

"Would you move your big-ass head out of my way so I can see the screen? I'm trying to add my number to your contact list."

Stumped, she actually drops back. "What for?"

I finish punching in the number and then hit call. Now I have hers as well. "So that the next time someone sets you up on a blind date, you can call me and I'll come pick you up before the douchebag gets there."

I hand the phone back to her, and she smirks. "Well, I might as well just delete it again, then, because I'm sure as hell not going out on any more blind dates."

Her fingers fly over the screen, and I clasp my hand around them to stop her. "Keep it anyway. Use it. Don't use it. I don't care. But I want you to have it. Just in case."

This time her quirky little mouth holds still. No smirk. No mocking grin. Just her. Nodding.

• • • •

QUINN

I see her before I even step one foot inside. Kirsten. She's in my room, pacing back and forth with such force that she reminds me of a tornado ripping through my place. I'm kind of expecting to see the floorboards busted out and strewn all over from the impact.

"Where the hell have you been?" She lunges for me the second I open the door. "And don't give me some bullshit about being out running, because I've been in this room all night waiting for you. I know you haven't been home. And I know for damn sure those aren't your clothes."

I glance down at the oversize t-shirt and drawstring shorts I'm wearing. "They could be mine. You don't know what all I have."

"Don't give me that. You don't fucking own a Mötley Crüe shirt. And don't try to distract me!" I think she's a little extra pissed now because it worked. Even if it was only temporarily.

"Not that it's any of your business, but I was at a friend's house. And yes, he let me borrow some clothes so I wouldn't have to walk down the beach in the dress you got me." Which incidentally, I no longer own since I watched Riker throw it into the garbage can right before he dragged it out to the curb to be picked up.

"So it's true?" Kirsten looks like her head is about to explode. Then her arms start flailing around dramatically, and I can't help but wonder if she intends to use the force of the impending explosion to propel herself upward and become airborne. "You've been seeing someone behind my back this entire time? Damn it, Quinn! When will you ever learn?"

"I just told you, *he's a friend*." It never pays to meet Kirsten at the height of her anger, but it's taking all I've got to remain calm when she's basically accusing me of being the dumbest fucking girl alive.

"Stop. Just stop." She's holding up her hand for extra measure. "Carson called last night and told us everything. Said the two of you had just finished a really great dinner and were walking out to his car when your jealous boyfriend showed up out of the blue and attacked him! Did you know he broke his jaw? Carson spent the night in the ER thanks to your mistakes."

My blood is quite literally boiling. I mean, I can't be certain, so maybe literally isn't as accurate as I'd like it to be, but my skin is burning up and I might scream, so if it's not boiling, it's something pretty damn close.

"Are you fucking kidding me right now? *My* mistakes? How about *your* mistakes? And Nate's mistakes?" It's my turn to charge across the room and get in her face. "For starters, dinner sucked ass. Mostly because all he could do is talk about his damn self, which would have been fine if he had been even remotely interesting. Which he was not! Then I avoid dessert in hopes of ending the evening, only to wind up being mauled by him in the parking lot. Your precious Carson is one fucking date-rape away from a long-term prison sentence. Shit, it's probably already happened and he just found a way to convince the girls that he was doing them a favor by assaulting them because it would boost their bad reputations. At least that's the line he gave me. Be sure to thank your husband for that one, by the way. He told that asshole just enough of my business to get the completely wrong idea! Not that that would have made it any better. Even if I *was* the biggest slut to ever walk the face of this earth, I still would not have slept with him!"

I don't think I've inhaled since I started shouting because I'm lightheaded now. But I'm not done. "And as for Riker—yeah, it was him. He's the one I was with last night. He's the one I've been with *every night* since Sophie's birthday party, and he's the one who stumbled upon Carson attacking me in the parking lot and put a stop to it. Because that's just the kind of loser he is."

"You're lying." But I can tell from her tone that she doesn't think I am. She just needs me to be. Because otherwise I was attacked last night. Again. And this time she was the leading force behind it.

"I'm not." The boil has subsided to a slow simmer, and now that I've said all there was to say, I'm wondering if it would have been better to just keep my mouth shut.

She shakes her head. "Carson is a decent guy. He comes from a good family. Nate knows him. They play golf together. I wouldn't set my baby sister up with someone who could hurt her."

"I know that, Kirsten." I can't be mad at her. She's going to rip herself to shreds over this one for a long time and that's the last thing I want. "I shouldn't have said it was your mistake. I was just . . . pissed. Because for once it wasn't mine either. Everything that went wrong was Carson's doing. And if I was anyone else, I would have called the cops. I wouldn't have put Riker in a position to have to handle it for me."

She looks up at me, still cringing at the sound of his name. "Why him, Quinn? I know what he did last night was to save you . . . but Carson sent Nate pictures of his face. That man has a violent streak. What if he turns it on you one day?"

I close my eyes because hearing her say those words about the man who held me in his arms last night, showing me more care and kindness than any one person on this earth ever has, makes me hurt. An almost unbearable hurt.

"He won't, Kirsten." I exhale and feel the emotions trickle out with my shaky breath. "You don't know him. The version you've seen . . . that's not even him. That's just his job. The clothes and the environment you associate with Jackson aren't even attached to Riker outside of his work. And even if they were, that's a pretty heavy stereotype to put on people. You really think every guy who works outdoors wears jeans, boots, and a backward baseball cap, then goes home and beats on their woman? You can't possibly believe that. Any more than I think every guy who looks like Carson is a rapist. Because that would make Nate one too. And we both know nothing could be further from the truth."

Gradually, Kirsten's demeanor is changing. She's not pissed anymore. But now I kind of wish she still was, because the agony creeping in and taking over isn't any easier to bear. It's harder.

"He's not the one who makes me worry, Quinn." She turns and walks over to my bed where she sinks down on the mattress. "You are. You're sneaking around. Lying. Keeping him hidden. Why would you do that if you thought there wasn't anything wrong with this relationship?"

I sit down beside her, feeling a lot calmer in spite of the fact that I'm now having to put into words something that was so much simpler in silence. "Because it's not a relationship." I watch and wait for her to get the point I'm trying to make. It takes a second, but the understanding starts to filter in.

"Oh." She rolls her eyes at me. "Well, that's charming."

"Would you make up your damn mind? Shit, Kirsten. One minute it's all *he's not good enough for you. Don't get involved with him, he'll treat you like Jackson did. Stop falling for losers, Quinn.* And then when I tell you, hey, no biggie, I'm not attached, not involved, and that there are no feelings to speak of, somehow that doesn't work for you either." I bump her shoulder with mine, trying my best to make her lighten up.

"So it's just sex. That's all?" Her left brow is cocked, displaying her skepticism.

"Well, really, really good sex. Kind of mind blowing, turn your world into a wonderland and teach you how to fly sort of sex. I wouldn't haul my cookies a mile down the beach every night for 'just sex.'"

Finally, the flat line taking the place of her mouth gives way to a small smile. "That's something, I guess. I'd hate to think you were 'just' a whore. But no, you're a whore with standards."

"A girl's gotta have those." I nod. This is the closest we've been to being *us* in a long time. I've missed it. I've missed her.

"I guess I'll let you get cleaned up." She stands up and starts for the door. "I'm making waffles. With chocolate chips."

I smile at her. She knows those are my favorite. "I'll be up in a few."

And then the door closes and she's gone.

Feeling unusually well rested after a night of solid sleep, I'm not tempted by my comfy bed and manage to jump right to my feet to start getting ready for the day. I'm at my dresser about to dig around in it for something suitable to wear, when my door comes flying open again and my sister runs toward me, wrapping both arms tightly around me.

"I'm so sorry. So, so very sorry, Quinn." Her voice is choked up and choppy from crying. "I was so busy worrying about you repeating the past that I completely missed the present." She pulls back, placing her hands on the sides of my face. "Did he hurt you? Did he . . . do anything before Riker showed up?"

I shake my head before I can find the words. "Just kissed me. And over-the-clothes stuff. Nothing that will leave scars any uglier than the ones I've already got."

She presses her lips to my forehead before she releases me. "Next time you see Riker, tell him I said thanks for looking out for my baby sister." She's at the door again. She wipes her eyes, preparing to face Nate and Sophie, who are probably sitting right at the end of the stairway in the living room. "And tell him that in the future it wouldn't hurt to break more than a measly little jaw on a man like Carson."

"I'll be sure to mention it." In a month or so, when we make the effort to have another conversation.

As it turns out, it takes less than twenty-four hours before I'm back at his place and we're *talking*.

"And now your sister knows? And she's cool with it?"

We're up on the rooftop deck, lying on the chaise lounge, me on top of him, both of us naked under his quilt and staring straight up at the night sky. It's beautiful out.

"Mostly. She likes you now, but I don't think she's all that impressed with our arrangement."

His hand reaches over to cup my breast. "What's wrong with our arrangement?" I can hear the grin in his voice even if I can't see it.

"Not a thing. It's pretty perfect if you ask me." I snake my arm up out of his hold and around the back of his head to play with his thick hair. It's got a slight wave to it now from the moisture in the air. "My sister did throw the word 'whore' around a time or two, though."

"That seems a bit harsh. I mean, *easy*, maybe. But whore?"

I grab a fistful of his hair and hold it hostage. "What was that?"

"I was kidding. I swear. Ow!" He dramatically rubs the spot on his scalp.

"You're such a wuss. Men, I swear." I roll onto my chest, carefully balancing my weight so I don't fall off of him and the chaise. "Meanwhile, I'm hungry."

Riker stretches into a more upright position, taking me with him. "I've got some shrimp fried rice downstairs."

"Hmm."

He squints at me, a shadow coming down over his handsome face. "What?"

I flick my wrist casually like it's no big deal, only it totally is. "It's nothing. I just seem to recall someone mentioning providing an actual meal with actual plates and actual silverware . . . from time to time."

His brows lift again, and the corner of his mouth inches its way upward as well. "And I take it, time to time is right now?"

"Oh, well, if you insist. I mean, I would have been fine reheating old takeout—"

He dives in to kiss me before I even finish. "Shut up, Quinn," he murmurs, his mouth hovering right over mine.

"Okay." I close my eyes and let my lips find their own way back to him. They always do.

CHAPTER TEN

RIKER

I lock the door and head back down the cobblestone driveway. This is the fifth house I've checked on so far, and I've got eight more to go before I can head home. I'm tempted to call Quinn and have her come out and meet me for the night. This time of year, almost all the rentals are booked, but I've got one that won't be occupied again until next Friday. But an overnight trip out of town doesn't sound like something you invite your fuckbuddy to do. And that is, after all, what she is. Or what she thinks she wants to be.

Climbing into the driver's seat of my truck, I hear my phone vibrating on the dash. I don't know why I can never remember to stick it in my fucking pocket. Maybe because I'm never expecting any calls I really want to answer.

I don't even bother looking who it is.

"Yeah?"

"Nox is in trouble. You need to come. Now." It's Sid.

"What's wrong?" I slam the door shut and start up the engine. Then I turn the key again and stop what I'm doing. I'm three hours out.

"He's hurt. He got spooked out in the pasture and started running. Next thing I see, he's falling, crashing into the ground at full speed. It was horrible, Riker. I couldn't move. I just stood there, waiting and praying, hoping he would stand up again." I can hear her sniffle. She's crying. This is bad. Sid doesn't cry. She just doesn't. "I couldn't take it. I had to make Harrold go check on him. I thought for sure he was lying out there dead. Broken neck. Something. But he's not. He's alive. Just in really bad shape."

"What the hell happened, Sid?"

"There was barbed wire hidden in the tall grass," she wails. "I don't know where it came from. Must have blown over from the neighbor's during the last storm. There's still half a fence post attached to it. The rest is wrapped around his legs. He can't get up. I have no idea how badly he's been hurt, and he won't let anyone near enough to help him. Every time we try, he starts kicking his legs, tightening the wires around him more. It has to be you. You have to get here. Now."

I drop my head to the steering wheel. This can't be happening. "I'm out checking the properties. I'm three hours down the coast."

Sid sucks in a loud breath. She's counting on me. Nox is counting on me. My fucking grandfather is counting on me. *Fuck me.*

"Listen to me, Sid. You need to call Kirsten Bernheimer. Tell her to bring her sister down. Nox likes her. I don't know why, but he does." And right now she's the only chance he's got.

"Quinn? The cranky one who never smiles? When has she ever been around him?" I understand why she's skeptical. Nox matters to her as well, but that's precisely why she shouldn't be wasting more time than necessary.

"Yeah. The cranky one. Just fucking call her. I'm telling you, she'll be able to help him. At least until I get there." This time, I hang up before she can argue with me anymore. I start the truck up again and back out of the driveway, still searching my phone for her name. She's the last one in my contact list.

"I'm sorry, I don't do barn calls. I'll be over when you're home. And showered." Outside of her voice, there isn't a single other sound on the line, and it occurs to me that I have no idea what she does all day.

"I'm calling about Nox." I pause to merge into traffic. "He got tangled up in some barbed wire and won't let anyone near him."

"Shit." I hear the squeak of an office chair.

"Look, I'm sure this is going to sound crazy, but I think you might be the only one who can help him. He doesn't like people. He barely even tolerates me, but I'm three hours away. And he needs help now. And that day of Sophie's party . . . he likes you. He'll let you get close enough to help him."

She's quiet on the other end. Then there's the sound of a door opening, and I hear her sister's voice. "Quinn. Sidney called. They have a horse in trouble and for some reason they think you might be able to help?"

"I'm going to need to borrow the Beemer." She gets back on the line with me. "I'll be there in fifteen minutes. And I won't even tell Sidney you called."

"Thank you." The line goes dead, and I throw the phone back onto my dash. Where I'll probably find it again sometime tomorrow morning.

• • • •

QUINN

"That was . . . amazing. It really was. I don't even know how to thank you, Quinn." But Sidney tries anyway by throwing her arms around my shoulders and drawing me in for an awkward hug. It's only awkward because I'm not hugging her back. I should. I just suck at this stuff. By the time I manage to return the gesture, it only gets more awkward because she's already letting me go.

"It was nothing. I mean, it's just a fluke he happens to like me. I'm just glad he's going to be alright." By some miracle, Nox walked away from the incident with all of his bones still intact. His legs are cut up pretty bad, and there'll be scarring, but the vet seems to think that's the worst of it. Of course, he won't know for sure until all the swelling goes down. There's still a chance he has a sprain or damaged tendon; however, at this point, everything is treatable.

"Yeah. A fluke." Sidney shakes her head like she's still trying to make sense out of everything. "You know, once upon a time, he was a completely different horse. Then Old Willie died, and he was never the same. Only lets Riker handle him now." She chuckles quietly. "And Riker hates him, so I guess Nox really does pick and choose the people he accepts randomly."

"Well, for what it's worth, I'm glad he chose me." I smile. Once upon a time, my Jazz had chosen me too.

Sidney's still standing a bit closer than necessary after our little hug, when something catches her eye and she sidesteps me on her way to something, or someone else.

When I turn around, I find her holding tight to Riker, and he's returning the hug. And it's not at all awkward. Although, I suddenly really wish it was.

"He's going to be alright," she tells him, moving out of his embrace only to land at his side still holding onto him. She wipes her eyes, leaving dirt smears across her cheek from the sand and dust on her face and hands.

"I told you she'd be able to help him." His eyes cut straight to mine. And that thing happens. That thing where two people can suddenly have entire conversations by exchanging a mere glance. And it freaks me the fuck out. Because those word-filled glances don't happen to just anyone. They happen between people who know each other. Intimately. And not physically. Emotionally.

"Um, I'm going to go ahead and take off." I start walking toward the large barn doors. It's suddenly really crowded in here.

"Thanks again, Quinn." Sidney reaches out and squeezes my arm as I go by. She's really touchy feely, that one. I'm kind of surprised Riker doesn't seem to mind it.

I'm all the way to the parking lot when I hear footsteps running up behind me. "Hey. Wait a sec."

I turn around and lean back against the Beemer. "What's up, Cowboy?"

He smirks as his eyes narrow briefly. "You tell me, Boots."

"Just trying to get out of your way so you and Sidney can handle your business." I mean for it to sound casual. It doesn't. It sounds like I'm jealous. And catty.

He takes a step closer and rests his hands loosely on my hips. He's dressed unusually nicely today. No suit or tie or anything, but these jeans don't have any dirt stains on them, and the fitted shirt he's wearing is tucked in. With buttons. And it's not made out of flannel. And now that he's standing so annoyingly close, I can smell him. It's not the usual straight from the shower soap scent. He's wearing cologne. And *Oh my GOD!* He smells good enough to eat.

"What's going on in that twisted brain of yours now? Huh?" He tugs at my belt loops, bringing my hips in to meet his. Like I really need to get any closer to him right now.

"I don't know. It seems like things are . . . overlapping. And I don't like it." I turn my head to keep from having to maintain eye contact. I'll be completely at his mercy if I let those teal-blue eyes of his bore into me a second longer. I'm already not doing so hot in that department as it is.

He takes advantage of my face being turned away and moves in close beside my ear to whisper, "Getting confused, are we? Having . . . feelings?"

I press the side of my head into his and lower my face into the crook of his neck. "Just one."

"And what's that?"

I mold the rest of my body to him and let his arms take me in. "Hope." And it's both the best and most frightening thing I've experienced in a long time.

"Hope," he repeats quietly. "I think hope is going to go a long way for us."

"It might never go anywhere other than here." I start to step out of his embrace, but he stops me.

"Or it could take us to death do us part. That's the thing about hope, Quinn. It comes with possibilities. And I like that. Whatever they are. I like knowing they exist." He bends down and kisses the top of my head. Then he reaches for my door handle with one hand, while still holding me to him with the other.

"I'm going to finish up here, help Sid with the night feeding and then I'll be home. You gonna be there?"

I unravel my way out of his arm and the safety of his broad frame and slide into the front seat of Kirsten's car. "I'll be there. Now that I don't have to fake going for a run, I might even show up wearing something nice and girly like."

"And yet another thing to hope for." He winks and flashes me a mischievous grin, making me blush like a teenager. We're flirting. And not dirty flirting, but cutesy flirting. It's a whole new side of him. And it's freaking adorable.

"Okay, you need to stop that right now." My stern tone goes entirely to waste since I'm smiling from ear to ear. "Don't get all sweet and charming with me now, mister. It won't work. I already know you're an antisocial asshole, so just stick with that. It makes me less wobbly in the knees and pink in the cheeks."

He comes down into the car and kisses me square on the lips. Right there. In broad daylight. "Bye, Quinn."

"Bye, jackass."

He closes my door, still smirking, then taps the roof before he steps away from the car, giving me the final go ahead, and I take off, but not without watching him in the side mirror the entire drive down the driveway until I turn off on the main drag. And he stands there the whole time, watching me too.

When I get back to the house, Kirsten is in full-on dinner-making mode and Sophie is busy playing with her dolls in the family room just off the kitchen.

"Save the horse?" She's staring at me expectantly over a pot of boiling spaghetti.

"Yep." I plop down on one of the barstools across from her.

"Then why are you so mopey?" She sets down the wooden spoon she's holding and comes to take a seat beside me. As soon as she reaches me, her nose crinkles in disgust. "You stink, by the way. Is that what's depressing you? Because it's definitely having an effect on my mood right now, I can tell you that."

I lift my shirt up to my face and inhale. I smell fabulous. Like horses and fresh hay. "You're crazy. This scent is amazing."

"Quinn."

"I don't want to lose him." I bury my face in my hands to avoid having to see whatever expression will show up on her following those words.

"Why do you think you're going to lose him?" she asks calmly, and I venture a peek in her direction. She's not mocking me or looking at me like I've lost my mind. She's seriously asking.

"Because." I let my hands fall into my lap. "We're not together. But we're something. And I think maybe he wants the something to become a together thing, only I don't know if I can do together. I just know I don't want to do apart. You know?"

Kirsten laughs. "Do I know? Jesus, Quinn. *You* don't even know."

"Thanks. That's helpful. I'm really glad I opened up to you about this." I go to get up but feel her hand on my elbow.

"You really want to know what I think?"

I turn around to look at her again. "Kind of. Tell me what it is first and then I'll decide."

She grimaces but tells me anyway. "I think you want to have your Riker cake and eat it too. You're used to having him all to yourself without having to invest any feelings or offer any kind of commitment, and that suits you just fine. And maybe it suits him too. Except now . . . now you're having some sort of tingling sensation in the hollow hole in the pit of your chest that used to house your heart, and you're starting to remember what it means to have feelings and you don't like it. And now you don't know which is worse. Leaving the man you want dangling out there for someone else to come along and snatch right out from under you—literally, given what the two of you do with your time—*or* taking a trip down memory lane to retrieve what's left of yourself in hopes of someday handing it over to him." She clicks her tongue at me. "I don't know, Quinn. Tricky shit, this falling in love crap, when you claim you've no longer got a heart to do it with."

"No."

Her brow raises. "No, what?"

I press my bottom lip out into a pout. "No, I don't want to know what you think."

She shrugs. "Too late." Then she has the audacity to laugh again as she climbs off of the barstool and returns to her pasta.

"I think I liked it better when you thought he was a redneck loser I needed to stay away from," I grumble as I get up and start to stalk off.

"Oh, I see. You want to have your Kirsten cake and eat *that* too. Man, that's like your thing now."

I turn around before I reach the stairs. "Stop talking about cake. You're going to ruin pastries for me altogether if you keep it up. And then what joys will there be left for me in this life?"

She giggles. "There's always sausage. You do seem to be rather fond of that these days."

"You're disgusting. And stop comparing Riker to food. It's making me hungry." I'm halfway through my door when I call back, "And not for your damn pasta!"

Harley greets me as soon as I walk in, and together we stroll out through the back, straight down to the sand where he spends the next twenty minutes chasing waves to his heart's content. Days like today I watch him extra close, and I wonder how often he thinks of the night that changed us both. People like to remind me how time will heal me. How it will somehow mend all that is broken within, just by passing me by. But then I look at Harley. I see his missing limb and I think, no amount of time will ever bring it back. He will bear the scars and the loss of that night for the rest of his life. Why would I be any different? Why would time return what that night took from me? It wouldn't.

Back inside, I finally decide to part with the scent I've thoroughly enjoyed these last few hours and jump in the shower. I pay an unusual amount of attention to detail today, and then scold myself for acting as if tonight will be the first time he's ever seen me naked. Considering the circumstances surrounding our first time together, now is really a ridiculous time to start worrying about whether or not I missed a spot on my kneecaps while shaving my legs.

But I'm on a roll. So after I dry off I decide to dig through the old makeup case Kirsten passed down to me when I moved in here. I locate some hot-pink nail polish and have a go at my neglected toenails. For a split second, I consider doing my fingers as well, and then I remember whose hands they're attached to and don't bother. In twenty-two years, the only times I've ever had a fancy manicure were when Kirsten insisted on giving me one. So even if my efforts went unnoticed or wound up being deemed as insignificant by Riker, my sister would definitely see the unnatural aspect of my behavior and bust me for it.

However, since I did sort of mention looking more like a girl than a sweaty gym towel when I arrive tonight, I allow one last moment of vanity and put on a skirt. Nothing fancy. Just a denim cut-off mini with a long-sleeved tee and my boots. Still, it's about as dressed up as I get, so I do kind of hope he appreciates it. Just as long as he doesn't read anything into it. I'm sure he won't. Just as sure as I am that I will. Because I'm a fucking wreck. I nearly change my clothes seven times before I'm back in outfit number one and force myself out through the front door to borrow Kirsten's car for the second time today.

Parking in his driveway feels weird, and I'm tempted to drive back home and then walk back along the beach. But that would take forever. And I would definitely chicken out of wearing a skirt. So, I stay. Because that way I can make the skirt stay. At least until I get inside and Riker chooses otherwise.

I'm bending over inside the passenger seat, retrieving some items that fell out of my purse—yet another aspect of this evening that's new and unfamiliar, given the fact that a purse doesn't tend to go with running shorts—when I hear a loud whistle from behind. I stand up straight, nearly bumping my head on the car roof as I do.

"I like this look on you." His hands glide smoothly down my hips and reach around to the front of my thighs as he comes up right behind me. "I like this look on you *a lot.*"

"Well, don't get too used to it. At least not until I get my own car. Kirsten's not going to let me hijack hers every night, so there will still be plenty of occasions I show up in my sweats."

He turns me around to face him and greets me with a kiss. "I'm pretty sure you already know how fond I am of the way you look in your sweats."

I smirk. "Can't like 'em too much. You pretty much rip them off of me the second I walk through the door."

"Mmhmm," he murmurs, eyeing me up and down, this time from the front. "And don't think for one second this little number will fare any better."

And he's not kidding. I'm barely through the door before I'm wondering why I bothered stressing so much about an outfit I literally only wore for the drive over here. Well, that and his reaction, which, honestly, was totally worth the anxiety.

An hour later and I'm wearing one of his t-shirts and sitting perched up on his kitchen counter watching him cook for the second night in a row. It's just scrambled eggs, but still. I can't not appreciate the effort.

"Can I ask you something?" He's stirring the eggs, making sure the cheese he just added doesn't burn and get all brown and crusty. "Something personal?"

"Since when do you ask my permission to ask me something personal? And while we're on that, when have you ever asked me for permission period?" I rip off a piece of the tortilla he was planning to load my scrambled eggs into and shove it into my mouth.

"Good point. Forget I asked and just answer. What the hell do you do all day?" He's turned toward me now, flinging his wooden spoon at me as part of his interrogation technique. It's lacking, and I want to laugh at him, but I hold it in as best I can.

"What do you mean, what do I do? I spend all day staring at the clock and counting down the seconds until I can race over here and see you again."

His lips are tightly pursed, and I know he's not nearly as amused as I am. Although he's also not nearly as put off by my sense of humor as he'd like me to believe. "I'm being serious. You know what I do. I want to know how you fill your time. And why you don't need a car." He cocks his brow on the second half of his statement. I guess anyone would wonder. It's not like I never had a car. Just haven't had a need for one in a while.

"First of all, I only sort of know what you do. For example, I'm still not clear on where you were today that it took you three hours to get back." I'm stalling, but I also really want to know.

He takes the pan from the stove and starts fixing two plates for us. "You don't sort of know what I do. You know exactly what I do. I help out Sid at the ranch and I take care of the rental properties. The Shepherdson Realty Group owns properties all up and down this coastline. Some are even out of state. Sometimes that means I have to drive a ways to check on things."

"You have to take care of all of them?" For some stupid reason I'd thought it was just this one.

"Yep." He places the empty pan in the sink and runs water over it before he comes back and hands me my dinner. He doesn't sit down himself, just leans against the counter beside me. "Okay. Your turn."

I tip my head back and forth between each shoulder a few times, debating on how detailed I want my answer to be. "Well, the reason I don't need a car is because I work out of the house. I help run this website. I'm responsible for everything from answering emails, to writing content, to dealing directly with the public and offering them whatever assistance they require depending on their situation."

He stares at me for a second, unimpressed, his tongue sort of stuck in the corner of his mouth. "That was vague." He shakes his head, stabs a piece of egg with his fork, and then points it at me before he takes a bite. "Now try that again. And this time tell it like you want me to actually know what you do."

Half of my face gives way to a smile. The other half is still perturbed by his need to override every single emotional barrier I've tried to put in his path since meeting him.

"Fine. I work with a nonprofit organization called Warriors for Women. We help women and children who deal with varying degrees of domestic abuse. We offer them everything from legal advice to counseling, and a few other services I won't go into detail about. Everything is online and it's all anonymous." I don't repeat what part I play in all of it, because I already covered it.

This time, he genuinely *is* impressed. "Wow, Quinn. That's amazing. Is that something you always wanted to do? Or did your personal experience lead you there?" He's asking a question to which he already knows the answer. He's doing it because it would almost be awkward to assume. And even more awkward to say, "*Well, Quinn, that's really admirable, but what did you really want to do with your life?*" So I skip answering the first one and go right to the real question.

"When I was younger, I was really into the rodeo circuit. My mare and I were steadily working our way up to the big leagues in barrels. Horses. Rodeos. That was my life from the time I was five. Kind of always thought I'd do it until I was ready to settle down, have a ranch of my own, and raise a few babies and foals." I shrug. "When that didn't pan out, I switched gears completely. Got my bachelor's degree in social work and wound up working for Warriors."

Riker's watching me intently, hanging on every word I say. "So do you eventually want to be a social worker and be more hands-on?"

I shake my head. "I didn't choose the degree to learn the job. I chose it to learn the system so I could work around it. Not with it." I shrug. "But I do want to eventually be more involved in something. My own thing."

He sets his plate down and smiles. "You already know what it is, don't you?"

I nod. I haven't told anyone. I can't believe I'm going to tell Riker. "I'm working on putting together a program that would match up dogs in need of adopting with women in need of saving."

"I'm intrigued. Let's hear it." And because his blue eyes are so damn beautiful and so damn focused on me, I tell him.

"It's no secret that most women who are in abusive relationships tend to struggle with breaking the cycle. Even if they do muster up the courage to leave once, nine out of ten times they go back. The reasons are endless, and often seem just as minor and illogical to those on the outside as they seem life-and-death major and completely logical to those on the inside." I'm tempted to expound on this. I really, really want him to understand why the inside looks so different, but I don't. Because I don't want him to ask me why I know what the inside looks like. "What I would like to do is work directly with women's shelters. Bring in dogs that have gone through the shelter system and have been to the death chamber's door and back and connect them with women who are just as desperate to stay alive as they are. So that if they go back, or *when* they go back . . . they don't go back alone. They go back with a friend. The most loyal friend they'll ever have. A friend who will fight for them when no one else is around to hear them cry for help."

Riker's not smiling anymore. His expression moves back and forth somewhere between sadness and anger, and his voice is a new kind of low when he asks, "Like Harley did for you?"

It's not really a question. We both already know the answer is yes.

"He saved my life that day. Not just because he went after the man who was attacking me, but because he gave me the courage to fight back. He gave me something, someone, to fight for. Because I couldn't do it for myself." I move my plate out of my lap and stack it on top of his on the counter. Now that I've heard myself say it all out loud, I'm wondering if it's kind of silly. Maybe the whole thing is a stupid idea and I just want it to be more so Harley's sacrifice counts for more. I don't know.

"Hey." Riker's hand slips under my chin, gently directing me to face him again. "You're amazing. You know that?"

I start to roll my eyes, but he catches me and shoots me a threatening glare. "Take a compliment, Quinn. Especially one that comes from me. I don't hand that shit out to just anyone."

"I just don't feel all that amazing." I pull my knees up to my chest, then rest my cheek on them. "But I think I might if I saw myself through your eyes," I whisper. Because the way he looks at me, sometimes I think he's face-to-face with something utterly remarkable. Like maybe he's remembering something spectacular he saw once upon a time. Until I look again, and I notice how his eyes are locked directly on mine and I feel how they pull me in and pry me open, and I realize I'm the spectacular thing he's seeing.

"Come here." He takes my hands and helps me down from the counter. Then, without letting go, he leads the way out of the kitchen and through the small studio until we're both standing in the bathroom facing the mirror. He's behind me, his arms wrapped around my chest, his hands folded right in the center of it.

"See this, right here?" He's putting pressure on my skin, right below my collarbone. "The first time I saw you interacting with Nox, I knew whatever was under here was exceptional, that you were special, because Nox doesn't stand for ordinary. Then I watched you with your niece, and even though you were nervous and visibly uncomfortable trying to manage all those kids, you put your own feelings aside and focused only on hers. And I knew you were selfless." He lowers his head down to mine, touching my cheek with his and brushing my skin with his soft stubble, and still staring straight ahead at the mirror. "Then I met Harley. And I saw how you view him. Not as broken. Or damaged. Or less. You look at Harley and you don't see what he lacks physically. You see his strength and his courage. His unwavering fight for life. He's your hero. You look at him and you see more dog than you'll ever see looking at one with all of his limbs perfectly intact. And because you see him that way, you make other people see it too."

His words are making tears sting my eyes. I'm not even sure why. Because most of the things he just listed, while important to me, should mean nothing to him or anyone else. And yet they do.

Riker's hands move down to my waist, and he brings me around to face him. "I saw the way you looked at Harley, and I knew you were different. And that's just what I knew after one day with you. I knew you could see light where others see nothing but darkness. Only you can't seem to see it in yourself. It's a gift you only give to others." He presses his forehead to mine and closes his eyes as he continues, "You know what the irony is, Quinn? Hearing you say you wish you could see yourself through my eyes, when all this time all I've wanted was to be the man you see through yours."

CHAPTER ELEVEN

RIKER

I'm lying with my head in her lap staring blankly at the ceiling. I don't see the water damage from where the washer was leaking in the laundry room directly above the bed. I don't notice the cobwebs in the corner over my recliner where I never bother to reach up and dust. I can't even tell that the fan blades, which are currently still, are entirely covered in a thick layer of dust, and now thanks to Harley's frequent visits, dog hair.

I know they are. Same as I know about the cobwebs and water damage. Because I've spent countless hours lying here without her, staring up at those very things, unable to see anything else and unwilling to pick my ass up and do anything about it.

Tonight is different. Tonight, no matter where I direct my attention it keeps coming back to her. I'm completely devoid of the ability to focus on anything outside of her. She consumes me, like a riddle I am desperate to solve but no matter how I approach it, I just can't. And for every clue I unveil along the way to cracking her code, I find myself only more and more confused. Somehow figuring her out was easiest when I knew nothing about her. Now, the more I know, the more I discover how much I *don't* know. And it's driving me out of my fucking mind. Not because she isn't entitled to her secrets. We all are. But because I have a feeling not knowing hers will wind up costing me what I want. What I'm starting to need. *Her.*

She's ruined me. She's destroyed the man who didn't give two shits about his life and left behind a pile of rubble determined to rebuild itself into something better, a man more worthy than I've been these last few years.

Her hand is gently stroking my hair as she tips her head to smile down at me. "Comfortable?" Her smile turns almost childlike as she reveals her silly side by stealing the covers and leaving my naked ass bare on the cold hardwood floor. We'd started on the bed. We just hadn't finished there.

"Hey! It's cold over here. I'm not the one with a human heater lying in my lap."

She giggles. "Oh, so you're a hothead. That's good to know." But she returns the blanket and covers the both of us again.

"Only when dealing with assholes. Never with you." I'm not necessarily looking to turn this into some sort of a moment, but I need her to know it. To believe it without a doubt. Because her trust in me depends on it. And moving forward with her will be impossible without that trust.

She bends down to kiss me, gradually deepening the kiss as I open up and let her in. My hand moves up around the back of her head, my fingers roaming through her thick, wild hair. I'm still twirling a long strand of it when she pulls back.

"Quinn?"

"Yes, Riker." She's smirking because she knows how much I like it when she says my name. I'm tempted to tug at the hair still in my hand to bring her back down where I can kiss that sweet mouth all over again. But I don't.

"Remember the first night you came over?"

She scrunches her eyes together. "Vaguely."

She's a brat. "Yeah, same here." I yank at her hair. Not hard, just enough to remind her I'm not the only one with vulnerabilities between us.

"Ow! Fine! I remember. You were a stud and a half and delivered five happy endings before I went running back home, delirious and exhausted. What's your point?"

Between the way her lips move when she speaks and the words *stud* and *happy endings* still ringing in my ears, I almost forget I have one.

"You said you'd never fall for another loser who didn't have his shit together." I spit out the words before I fully remember why I'm bringing them up again.

Her brow curves, and I can tell she's not sure why either. "Actually, I said that the *second* time I came over. But what's your point?"

I laugh. "Sorry, that whole first week sort of blurs together for me now, what with all the lack of sleep I was experiencing." I pause, trying to focus on my original topic again. "Anyway, I've just been wondering what you meant by that. I mean, I know my place is kind of a shithole compared to the house you live in. And my truck is about three decades older than anything sitting in your sister's garage." I have a whole list I've been making for a while now, but she's shaking her head at me and I'm pretty sure she's fighting the urge to smack me, so I stop talking.

"You're a dumbass." Yeah. She was definitely thinking about slapping me. Even if it was just to startle some brain cells back into action. "Having your shit together has nothing to do with money or the amount of fancy crap you own. It's knowing the difference between having a bed to sleep in and a home to come to. The difference between taking care of yourself and eating ramen noodles for dinner every night of the week. And the difference between having a random job to get you by and doing what you love and want to be doing for the rest of your life, or at least working toward doing that. If having your shit together had anything to do with money, I couldn't claim to have my shit together. Which, clearly, I do." Her hand drops to her chest, indicating herself.

Between the gesture and her haughty expression, I can't help but laugh again. "No, you don't."

"Um, I resent that. I totally do." But the underlying sarcasm in her voice suggests otherwise.

"You live with your sister. You eat leftover shit out of my fridge, and on occasion you've even nuked a cup of ramen noodles. The only one I'll give you is the job one. No one can argue the fact that you're pursuing something you're passionate about."

Her index finger shoots straight into the air like she's about to make her argument, and I can't wait to hear what it is.

"Excuse me, but I said nothing about actually doing one over the other. I simply stated one would know the difference between the two. Which I do. And, someday, when I get bored with the amazing sex I have over here, I can move out of my sister's conveniently located abode to one farther away, and then I'll stop being able to run over here on a daily basis to eat your shitty food."

I lift myself up out of her lap and prop myself up onto my side. "So that's why you come here. Just the sex."

Her eyes flit back and forth as the corners of her mouth twitch playfully. "I believe I said 'amazing.'"

"Hm. And here I was starting to think it was my shitty food." My hand slips up behind her neck to bring her to me. Not that I need to. She's moving toward me all on her own. I'm about to pick her up and put her back in the bed so I can do all the things that make her forget the shitty food I feed her, when there's a knock on the door.

"What the hell was that?" Quinn's face is both confused and frustrated, and I'm pretty sure mine is a mirror image.

I'm about to answer when the knocker repeats the offense and does it again. "Riker? Get your lazy ass out of bed and open the door. It's cold out here."

It's Sid.

And I'm not the only one who recognizes her voice. "What is Sidney doing here at ten o'clock at night?" Quinn hisses, definitely unimpressed with our late-night visitor. And I don't think it's only due to interrupting what we were doing. Or about to do, anyway.

"I need you to do me a favor and go wait in the bathroom while I get rid of her." Even as I hear myself say the words, I know how horrible they sound. "Please. I promise I'll explain as soon as she leaves."

"Are you fucking kidding me right now?" But she's already up on her feet, so I'm hoping she's just letting me know how pissed she is while doing what she's pissed about.

"I'm sorry. I swear to you I'll answer every question in a minute." I reach for the closest pair of sweats and start to pull them on while she huffs her way to the bathroom. Then, as soon as I hear the door shut behind her, I go to let in Sid.

• • • •

QUINN

I didn't have time to grab any clothes on my way in here. Something I'm now annoyingly aware of as I'm standing naked in front of the mirror. The same mirror I was so enamored with a couple of hours ago. Now I kinda hate it. I hate it even more when I see my face. It's ugly, painted with disgusting feelings like shame and jealousy, and I have half a mind to bust out of here buck-ass naked to confront Riker and Sidney. But then I'd have to add humiliation to the list of ugliness, and I'm all tapped out already.

Since causing a massive scene is out of the question, I opt for the next most appeasing thing and eavesdrop by pressing the side of my head to the door as tight as I can.

"What the hell happened in here, Riker? It looks like a fucking bomb went off. You've got half your bedding on the floor. There are clothes everywhere. Why don't you use some of the money you're not spending on car payments or rent and hire a maid? You could definitely use one." She sounds like she's trying to make a joke while still being completely serious. I'm familiar with the tactic. Kirsten uses it on me all the time. Like the humorous delivery somehow makes the condescending message less offensive. It doesn't.

"I can manage doing a load of laundry without hiring someone." He's moving around, probably picking up the scattered clothes before she notices they're mine. I don't get it. I don't think they're together. After everything that's happened in the last couple of days, I can't imagine he would have lied to me about that. Besides, when would he have time to see her? I'm here every night.

"Sometimes I wonder. You do wear that same damn flannel shirt almost every day." She giggles at her own comment, and I'm pretty damn sure this is her attempt at flirting.

"I bought a pack of five. They're different shirts. They just look the same." He exhales loudly. "Can you just get to the point and tell me what you're doing here so late? Because I seriously doubt it was to hassle me about my lack of housekeeping skills." I'm oddly satisfied by how annoyed he sounds right now. Even if she's into him, he's not feeling it. Although that still doesn't explain why I was shunned to the bathroom like his dirty little secret. Especially given how unconcerned he seemed earlier at the ranch when he was kissing me goodbye for the entire world to see. Of course, Sidney had been in the barn for the whole thing and no one else had been around.

"Honestly? I couldn't sleep. The whole thing with Nox today. I don't know. It just got to me. I don't know what I would have done if we had lost him." Toward the end, her words are muffled, and I know there's only one reason they would be. He's holding her. Right there. Outside this door. And I hate him for it. And then I hate myself for hating him for it. Because he's a good man. And she's hurting. And of course he would console her. He would do whatever he could to make the pain go away. I know that. Without a doubt. Because that's precisely what he does for me.

"He's going to be fine, Sid. I'm not going to let anything happen to him. You know that. Same as I'm not going to let anything happen to you." I hear something that sounds unsettlingly similar to a kiss. "I'm here for you. You know that."

"Yeah, well. Next time don't take so long answering the damn door. It makes a girl wonder," she grumbles, but it's not muffled anymore so I'm going to assume she's no longer in his arms.

"Won't happen again. I'm sorry." He chuckles, that deep, quiet chuckle. The one I stupidly thought belonged to me. Why the hell I thought that I don't know. I guess because until now we've existed in this tiny bubble where I never heard him interact with anyone else. Of course he would chuckle around other people. Other women. Women he was promising to look after for all eternity. Why is that making me want to claw my way out of my own skin?

"Okay. I think I'm good now." I hear footsteps, hopefully headed for the door.

"You sure? You could stay a while if you wanted." Like hell she could. How fucking long does he plan on keeping me stashed in here?

Thankfully, she's ready to leave. "I'm good. Really. I just needed something to snap me out of the funk. So thank you." The door opens. Then it closes. And I come flying out of the bathroom like a bat out of hell riding a broomstick.

"Quinn." His hand draws out to catch me.

"Get off of me." I shrug out of his grip. "I have to go."

He steps into my path but doesn't touch me again. "Just let me explain." He hands me one of his stupid flannel shirts, and I slip it on.

"Fine. Explain. But I'm telling you right now, chances are good I won't give a shit. I don't much care for being trapped and locked away out of sight."

He squints at me for a second longer than I'd like, and I'm sure I emphasized the word trapped more than I should have.

"I'm sorry I asked you to wait in the bathroom. I'm even more sorry you felt trapped. I wasn't trying to confine you . . . just keep things from getting complicated."

I twist the shirt tight around my body. "I don't know, Riker. Sounds like you and Sidney are already pretty fucking complicated. You obviously care about her. What's the problem? She won't get involved with the help? Doesn't want to deal with your half-assed way of living? Or maybe she just can't stand wading through the constant pool of self-loathing one has to cross to get to you." I'm raging at him now. Hurling every hurtful thing that comes to mind in his direction. And I don't even know if he really deserves it or not.

"Are you done?" His hands are hanging listless at his sides, and his eyes, God, his eyes. They're so dark and deep I'm certain he's in there drowning. And I don't know what to fucking do to save him because I'm going under myself.

"Yeah. I'm done." I nod. "We're done." I start to walk away, but his hand comes out and touches mine, his fingers lacing into mine until our palms are connecting.

"She's my sister-in-law," he says sadly. "Or she would have been if Hannah hadn't died before they were able to get married."

I turn around, speechless.

He shrugs, the agony casting a shadow over his face. "They were engaged for seven years. They built a life together. Were planning on children. And grandchildren. Now I'm all she has left. Me and that damn horse."

"Oh." That, I did not see coming.

His hand still twined with mine, he brings me to him until he's completely invading me, eyes tied to mine, so close we're breathing the same breath. "I'm sorry I didn't tell you. And I'm even more sorry if I made you feel like I was hiding you from her. I was actually trying to keep her from *you*. She's protective of me. And overbearing now that she doesn't have anyone else to worry about. She means well, but sometimes she's harsher than she intends to be. It changed her, you know? Losing the love of her life. It took something from her. Something more than just my sister. It took a piece of Sid. The piece that belonged to Hannah, I guess."

I rest my forehead to his stubbled jaw. "Please," I whisper. "Stop. You don't owe me any more explanations or apologies. I'm an asshole. I shouldn't have freaked out like that."

Riker's free hand tilts my head back to look up at him, and the pain in his eyes tears through me like a knife. His lids close, saving me from the hell he can't escape, and his lips come crashing down on mine, ravishing my mouth with a desperate urgency. He's almost frantic as he rips the shirt from my body and carries me to his bed, and I'm prepared to give him whatever he needs to ease the ache within him.

He's on top of me in no time. Then inside of me. Thrusting hard and fast, as if he's racing the demons. And I want him to win, so I match him move for move, never once letting up until I know he's beat them.

He's still breathing heavy when he rolls over onto his side, gripping me tightly to his chest. We're both so wrapped up in the emotional and physical aftermath of what just transpired between us, neither of us hears the knock at the door until it's too late and the door opens.

"I fucking knew it!" Sidney.

"What the hell?" Riker bolts into an upright position. "You can't just come bursting in here like you own the goddamn place, Sid." In an instant he's on his feet, and while he was courteous enough to cover me up before he jumped out of bed, he's not hurrying as he moves to the recliner in search of a pair of pants.

"I knocked!" Sid throws back. "You know I was halfway home before I registered the fucking BMW in your driveway? That's how out of it I was when I showed up here. Took me the whole drive back to figure out whose it was. Kirsten Bernheimer." She laughs, but she's not hiding her insults in humor this time. "Well, wasn't hard to narrow it down from there." She stares at me, blasting daggers straight at my heart, but the joke's on her. Nothing left there to hit.

"This is none of your business, Sid." Riker steps in front of me to shield me from her murderous glare. "I don't need your approval. Not for this. Not for anything."

Sidney doesn't seem all that interested in hearing his arguments. She flies at him again. "You're out of your fucking mind if you think I'm just going to sit back and watch you fuck up your life a second time. God! You really only know how to attract one type of woman, don't you!?" She pauses briefly to deliver the most depreciating sneer I've ever witnessed, and I've been on the receiving end of plenty. "You know how this is going to end, don't you? I mean, you've met her sister."

"Whoa!" Now it's my turn to leap to my feet. Although not from the bed. I'm liking the higher ground. Besides, at five foot three I'm the shortest person in the room. I need the extra edge. "What the hell does my sister have to do with any of this?"

Riker spins around to address me, but Sidney beats him to it. "Nothing much. Except she's a money hungry gold digger and considering I already heard all about how she's been fixing you up with the likes of Carson Winn, I'm guessing you're no different."

Riker's attention is back on Sidney one hundred percent. "Shut up, Sid," he snarls. "You don't know what the fuck you're talking about."

"No fucking kidding." Standing on the bed doesn't feel right anymore. Still wrapped in the sheet, I march straight off the edge for Sidney, but Riker catches me halfway. "You don't know the first thing about my sister."

"Oh, please. There isn't a person in town who *doesn't* know about your sister. Or the misery she put every real estate agent in the state through trying to make sure she had the fanciest, priciest house in the land." Her mocking tone makes me want to rip out her tongue. My sister's a handful and a half on a good day. And yeah, I talk my share of shit about her, but I won't stand for it from anyone else. Not even a grieving woman who's too broken to see that she's pushing away the only person she has left in her life.

"So what? So what if she wanted to buy the most expensive house she could find? Who gives a shit?"

Sidney throws her arms up at me like it's obvious. "Um, I don't know. Nate might."

Gotcha, bitch. "Guess again. It's not his fucking money she's spending. It's hers." Both Riker and Sidney are so caught off guard by this news, I have free reign to just keep going. "Kirsten has more money than Nate's entire family. When they got married, *he* was the one my parents wanted to sign the prenup, but Kirsten refused. So tell me again what a fucking gold digger she is. Because you don't know shit about it."

Sidney's slowly processing this new information, but she clearly isn't prepared to admit she was wrong just yet. "If your family's so loaded, what's your fucking deal? Why don't you have your own beachside mansion instead of moving your way through this town like a fucking leech?"

"Because my family isn't loaded. Kirsten is." I'm about to reveal her most personal private history, and I shouldn't. But I'm so tired of keeping secrets. And I can't stand any more rumors about our family and who we are. Especially when they're always so fucking hideous. "Kirsten was married once before, right out of high school. She and Levi grew up together. Knew each other since kindergarten. Shared their first kiss in middle school. Fell in love in high school. By the time they were sixteen, everyone knew they'd be together forever. Only forever wasn't quite as long as they planned."

I stop. Last chance to back out. I don't take it. "Then Levi got sick. Wasn't the first time. He'd battled childhood leukemia once before and won, so they were confident he would do it again. Then, senior year, three months before graduation, doctors told him they were out of options. Nothing was working. The cancer was spreading." I clear my throat. In the sudden silence of this room, it sounds like a lion's roar, and I almost startle myself. Probably because I know Kirsten would kill me if she knew I was talking about this. "Everyone was devastated. His family. Our family. It was the last thing anyone ever expected. But, in spite of everything, Levi was determined to marry my sister. And so he did. Two weeks after they graduated, they had a little ceremony at his parents' house. It was beautiful. I've never seen two people so truly in love with one another." I sigh painfully. "Levi died three days later."

"Shit." Tears are pooling in Sidney's eyes now, and I know she's connecting with my sister in a way she didn't even know was possible.

"Levi was a trust fund baby. He left it all to Kirsten. She didn't even want it, but his parents insisted she keep it. He was their only son, and she was the only woman he ever loved. That meant something to them. So much so that someday when they pass, Kirsten will inherit all over again. And she's terrified of the day it happens. Kirsten hates money. That's the reason she spends it all the damn time. Because she's trying to get rid of it. If it wasn't for me and the fact that I'm an ongoing charity case, she would have just chosen a random cause and donated the bulk of it, keeping only a sliver of it to secure Sophie's future. But she can't. Because of me. Because she refuses to let me fall on my ass, even if I deserve to." I'm feeling oddly deflated after all that. Maybe pain and anger really are my life source and releasing some of it wasn't such a bright idea after all.

"I'm really sorry, Quinn." Sidney shifts a desperate glance back and forth between me and Riker, waiting for one of us to tell her it's alright. I can tell he's not ready. So I do it for him.

"Forget it. Seriously. Kirsten would prefer if you did." I force the corner of my mouth upward. "Honestly, she'd probably rather you just went on thinking she was a money hungry gold digger."

She nods. "Don't worry. I get it. No one likes to walk around with the dreaded 'W' word following them around." She turns toward Riker one more time. "I owe you an apology as well."

"Sid." It's all he says as he shakes his head at her. I've never seen him like this. He's cold, like he's standing behind an ice wall that can't be penetrated by her pain or anyone else's. "You should go. I'll see you in the morning."

Sidney gasps loudly, then bites down on her lip, probably trying to force back the tears I imagine are making their way up to the surface again. Then she just turns and walks out, closing the door behind her.

"That was a bit harsh, don't you think?" I don't know why I expect to be on the right side of his stupid ice wall, but I do. And surprisingly, I am, because his expression is filled with concern and care when he turns to face me.

"She crossed a line. Besides, she knows I love her. My being pissed at her changes nothing." His hands reach up to rub my shoulders and arms. "Are you okay?"

"I'm fine." I shrug. "I don't think any of this was really about me." He smirks. "Just your money-grubbing sister."

"That gold-digging whore." I laugh. "Incidentally, I couldn't quite follow why searching for a sugar daddy would have led me straight to this shithole. Unless, of course, I was just slumming it here with you until I locked in a better prospect." Then it hits me. "Wait. Is that what happened to you before? You were with someone and she left you for a guy with more money?"

"That's not exactly what went down; although he's a pilot, so I'm sure he's doing pretty well for himself." His hand glides down my arm to land in my palm. "Come sit with me."

In an instant, mini explosions blast off in in the pit of my stomach warning me not to go any further. "Why?"

He smiles, but his eyes don't. "Because. It's time I tell you some things."

I shake my head. "No. Please. You don't owe me any explanations."

His hand gently tugs mine to follow him to the bed. "I know that. I want to tell you." He glances back at me over his shoulder. "It's nothing scary, Quinn. I promise."

Only his scary and my scary probably aren't the same thing. But that's not even why I don't want to know. I don't want to hear his story because then I'll have to tell him mine. And I'm nowhere near ready to.

"No. I'm serious, Riker. Whatever shit you have buried in your past, leave it there. Because that's where I'm keeping all of mine. I don't want to dig it up. Not even for you."

Riker watches me like he's contemplating his next move. He grinds his jaw back and forth, and I know he's carefully choosing his response. At last, he nods. "Alright. No digging tonight. But I am going to get back in that bed with you and make up for the speed sex we had earlier. I know I can find more satisfying things to do to you before the night is over."

"Now this is a conversation I could get into." Except we both know there won't be any talking once we hit that mattress, which is fine by me. Actually, after all the talking I did tonight, it's probably a good thing if I limit my mouth to other activities for a while.

CHAPTER TWELVE

RIKER

"Are you still mad at me?" Sid's standing next to Nox's stall door. I've barely been here three minutes. I actually expected her to show up sooner.

"No." I scoop the soggy strands of hay out of his waterer and snort at him in disgust. He's sloppy as all get out.

"Are you sure? You kinda look like you might still be mad." She's rubbing the crease between her brows with her fingers. I hate when she stresses over stuff she doesn't need to.

"I'm pissed because it's seven a.m. and I'm in here cleaning slimy crud out of a water bowl and picking up his nighttime shit like I'm his little bitch. Because I am. Every day. For the rest of my life. Or at least his." And because Nox is smarter than most humans, he whips his tail just right to catch me straight across my face.

"You know, you really shouldn't insult him when he can hear you," Sid says, pointing out the obvious.

"And you should keep some of your dialogue internal," I shoot back.

"I'm guessing you're referring more to last night and less to just now?" She's still holding onto the stall door, but she's leaning back as if she's attempting to achieve a safer distance between us.

"You had no business saying half the shit you said." I finish up with Nox and walk past Sid into the aisle.

"I know that. And I said I'm sorry like a hundred times." She has a flare for exaggerating. And she knows it. "Okay, maybe like five. Whatever. I've said I was sorry. What else do you want?"

I turn to face her full on. "I want you to be okay with this. I want you to stop worrying. And I want you to be nice to her. She's not who you think she is."

She bites her lip, presumably fighting the urge to argue. "Fine. I'll do all of those. Just tell me one thing."

"What?"

"Are you sure she's who *you* think she is?"

I can't answer that. Sid knows I can't. It's why she asked it.

"She makes me happy, Sid. Whoever else she is, she's someone who makes me *happy*. And that's all I need to know right now."

• • • •

QUINN

"You look guilty. What did you do?" Kirsten hands me a cup of hot tea alongside her morning accusations.

"Nothing you want me to tell you about with your five-year-old sitting three feet away." It's an open-ended question and I'm well within my rights to give an equally unresolved answer. Even if I am misleading her slightly by sort of insinuating that I feel somehow guilty for my various sexual escapades, which is clearly not the case. Nevertheless, she wouldn't want me talking about Levi in front of Sophie either, so I'm not exactly being dishonest. Merely crafty in the interest of self-preservation. Which telling her what I told Sid and Riker last night would not be. Because she'd kill me if she knew.

Regardless, she's right. I do feel guilty. And not just because of all the personal stuff I shared on her behalf last night. It's all the personal stuff I chose to omit when the time came for one-on-one sharing with Riker.

Kirsten's still giving me a dirty look, and I'm pretty sure she's racking her brain of every heinous sexual act she's ever seen or heard about and wondering if I enacted it. I'm quite sure I haven't. I'm horny, and I have a lot of sex these days, but it's pretty basic stuff. Fun stuff. But nothing that would get me invited to a BDSM party anytime soon.

"Would you stop staring at me? Sophie's going to start thinking there's something wrong with me the way you keep glaring at me like I have a rainbow bursting out of my forehead."

She brings her own tea mug to her lips and pauses. "There *is* something wrong with you." Then she takes a drink, and I know damn well she timed it that way so I wouldn't see her smile.

"Ha ha." I decide to pass on returning the insult and instead count the previous secret-spilling as my silent retaliation. "Anyway, what do you two lovelies have planned for today?"

Kirsten tilts her head like I should already know the answer. And she's probably right, but I don't even know what day it is, so I can hardly keep track of what she's doing with it. "Well, it's Tuesday." *Tuesday. That sounds right.* "So, Sophie has school today."

I nod, putting it all together again. "That's a Tuesday and Thursday thing, right?"

"Yes. It's been a Tuesday and Thursday thing since you got here. Almost four months ago." She walks around the counter to clear Sophie's dishes. Sophie's been watching us over her empty cereal bowl for the last few minutes. Sometimes I wonder what goes on inside her head. She's super quiet. A lot like me. And that makes me both sad and worried for her. It shouldn't. She's not me. But it does. Because she has all kinds of potential to turn out like me. And none of us want that.

"Hey, Soph. What sort of stuff are the kids doing in school these days?" I prop myself onto my elbows right beside her at the breakfast bar.

"I learned to say the whole alphabet. And I know a song about all the colors of the rainbow. Want to hear it?" Her big blue eyes are gleaming with excitement, and a sharp pain ricochets straight through my heart. I'm the shittiest aunt ever. I can't even recall the last time I had a real conversation with her.

"I would love to hear it."

Kirsten cuts in between us to usher her out of her seat. "It will have to wait until this afternoon. Come on, kiddo. Time to get your shoes on."

"Yes, Mama." Disappointed, Sophie walks off with a noticeable slump to her shoulders.

"I'm a crapshoot for an aunt. You should trade me in and get your kid a better one." I plop into her now vacant seat at the counter, the same bummer slump in my posture.

"I would, but the market's bad right now. No way I can get out of keeping you without taking a major hit." Kirsten smirks. "Besides. Even if I got her another aunt, you'd still be her godmother. And there's no trading out on that gig."

"What? You didn't change that? Appoint someone new?"

She looks at me like I'm the crazy one. The irony here is priceless, but, apparently, I'm the only one aware of it. "Why would I appoint someone new? You're my sister. You were there when Sophie was born. You were the second person to ever hold her. The only one who could get her to stop crying when she was teething, and the last person to leave when she was admitted to the hospital with an allergic reaction so bad I thought she might die."

"All of that was a long time ago. Think of everything I missed in the meantime. I'm like a stranger to her now." Three years is a long time when you've only been around for five.

"Don't be ridiculous, Quinn. She loves you. You love her. Time hasn't changed that. Even if it's changed you." She pulls me in for a hug, and we're not huggers, so this is a big deal. "Now more than ever, I know without a doubt that you, and only you, are the person I would trust with my daughter's life. If ever there was a day that I wasn't here to be her mother anymore, I would find peace in knowing she still had you."

"Kirsten." I have to take a deep breath and swallow several times to push back down the emotions she so skillfully wrung to the surface. "I would fuck up your kid faster than they could give you entry to heaven. So just do whatever you have to, to stick around and finish the job yourself."

She pinches my side and laughs, but she's wiping her eyes with the palm of her free hand. "Deal."

Sophie comes back, shoes on and backpack in hand. And just in the nick of time. Who knows what other depressing sort of conversations Kirsten and I would have started without her presence to remind us that they were running late for school.

After a round of goodbye waves, they're both out the door and I'm left sitting alone in the kitchen.

I'm about to get up when my phone rings and my heart drops. My phone hardly ever rings. When it does, it's usually Devyn. And I'm not ready for more bad news just yet.

I bring it out of my pocket to send the call to voicemail when I see the name.

It's not Devyn.

It's Riker.

Again.

"Am I going to need to assign you your own ringtone? Like, will you be calling me often enough that it would be handy?" There's a reason barely anyone calls me. I have zero phone etiquette. Just never saw the point in starting the conversation with "hello." I mean, you're calling me. As far as I'm concerned, the conversation opens when my phone rings.

"Yes. And I want a good one. And don't think I won't test that shit out and call you when I'm sitting next to you just to hear what plays." He's completely serious. And my belly does a weird flip-flop thing. He does that to me. He's not supposed to . . . but he does.

"Fine. But I'll have to put some thought into it now. Jeez. Talk about pressure." I even roll my eyes. Just because I believe in following through.

"Good. I wouldn't want you to just pick the first song that comes along." He chuckles, and the sound sends a sea of goosebumps down my body. "Anyway, since everyone pretty much knows about us . . . what there is to know, at least, how do you feel about doing something *not* inside my apartment tonight?"

I pick at a crusty, dried piece of frosted flake that has glued itself to Kirsten's kitchen counter. "You mean like on the rooftop terrace? I don't know, it's kind of overcast. I'm not sure I'd be into that in the rain."

"No. I mean, like, out. Away from my place. With clothes."

I stop what I'm doing. Things just got serious. So it's clearly time to deflect. "With clothes? That doesn't sound like much fun."

"I'm going to take that as a yes." He would.

"I'm going to take *that* as a refusal to accept no," I mumble. I don't know why. I'm actually pretty excited. In spite of myself.

"Take it however you like. I'm coming over at seven. Be ready. And dressed." He hangs up before I can say anything else. Like, "don't come to my sister's house." Or . . . no, that first one would have pretty much covered it.

Since Nate left for work sometime before I even woke up this morning, I abandon the greater part of the house and head downstairs to my own little sanctuary, where I spend the day with Harley curled up at my feet and laptop propped up over my knees while I work out of bed. I love what I do. Maybe love is a strong word. I find it satisfying. Redeeming, even. And I need that. I need things that grant me some sort of redemption for the things I've done. I can't say that out loud. Not in front of Kirsten. Or Devyn. Or even my parents; although, I think there are days they wonder about the girl they raised and how it happened that she vanished right before their eyes. But not saying it to any of them doesn't keep me from feeling it. And it doesn't keep me from hoping against all hope that someday, just maybe, I'll be able to give back what I took.

The day takes turns flying by and moving slow as molasses. Somewhere along the way, Kirsten comes down and insists I come out of my cave for a meal, and I wind up sharing some celery and peanut butter with Sophie while she sings me her rainbow song. Then I creep back downstairs for the simple solitude my soul craves so much of the time.

I get so involved in working, I don't notice when time switches back into flying mode, and before I know it, six thirty has rolled around and I'm still sitting on my bed in the same clothes I wore last night. My computer nearly meets an untimely end as it almost falls from the bed after I jump up in a panic. I catch it just in time and then hurry over to put it back in the safe zone (aka, my desk), before I run for the shower.

Even in record time, I'm not getting ready in under thirty minutes, and my level of anxiety gradually climbs. When I hear the doorbell at seven, I'm still rushing around my room in my underwear.

Ten minutes later and I'm finally taking the steps two at a time to reach the main level, where I find Kirsten and Riker sitting casually in the formal living room having what appears to be a fairly pleasant conversation.

My sister sees me first. "You didn't tell me you had a date tonight."

I shrug. "Is it a date? I don't know. Are we calling it that?" I glance over at Riker, expecting him to follow my lead and downplay the whole thing.

"Yes. We're calling it that." So much for downplaying. Then he makes matters worse by getting up from the couch and walking straight across the room to where I'm standing. "You look beautiful, by the way." He pauses a second, then mumbles "Screw it" and kisses me. Right there. In front of my sister. And I melt, completely forgetting where we are.

Until I hear Nate's voice. "Shep?"

Riker breaks away instantly. As soon as he sees Nate, his hand extends to him. "Hey, man. It's been a long time."

Nate shakes his hand longer than necessary, but he's smiling, so I'm assuming everything is okay. "It has been a while." He laughs. "So, you're Quinn's mystery man. Makes sense now. You guys meeting out at the ranch." He finally lets go of Riker, who seems oddly interested in the floor.

"Yeah. I guess it would."

Meanwhile, Kirsten and I have both been flipping our heads back and forth as if we've been watching a Ping-Pong match. And while I could continue watching to see how this plays out, Kirsten isn't nearly that patient. "You two know each other?"

Nate nods. "Oh, yeah. We go way back. What? Third grade?"

"Sounds about right." Riker's keeping things more at eye level now, although he's still not looking at me.

"How crazy." Kirsten's tone shifts gears. "Well, you two should get going. Don't want to keep you from your date any longer." She's practically pushing us out the door, and I know it's just so she can pump Nate for more backstory the second we leave. I'm sure she's assuming I'm eager to do the same thing. Only I'm not. Because I got more backstory than I bargained for the second Nate saw Riker and called him "Shep."

We're not even touching while we walk out to his truck. It's ridiculous, because he looks amazing in his worn and slightly ripped jeans and fitted button-up shirt. He's got the top buttons undone, revealing his usual white t-shirt, and the sleeves are rolled up to just below his elbows, showing off his tattoos. Normally, I'd be all over him.

"He called you Shep."

Riker nods. "He did. Most people I went to school with do."

We reach his truck and stop.

"You're James Shepherdson." I'm not asking. I already know he is. Frankly, I'm a little embarrassed I didn't realize it sooner. Of course, I wouldn't have. I didn't want to know.

"Riker's my middle name. I've always used it. I wasn't hiding this from you." He sounds worried, and I get now why he was so busy studying the tile work in my sister's living room. He's wondering how I'll react.

"You can't hide something I deliberately ask you not to show." After all, I'm the one who refused to listen last night when he wanted to talk. Clearly, this was on the list of things he wanted to share.

He turns toward me, drawing me to him until I have no choice but to look him square in the eyes. "When I first told you this thing between us couldn't be more, I meant it. I never had any intention of telling you about my past. I was happy going with the fact that you didn't need anything from me in the present, and I was depending on you never expecting anything from me in the future. Because when you showed up, I didn't have one. All I had was a fucked-up past. And a dead-end present." He brushes his thumb softly over my cheek. "And now? Fuck. I don't know what now. All I know is I don't feel like I did before that day I first saw you. My past is still fucked up. But my present is changing. And maybe that means the future is something I can dare to think about again."

I shake my head. I don't mean to. The second I do, a darkness rolls over his eyes and I know I've hurt him. It's the last thing I'm trying to do. The opposite of what I want. I take his face in both my hands and kiss him. Deeply. And so long that I'm out of breath when I finally speak. "I'm not saying no to you, Riker. I'm saying I can't say yes." The quiver in my own voice shocks me.

"So say maybe." His deep voice is husky and slightly strained. This is getting to him as well.

"I can't. I want to. I just can't." I wrap my arms around him and rest my head against his chest. "I'm not staying, Riker. I have to go back home in August."

"For good?"

I nuzzle my face into his shirt and nod. "I have some things to take care of there. Things I knew I would have to do long before I met you. I just didn't know when."

His chin comes down to rest beside my ear. "Is this some of the stuff you didn't want to dig up last night?"

"I still don't. Can't we just take the next two months and spend as much or as little of it together as we want? Can't that be enough?"

He sighs and his breath moves through my hair until it touches my skin with its warmth. "No. It's not enough." He moves back, taking me from the safe spot I'd carved out for myself on his chest. "But I'll take it." He kisses my forehead. Then the tip of my nose. "I'll take whatever you're willing to give me for however long you give it." He doesn't have to move in for my mouth because I'm already reaching for his, my lips open and starving for him as if it's been weeks since I've kissed him, not minutes.

When we finally separate, I'm not sure how long we've been standing in my sister's driveway anymore, and I'm fairly certain she's spying on us from the kitchen window.

"We should probably get out of here," I say. "Provided you still want to take me on this date thing."

"Are you kidding? For the next two months, this date thing is going to be the norm. I'm going to cram everything I can possibly think of into every second between now and August." He takes my hand and leads me to the passenger side of his truck.

"Why? What was wrong with how we've done things up until now?"

He opens the door for me and even helps me up. I'd almost forgotten guys in pick-up trucks did that. Then he hurries around to the driver's side and gets in as well.

"Nothing. Nothing was wrong with it. And we'll still be keeping that stuff the same. We're just adding to it. Because when you leave here, I don't want to just be the guy you were screwing in North Carolina."

My face snaps to his, and I quirk up an eyebrow. "Who do you want to be?"

He just starts up the truck and grins like he's about to get me good. "I'm not telling you. But you'll figure it out when I'm no longer just the guy you're screwing in North Carolina."

"What, are you planning on taking me over state lines and screwing me there too?" I'm doing it again. Using stupid jokes to avoid the stuff that scares me. The feelings. Well, it's not the feelings that scare me, really. It's finding out whether or not I actually have any. And finding out I have them is not what terrifies me. It's finding out I don't. Because if I can't feel something for him, I'll never feel anything for anyone. It's an ugly truth I live with day in and day out, but it seems magnified now, and harder to bear with every day Riker continues to be in my life.

He doesn't say much of anything the entire drive, just holds my hand, rubbing the top of it with the inside of his thumb. It's such a simple gesture, and yet it's a gesture he's making for no other reason than that he wants to, which sort of takes it from simple to significant.

"Are you going to tell me where we're going?"

"Nope."

I'm not particularly fond of surprises. They rarely seem to work out for me. "Can you at least tell me if I'm dressed appropriately?" I went with jeans this time. And the boots he was so eager to show his disdain for the first time we met.

"Nope."

"You're not giving up anything, are you? Not one itty bitty clue, even?"

He briefly takes his eyes off the road to flash me a satisfied smirk. "Nope."

"Fine." My inner two-year-old is tempted to yank my hand from his out of spite, but then I'd have to come cowering back a second later, my fingers creeping past his palm to lock in with his. Pouting wouldn't be worth the humiliation.

Thankfully, it isn't much longer before he turns down a small dirt road leading away from the main drag. Shortly after, a house becomes visible at the end of it.

"What is this place?"

"It's the Butterfly Inn. Don't worry, we're not staying the night." He parks the truck and kills the engine. "We're just here for their chocolate fondue. They have other food, too, obviously, but why ruin a perfectly good appetite with real food when we can go straight for dessert?"

I slant my eyes at him. "Who are you? And what woman has been telling you all of our secrets?"

"I grew up with a sister, remember?" He winks and tugs my hand to slide me across the seats to follow him out of the driver's side door, before either of us can dwell on the part where his sister is no longer here.

Still holding hands, we walk up to the most charming cottage-style house I've ever seen. "You know, it's kind of funny they call you Shep."

He peers at me out of the corner of his eye. "Oh, yeah? Why's that?"

"Because Quinn is short for my last name as well." Then, before he can ask me what it is, I reach for the door handle and hurry inside where I'm welcomed with a wealth of new conversation topics, from the adorable décor to the heavenly scents wafting toward us from the dining room.

CHAPTER THIRTEEN

RIKER

Time is passing too quickly, and I don't know how to stop it. Two weeks. Two weeks is all I have left, and it isn't nearly enough.

I stroke her hair and watch her sleep, her head on my bare chest, her warm breath sweeping over my skin. I don't want to give this up. I don't want to give *her* up. But she's still leaving. It doesn't matter how often I try to bring up staying, she won't talk about it and she won't tell me why. And I know it's killing her. Whatever it is. It's eating away at her. Taking small pieces of her soul and destroying them with every day that passes us by.

Several times I've wound up standing on Kirsten's doorstep, fully prepared to demand a fucking explanation for Quinn's secretive behavior. And every time I've turned back and left without ever ringing the doorbell. Because those secrets aren't Kirsten's to tell. And they aren't mine to know. Not until Quinn decides they are.

She moans in her sleep, and my gaze drops to her mouth. She's smiling. And I'm smiling. It's been weeks since she had a nightmare. Weeks since she cried in her sleep or woke up screaming. When she first started staying over it happened all the time. Now, even if I can't keep her nightmares away forever, I can at least hold onto the fact that she felt safe in my arms for a while. She found peace with me. The same peace I found with her. I just wish she would let me hold her longer.

She moves her feet, a sign I recognize now as the beginning of her waking up. I like that. Knowing these things about her. I want to know more. I want to know them all.

I press my lips to the top of her head, and she grins without even opening her eyes.

"Move in with me."

Her lids fly open so fast I'm surprised they didn't disappear in their sockets. "What?"

"Until you leave. Stay here with me. What's the point of going back and forth every day? You sleep here every night anyway. Why bother going to Kirsten's just to shower and change?" I'm hoping if I make it sound like it's motivated by a desire to be more practical as opposed to a desire to just be with her *more*, she'll actually go for it.

"I don't just change clothes when I go back there, you know. I have a job, for example." She lifts herself up on my chest, resting on her arms to face me.

"Yeah. On your laptop. Pretty sure those can go anywhere you do."

She peers around the room skeptically. "Do you even have internet here?"

"Yes, I have internet. I run a business, too, you know." Lately I've even been something one could consider proactive in that arena, doing more than just the basics required to keep my father and grandfather's empire afloat.

She rolls onto her side and scans the whole apartment. "With what? There isn't a single electric device in this entire place. You don't even have a freaking TV."

"I have an office. It's just not connected to the apartment. It's on the other side of the house. Used to be the third garage. In fact, there's a spare desk in there you could use." I trace down the middle of her exposed back. I want to memorize it—the way her skin feels against mine. The way her body moves under my touch. Every curve. Every freckle. Every scar. I want to brand them into my mind forever so I can keep her with me even when she's gone.

"You're serious about this. You want me to move in with you. A step which usually occurs when a couple is moving forward, making a commitment. Not when they're about to say goodbye." She's spelling it out for me again. Reminding me. She does that a lot. Honestly, I think she does it for herself.

"Yes. I'm serious. And why does it have to represent anything? Why can't it just be a fun way to spend two weeks? Not to mention, I could save some gas money not having to pick you up for our nightly outings." As soon as I stop talking, I realize that saving the environment with less exhaust pollution would have been a more reasonable argument. Especially considering she's been well aware of my abundant bank account ever since Nate outed me in his living room. The fifty cents it costs to cover the trip back and forth every day is hardly hurting me.

"You're weird." She smirks like she's made a joke only she knows is funny. "But I'm not going to let that stop me. I'll pack up my stuff and bring it over here in a bit."

It's taking all I've got not to shoot straight to my feet and start jumping up and down on my bed like a five-year-old. "Cool. That works for me."

· · · ·

QUINN

I've lost my ever-loving mind. Clearly. Why else would I agree to move in with Riker? Unless I've lost it. Every last little brain cell. Gone. Poof. Now I'm but one pair of ruby-red slippers away from representing the entire cast of *The Wizard of Oz,* because the second I break this news to my sister, I'll even have my very own good witch, all sparkling and shit, waving her wand to help matters along whether I'm ready for the trip or not.

"Hey, Kirsten." Took me almost ten minutes of walking around this giant-ass house to locate her in the laundry room.

"There you are. I went downstairs looking for you earlier, but you weren't back yet." She's busy folding the laundry straight out of the dryer. I wish I was organized like she is. I'm lucky if my clothes make it out of the laundry basket and into my dresser before I wear them and they land back in the hamper.

"Oh, did you need something?" I'm stalling. I know what she needed. To have her curiosities satisfied. She checks on me almost every morning now to find out what romantic date thing Riker cooked up the night before. And he's been on a roll, so the stories have been good.

"Just wanted to hear about last night." She smiles. As much as she hated Riker at first, I think she might be a little too enamored with him now. But I get it. I was enamored with Nate, too, when I first saw how happy he made my sister. Especially after I'd seen what she went through losing Levi. If Nate had the power to put light back into my sister's beautiful green eyes, he was a hero in my book. So I can see why Riker is riding high on a pedestal these days with Kirsten.

"I'm not sure you would have liked last night's outing. It was very outdoorsy." Not my sister's speed at all.

"Hmm. Well, you're into that sort of stuff, so I'm still liking it. What did you guys do?" Her voice echoes slightly as she's headfirst in the dryer searching for the missing socks to the two lonely ones she's holding.

"We went for a drive down the beach. Then he made a fire and we roasted marshmallows and made s'mores while Harley ran around chasing the waves in the dark. After, he lowered the tailgate and loaded the back of the pick-up with blankets and pillows he had crammed in the back seat, and we curled up in them and watched the stars." I sigh. Yes. An actual sigh.

So does Kirsten. "Aw. How cute is he?"

"I know." My eyes bug out dramatically. "And freaking smart too. You know he gave me an entire astronomy lesson while we were lying there. I swear, he surprises me all the time."

"He's really trying hard."

I frown. "What do you mean?"

She gives up on the socks and closes the dryer. "You know exactly what I mean. That man is in love with you. He doesn't want you to leave, and he's pulling out all the stops to convince you to stay."

"Don't say that. He's not in love with me. That's not even possible. Not when there's so much he doesn't know about me." I turn away and start pacing in the cramped laundry room. It's not an ideal space for pacing, but I'm antsy. "Anyway, it doesn't matter what he wants. Or even what I want. I can't stay. You know that."

Kirsten places her laundry basket filled with neatly folded clothes onto the dryer, and I know she's settling in to give me a good speech.

"First of all, I don't care what you think he doesn't know, Riker Shepherdson can see right to your core. I see it in his eyes every time he looks at you. So save me this bullshit about how he can't love you because he doesn't know about your past. Who gives a fuck about who you were? He's in love with you *now*." Her hands land on her hips, and I don't bother to interrupt because she's only just getting started. "Second, it always matters what you want. Even when you can't have it. It still matters. Because you matter. You matter to me. You matter to Mom and Dad. Nate. Sophie. Devyn. And you sure as hell matter to Riker. It's about damn time you start to matter to yourself." She takes a breath, and I brace myself for "third of all," since I'm pretty sure it's going to knock me the fuck out.

"Lastly, don't you dare let this thing with Jackson's family be the reason you lose Riker. Fine. You have to go home. And fine. You have no idea for how long. And fucking fine, you don't have a clue what will happen before it's all over and done with. But none of that means you have to give up the one thing that has made you smile, really, truly, genuinely smile, in over three years. It just means you'll have to put forth a little more effort, show a little more courage, and have a little more trust . . . in *him* . . . to keep it."

I'm not pacing anymore. I'm barely even standing. I'm just leaning against the doorframe hoping my knees don't buckle and I end up a puddle on the ground weeping like a baby. She hit me good. Right in all the scary shit. I knew she would. Kirsten always does. She's a good sister like that.

"He wants me to move in," I mumble.

She grabs her basket and nods. "Good. I'll help you pack." Then she comes at me, practically pushing me through the door with her load of laundry.

"You do understand that it'll only be for two weeks, right?" I stumble slightly, still being moved along by the basket rammed into my lower back.

"I understand that you need to go downstairs and start emptying your closet." She stops, straightening her arms and letting the laundry basket dangle over her thighs. "Please, Quinn. Just go and get packed. Don't take the time to think it through. Just do it. I promise you, it won't be a mistake. He's not going to hurt you. You know that, right?" Her earlier conviction is turning to concern, and I'm not sure if I feel better or worse about it.

"I do know that." I bite the inside of my lip, trying not to let fear and guilt get the best of me. "But what if I hurt him?"

"That's a risk he's willing to take." She holds my stare for as long as I need her to. Until I know she's right. Until I believe that everything will work out. Not just for me, but for Riker as well. Then I turn and go downstairs and pack. Just like she instructed me to.

Even though I showed up here with everything I own in the world, it takes all of two hours before the downstairs game room looks like I never even lived in it. To make matters even more depressing, it only takes one trip with Kirsten's little car to get all of my stuff moved over to Riker's.

He's not here when we pull up, but the door's never locked anyway and I've been letting myself in for weeks now, so today is no different.

"This is . . . cozy." I'm sure it's the nicest thing Kirsten could think to say. And she can't say anything bad since she doesn't want me to come back home with her.

"It's Riker." I figured this out a while back. One of the nights I was too wired to sleep, I just laid here in the dark, scanning the room over and over again until I started to really see what I was looking at. Everything in this place is something he has repurposed in some way. The old wicker chairs. The turned over milk crate. I'm sincerely hoping the mattress is new, but I'm not asking for confirmation on this because I may not get the answer I'm looking for. Then there's the dingy paint and water-damaged ceilings, and a wardrobe that consists of clothes that are so old they are falling apart and flannel shirts he buys in five-packs at Walmart, and only when he absolutely has to.

Riker grew up with everything he could possibly want or need. Ever. Then he lost what couldn't be bought and realized *things* mean nothing. It's one of the qualities I like best about him. So when I walk in this apartment, I never see the shitty-looking sheets or the busted blinds that probably cost five dollars at Home Depot to replace. I see him. I see what he places value on. And judging by the new dog bed in the corner and the Post-It on his dresser marked "starving for some chick clothes," it's me.

Of course, these things go unnoticed by my sister, her nose crinkled as she stares at me, inspecting the dopey-ass grin I can feel on my face.

"Really? The sight of this place makes you *that* happy?" She shakes her head, smirking. "Alright. Let's get you moved in here." She drops the box she's holding onto the floor along the wall and heads back to the car. We go back and forth maybe five times between the two of us, and then it's done. My stuff and I are here. To stay. For now.

"So how about I take you to lunch to celebrate your new living situation?"

I peer over at the fridge, which is likely empty. "I think that's a wonderful idea. But I'm buying. It's the least I can do after you helped me move." And, you know, everything else.

"Deal." She leads the way back to the driveway, and I say a quick goodbye to Harley before I close the door behind me. I don't even feel weird about leaving him here. Probably because he looked so comfortable lying there in his brand-new bed.

After two hours of eating every appetizer on the menu and finishing the ordeal off with a shared death by chocolate cake, Kirsten drops me back at Riker's and then takes off to pick up Sophie from summer camp.

Since I've yet to even power up my computer today, I take my laptop and wander around to the other side of the house in search of the mysterious office. When I find it, it's actually locked, but the key is hanging from a hook beside the door. Don't ask me where the logic is in this, but I'm not complaining since I want in and I need the key.

Unlike the apartment, everything in here is brand new. Top-notch computers and printers. Fancy desks and leather chairs. There's even a really nice sofa in here. And, of course, a lovely corner desk all cleared out and waiting for my itty-bitty laptop. It's not really itty bitty. Just kinda looks that way now in contrast to everything else in here.

The chair is about the most comfortable thing I've ever sat in, and I have half a mind to tell Riker he'll be sleeping alone on that crappy old mattress from here on out, but then I settle in long enough to feel the cool leather against my skin and decide being flesh on flesh with Riker really is the more appealing way to go.

Once I get over the initial shock of being in an actual office, I get to work. I'm so focused on what I'm doing, I don't even realize how long I've been in here until I hear the creak of the door open, and the scent of Riker's shower soap fills the room with the breeze sweeping in from the ocean.

"This works," he says, sounding very satisfied with himself. "It really does." He comes over and kisses the top of my head. "Yes. I like it. Coming home. Finding you. Makes me want to come home more."

I want to tell him not to say stuff like that. To remind him of my impending departure. Not to get used to this. But I don't.

"Thank you for Harley's new bed. He really likes it. And the note on the dresser was cute."

He spins my chair all the way around to face him. "You're welcome. And I hope you don't mind, but I fed the beast since you didn't. All the clothes from the black duffle bag are now in the dresser. And not that I was going through your underwear or anything, but I may have held onto a few pieces I wouldn't mind seeing you in later tonight."

"Is that so?"

He leans in, a playful grin flashing across his lips right before he comes in to kiss me.

"How much longer before you're finished here?" he murmurs, still inches from my face.

"Oh, I was done the second you walked in. Who can concentrate on anything work related when you're in the room?" I laugh at myself. I don't say stuff like this. Even if I do think it. A lot. But I don't actually say it. Out loud.

"Well, Miss Quinn. I do believe you're blushing. Unless, of course, you're just getting hot and bothered thinking about what I'm going to do to you later." Oh my God. Why is he so much better at this than I am? I could have said the same damn thing and it would have sounded cheesy as hell. He says anything with my name in it and the words "I", "do," and "you," and I'm ready to melt right out of my clothes and into his arms.

"Does that mean we're staying in tonight?" I ask hopefully. Not that I haven't enjoyed all the ways he's found to entertain me night after night in this town. It's just that I'm starting to feel a little anxious about leaving. And I know in the end, it won't be any of the restaurants, or sights, or even romantic activities I'll miss. It'll just be him.

"It does." His arms wrap around me without warning, hoisting me up out of the chair and over his shoulder.

"What the hell are you doing now?" I start smacking his ass. Because it's a damn fine ass and it's right there for the smacking.

"Taking you home and giving you a little lesson in moving in. Just dropping boxes full of your shit randomly around my place isn't going to cut it." He gives me a good whack as well. "Now stop spanking me, crazy ass."

"Fine." I stop beating on him and resolve to simply cup each perfectly sculpted butt cheek with my hands while he walks me from one side of the house to the other, dangling headfirst over his shoulder the entire way.

"You don't think this is a little silly?" I ask, handing him books out of my box and watching him stack them on top of his shelf next to the front door. "Moving in. For two weeks? It's not like I'm going to be doing a lot of reading." I shoot him a dirty look. "I better *not* be doing a lot of reading."

He chuckles. The sweet chuckle. I kinda hate it. Because I kinda love it. And then I wonder who else gets to hear it. Secretly, I hope he keeps it just for me, but I'm guessing Sidney's heard this one too.

"No, I have no intention of giving you reading time," he assures me as he takes the last of my paperbacks and stacks them alongside the others. "I just like seeing your stuff in my place." Then he kisses me flush on the lips. Not long. Just a second or two to distract me from seeing it. But I do anyway. And not just now.

I see it more and more clearly every day. This part of him. The part he wants to give me. Only I can never take it from him. Because people like me don't deserve a heart like Riker Shepherdson has. In spite of what my sister would like me to believe, when it comes to Riker, what I want doesn't matter.

He sits down next to me on the floor and tugs over another load. "Where do you want these?"

He's holding two picture frames in his hand, and I realize in a panic that one of the boxes I keep permanently sealed is now open.

"Put those back," I snap, practically lunging for the cardboard flaps to close them again.

"Whoa." He hurries out of my path but makes no effort to return the frames he already has in his possession. "Why do I feel like maybe you should have marked this one Pandora's box instead of just 'Pics'?"

I try to snatch the pictures from him, but he moves too fast. "I'm not in the mood for smartass comebacks, Riker. Just put those back. Now." I'm not even pissed. I'm something. Scared. I'm scared. That box has been sealed for a long time. And for good reason. I'm not ready to face what's in it. I may never be ready.

Slowly, he moves the frames face down onto the closed box. "He's the reason you don't ride anymore. The reason you never talk about horses. Even though you clearly feel more at home in a barn than you do anywhere else."

"I don't want to talk about it." I slide the pictures in through the crack without looking at them.

"I know you don't. You never want to talk about anything too personal. Do you really think that it keeps me at some sort of a distance? That not talking about it somehow means I don't know? I know, Quinn. I'm not a fucking idiot." He leans his head back against the wall. He's not even mad at me. Just hurt. Which makes me mad at myself.

"Whatever you think you know . . . just forget it." I get to my feet and pick up the box to move it. Somewhere. I don't even know where. I just want it gone.

"Forget it." He laughs dryly. "Sure. I'll forget." His head drops back to catch my gaze again. "I'll forget the scars I've seen on your body. And I'll forget the way you scream in your sleep sometimes as if you're being ripped to pieces by some monster. Hell, maybe I'll even forget that look in your eyes when you wake up and think that I'm him. Or the one after . . . when you realize I'm not."

It's like he's just knocked the wind out of me. Months it's been. Months of lying beside him naked and never once truly exposing myself. Or, at least, that's the delusion I'd created for myself. Turns out he's seen me all along. All of me. Everything I thought was carefully hidden, right there in plain sight.

"I'm . . . sorry." It's all I've got. That and an instinct to bolt. Right now. "I shouldn't be here. You shouldn't have to . . . I shouldn't be here." It's like I'm on autopilot as my legs start marching for the door, still holding the same disgusting box that started all of this.

Behind me, Riker scrambles to his feet, and I move faster. But he beats me to the door anyway. His hand flies out over my shoulder to hold it shut just as my hand struggles to reach the handle while still balancing the box in the other.

He doesn't even say anything. Just takes the box from me and places it on the floor where he pushes it off into the corner. Then he cups my face with both hands, cradling my cheeks in his palms, and stares me down. Hard. Long. Unwavering. And I know. He's not letting me go. Not today. Not ever.

CHAPTER FOURTEEN

RIKER

Fuck me. Fuck me and my stupid mouth. Why did I have to push her? Now she's crying and I can't even help because she won't fucking tell me where the darkness hides or why it keeps coming back for her. And it always comes back for her.

I would give anything to protect her from it. Anything. Only this time I'm the asshole who woke it up and I've got nothing to fight it with.

So I hold her. I keep her shaking, sobbing body pressed to mine, and I'm reminded over and over just how fragile she is. She's strong, but she's broken. And the pieces that are left are hardly holding onto one another. All I've got is my love for her to put them back together, but she won't take it.

"Breathe, baby. Please, just . . . breathe." I kiss the top of her head. The side of it. Her forehead. Anywhere my lips can reach her. "I'm an asshole. I shouldn't have gone through your stuff. You have every right to your privacy." I stroke her back, my fingers moving through her soft, thick hair. Suddenly it feels like the most solid thing about her. Like she's dissolving right here in my arms. It scares me. "Keep your secrets. All of them. Just let me keep *you*."

She still doesn't say anything, but her breathing is getting calmer, and her hands are moving, touching me, holding onto me, because I'm her safe place. And that's all I'll ever need to be.

• • • •

QUINN

We didn't go out tonight. We didn't make love either. We just lay here. Entangled in one another, staring at each other. For hours we've been like this. Not saying anything. I don't think I've ever learned so much about another person without uttering a word.

He's been studying me too. But it's different than before. I don't feel like he's looking for the things I don't want him to know. He's not trying to understand. Just accepting what is. And that means more to me than I could ever tell him.

So I'll tell him what I can. What he wants to know. What I swore I wouldn't share. After he answers one question.

"Why do you hate Nox so much?"

He looks almost startled, as if I yelled it instead of the quiet whisper it actually was. I guess that's what happens when no one says anything for several hours.

"I don't hate Nox." He stretches his arm and adjusts his head a bit.

"Liar." I slide my hand under my cheek for extra cushioning. The pillow's losing its fluff from lying on it this whole time.

"Fine. I hate his four-legged ass." He laughs when he says it, though.

"But why? He's so smart." I don't think I've ever been around a horse like him.

"That's why I hate him." His hand moves up to take a fallen strand of hair out of my face. Sometimes I still find it strange how comfortable I am with him in my space. Like right now as he's tucking the hair behind my ear. It's such a simple thing. I should be doing it myself, but by some miracle I'm okay with him doing it for me. If only I could feel that way about everything.

"You hate a horse because he's smart. That seems like an odd reason. No?" I should drop it. After all, I would want him to if the roles were reversed and I was purposely not answering a question.

"You're right. It's bullshit." He sighs. "I hate Nox because he's a selfish son of a bitch who refused to let me wallow in my own misery when all I wanted was to stay in bed until I died there."

"Oh." Not the response I was expecting.

He grants me half of a smile, and then, even though I can tell it isn't easy for him, he continues, "He wasn't always like this. You know, how he won't let anyone handle him? When my grandfather was alive, he would put kids on him, and he would be just as calm and gentle as a fucking Golden Retriever. Nox loved people. He loved my grandfather. We all did." His gaze drops down to my free hand resting on the mattress near my stomach, and his fingers travel down to interlock with mine. "When he died, it changed Nox. He was still friendly. Just . . . sad. And it only got worse. Then more shit hit the fan, and I wasn't going out there anymore. I just needed a fucking break, you know? Some sort of an escape from everything that had happened. I took off in my truck one morning and didn't stop for two days. When I finally couldn't keep going, I was somewhere in the middle of Nevada. I stopped in some shady little motel, bought a bottle of bourbon, and went straight to bed. Didn't get up for a week straight.

"Then Sid called. Nox wasn't eating. He was destroying everything in sight and had nearly injured three people. Herself included. They'd tried everything. Nothing was working, and the vet insisted he wasn't sick . . . but that he wouldn't last long at the rate he was going." His eyes travel upward to find mine again. "He left me no choice. Just because I wanted to die, didn't mean I was going to let him go with me. So I got back in my truck. Drove another thirty-four hours straight to get home and fed him his supper. Then I spent the night in his stall, and I stood there with him, eye to eye, and I understood. He knew what I was doing. That I was giving up. And he wasn't going to let me. He saved me. And I've fucking hated him for it ever since. Until now."

I feel the pressure on my hand as he squeezes it.

"I'm glad he saved you," I whisper.

"Me too." His soft rumble warms me at the pit of my stomach and spreads up into my chest. "I'm even happier he brought me you."

"You think he knew what he was doing that day?" It seems ridiculous, really. "Think he was trying to save me too?"

But Riker's completely serious. "I do."

I do too. Sometimes I even think it worked.

"My mare's name was Jazz." I know I've changed the topic abruptly, but if I don't just spit it out, I'll never get myself to say it out loud. "She was stunning. Not the same way Nox is. Her beauty was different. Wild."

Riker smiles. "Like you."

A rush of heat floods my cheeks. "More beautiful than me. She was my partner from the time I was seven. My father bought her for me after I'd been barrel racing in junior rodeos for two years on my trainer's horses. He said I'd made my point by then. I wasn't going to be growing out of this horse phase anytime soon, so he figured it was easier to just cave and quit fighting the inevitable." I untwine my fingers from his and crawl out of the bed and over to the corner where the box is now hidden in darkness. When I find the frame I'm looking for, I slip back into bed beside him and hand the picture of Jazz and I over.

"We competed for twelve years. We were really good. At eighteen I joined the WPRA and was competing at a professional level. I had every intention of making a career of it."

Riker's studying the photograph in his hands. "What happened?"

I shrug. "Life. Things came up, things I couldn't avoid or change, and I had to quit."

His eyes are level with mine. "What happened to Jazz?"

I swallow several times. Back-to-back, trying to force down the lump in my throat threatening to suffocate me. Then again, maybe I should let it. "She died. Two years ago. She had a degenerative disease in her joints. All the years of competing took their toll on her and hit with a vengeance a year into what were supposed to be her carefree years of retirement. Treatment only worked temporarily. Eventually, she was carrying all her weight on her front legs and dragging the hind ones. She wasn't able to lie down anymore because she knew she couldn't get back up. She was dropping weight. It was just a matter of time before she collapsed or injured herself." The words are getting harder to find. "I wasn't even there for Jazz at the end. Kirsten had to go for me. She was the one who held her head in her lap while the vet did what he had to do to set her free." Pissed at myself, I wipe my eyes with one harsh swoop of the back of my hand. Riker catches it as it comes back down.

"What are you doing?" he whispers.

"I shouldn't be crying." I sniff loudly and know I sound disgusting. It's good. I should. Nothing about me should be remotely appealing or endearing right now.

Riker frowns. "Why shouldn't you be crying? You lost someone close to you. What, because she wasn't a person that makes it lame to grieve her? I know you don't believe that."

"Of course not." It's the exact opposite. "I shouldn't be crying over her, because I have no right to. She gave her whole life to me. And I let her down when she needed me the most. I don't deserve to grieve her, any more than I deserve to experience even an ounce of the joy a horse can bring you. I lost every right to that life the second I lost her."

"You can't seriously think that." He sits up, and I know he's going to try and set me straight the way he always does. Only it won't work this time. Not with this.

"I do. And nothing you're about to say will change my mind. So don't bother. That's not why I told you."

His expression softens. "Why did you tell me?"

"You asked." I nestle against his chest. "And you deserve to get an answer every once in a while."

His strong arms envelope me, and his leg slides between mine. Sometimes I lie here with him and think how being with him gives new meaning to being wrapped up in someone. Riker's not the center of my universe. He's not my whole world. Or even my guy. But things have changed. We're not the same couple of lost souls desperate to escape our reality and willing to fuck our way out. We're not even the same people we were two months ago when we were just enjoying a casual fun fling.

We're not fucking anymore. Or even having sex. Riker makes love to me now. And every time he does, it feels like he takes a piece of my soul with him and leaves a piece of himself behind with me. I'm afraid if we keep going like this, one day in the near future we'll stop and look at each other and no longer be able to tell one from the other. Too much of me will live inside Riker for me to survive without him after this all comes to a crashing end. And it will end. It has to. Every dream does. And most of mine end with me screaming in agony. Why would this one be any different?

When I wake up the next morning, I'm somewhat taken aback that I am lying here alone. There's a certain amount of irony involved in waking up alone for the first time ever on the first morning that I officially live here.

I'm about to call his name when I hear the thud of a cupboard door closing. He's in the kitchen.

Wrapped in one of the sheets toga style, I drag my feet over the hardwood floor and sleepily wander over to where he is.

"Looking for food you don't keep here?"

He stops mid search of the cupboards above the sink. "Ha! That's where you're wrong. I went to the grocery store yesterday. Bought everything I needed to make you a proper welcome to your new home breakfast, only now I can't find my frying pan." Which he seems to give up on, temporarily at least, to give me a proper welcome to my new home good morning kiss.

"I can think of things I'd enjoy having right now that don't require a pan of any kind," I mumble against his soft lips.

"Hmm?" His hands are already roaming down from my shoulders along my waist until they reach the back of my thighs, gripping them tight and lifting me up onto the kitchen counter. "This along the lines of what you had in mind?" His husky voice breathes into my ear as he nips at my lobe.

But I'm too far gone already to utter even a single syllable. So I grab a handful of his dirty blond hair to hold him steady while I devour his lips with mine and let my tongue send a resounding yes in response to his question.

By the time we finish the appetizer romp before breakfast, I really am starving and hoping he wasn't joking about having actually bought food for once. Of course, there's still no frying pan, so I'm not any closer to eating any of it than I was before.

"Fuck it." He slams shut the last of the unexplored cabinets. All of which wound up being empty. "I've got some upstairs. I'll just grab what I need. Be right back." He gives me a quick peck on the lips as he hurries from the kitchen.

"Wait. Upstairs? There's still real stuff up there?"

He stops, apparently confused by my question. "Yeah. Why?"

I follow him out into the living area. "I don't know. That first night we had dinner on the deck, the door was open and I caught a glimpse inside. I wasn't snooping or anything, but the place looked like it had been cleaned out pretty good. Just random trash left lying on the ground. I thought it was weird, but we weren't really doing the sharing thing back then, so I didn't bring it up."

Riker glances back and forth between myself and the door. He's contemplating something, and judging by his expression, it's something big. I'm suddenly sorry I asked. We've shared plenty already in the last twenty-four hours. I'm not sure I'm up for more monumental revelations.

"It's my place," he says slowly. "From when I was married."

Shit. Why didn't I see that coming?

"Oh."

His gaze drops to the floor. "I know. It's weird. I should have sold it by now. I just . . ." He exhales loudly, then lifts his eyes and stretches out his hand for me to take. "Come on. It's easier if I just show you."

Against my better judgement, I take his hand. Because somehow, I no longer know how not to. Whenever I see his hand, mine simply insists on being in it. So there it is—my palm resting on his, my fingers anchored to him and thereby tying me to whatever lies beyond that door and up those stairs.

He keying in the code on the garage door opener to gain entry to the main house that way, when I'm hit by my moment of truth amid all the lies I've been telling myself since the second I met him, and I panic.

"Wait. I can't do this."

He turns back to look at me over his shoulder, the garage door already in motion. "I'm not hiding any dragons in here, Quinn. Nothing's going to happen to you that I can't protect you from."

I start to pull back, putting a strain on the grip between our hands. "It's just . . . If I go inside here . . . if you show me this last secret piece of yourself, I don't think I'll ever be able to walk away from you. This whole time . . . all of my insisting I could just leave in two weeks and never look back . . . I was just pretending."

He moves in close, taking my other hand as well. "So was I." He smiles, but it's a sad smile, wrought with the possibility of loss. "How about we stop?"

"You might not like what you see," I mumble because speaking clearly and confidently is a luxury I don't have right now.

"It won't keep me from looking." Then he eases the intensity by tugging at the oversize t-shirt I'm still wearing from last night, and grinning. "You should see yourself right now, by the way. Wearing nothing but my ratty old shirt with your hair all a mess. I bet you haven't even brushed your teeth yet."

I yank my shirt back out of his grip. "Can't be all that disgusting. You couldn't keep your hands off me five minutes ago."

"Still can't." And he draws me in for one more kiss before he leads the way inside.

Now that he's diffused enough of my angsty tension, I notice the shiny black Mercedes SUV parked inside. It's probably not the most recent model, but it still has the brand-new feel to it.

"You have a Mercedes SUV?" Because I still can't wrap my mind around it. It's just not him.

"Isn't mine," he says dryly as we walk past it.

"Oh." Yeah. That makes more sense.

We're already at the next door, and I'm guessing this one leads to another set of stairs. I take a deep breath and brace myself. Since Riker's tightened his hold on my hand this time, I won't be getting a second chance to make a run for it.

"Hang on, let me get the light," he murmurs while we stand together in the dark. When he finally flips on the switch, there's an explosion of sparks at the ceiling, and then darkness yet again.

"You should really talk to your maintenance guy about this shit. This place is practically falling apart." Because bad humor always makes me feel better.

"No kidding. Where is that asshole when you need him?"

Always at my side. But I don't say that out loud. I just close my eyes and wait for them to adjust to the lack of light. When I open them again, Riker has already navigated us safely to the main level where we enter through the kitchen.

Since it's an open floor plan, the tour starts pretty much immediately, in what I can only assume is the dining area. It's hard to say considering there isn't a single piece of furniture left in the place. Just . . . stuff. Picture frames mostly. Some random knickknacks. A vase in the corner with a full bouquet still in it, only of course they're not so much flowers as they are dried-out zombie blossoms.

"So, this style of decorating . . . it's a minimalist thing?" I don't know why I can't just ask a direct question. But then I also kind of feel like this tour should be guided. He's here. Leading the way. Why isn't he pointing and explaining as he goes? *And to your right we have what was once the formal dining room before the Grinch came one Christmas and took it all away.* I don't know. Something along those lines.

"Miranda took all the furniture when she moved out. According to the divorce agreement, she was only allowed to take her personal items upon her departure. I'm guessing she and the judge had vastly different ideas about what constitutes a personal item. Regardless, I didn't give a shit about any of it, so I let her." He continues through the empty space and rounds the corner into a large living room spanning the entire side of the house and matched in size by a balcony visible through the wall of windows and glass doors.

Miranda. His wife. Why do those three words make me want to throw up?

"How long were you two married?" I ask. Because if we're doing this, we're really doing this. And I'm going to need to know. All of it. Otherwise, I'll just make up my own shit to fill in the blanks, and that's got bad news written all over it.

"Five years. Well, would have been that year, anyway." He stops in front of one of the glass doors and gazes out at the ocean. "We got married right after I graduated college. We'd been seeing each other off and on for a few months when she found out she was pregnant." He turns toward me. "At first I just figured we'd work things out as we went. I mean, I wasn't worried about finances, and even though I hadn't been planning on it at that particular time in my life, I wanted to be a dad, so it was easy to accept the news as good. But Miranda was in a panic about the whole thing. Said her father would disown her if she had a baby out of wedlock and that not getting married was not an option."

I get it. Miranda was a controlling, manipulative, whiny bitch and I already hate her ass. Of course, my opinion might be slightly tainted. "And what? You were like, that's cool. Fuck it. Let's get married?"

He chuckles. I think I actually surprised him this time. "Yeah. Something like that. I was barely twenty-two. What did I know? My parents got married at nineteen. Had Hannah a year later. The concept wasn't completely foreign to me."

We're having one of those awkward reality moments where he's old and implying I'm an ignorant kid without realizing it. So I remind him. "I'm twenty-two."

He shakes his head at me. "Only in this lifetime."

Fair enough.

Apparently feeling that he's answered my question about his marriage sufficiently, he begins to move again. When we turn the corner once more, there's some sort of family room. At least, the main wall is covered in family pictures, so whatever was in here wasn't a movie room. That one I can rule out. There's no wall space left for the screen.

It takes me a second before I realize this is the part of the house I stumbled upon that night in the stairwell on my way to the deck. Even though most of the frames are still intact and on the wall, several more are in pieces on the floor.

"What happened in here?" My voice is barely audible. Mostly because I'm a little scared to ask.

"Me." It's a straightforward answer, and he bends down to pick up the frame at his feet. "Just couldn't take it, you know? First my dad and sister die in that crash. Then my grandfather. It was already taking all I had to try and take care of the business by myself, not to mention Sid." He's staring down at the picture in his hands, but I don't think it's really what he sees. His voice sounds like he's ages away. Back when everything first happened. "The irony was priceless, really. Hannah and Sid putting off their wedding all those years in hopes that my mother would come around and attend the wedding."

"Your mom wasn't going to go to their wedding?" My parents hated Jackson. But they still would have shown up if I had decided to marry him.

"My mom hadn't spoken to Hannah in nearly seven years. Not since the day she told her she was engaged to another woman. My sister never gave up, though. Every Saturday morning, she would call her and leave a lengthy voicemail pretending they were having the same weekly chats they'd had all her life before my mother found out her daughter was a lesbian." The disdain is abundant in his voice. "You know, if my parents hadn't already been divorced, I think my father would have left my mother right then and there. Didn't matter, though. She was already gone. Already living in New Hampshire with her thirty-five-year-old boyfriend.

"Anyway, after the accident, my mother finally deemed my sister worthy of a visit. Even if it was just to attend her funeral. Honestly, I think Hannah would have preferred she'd just stayed away. She did nothing but make everything harder on everyone else. Especially Sid.

Then, after my mother found out Sid was set to inherit Hannah's trust and the shares she owned in the company, things only got worse. My mother flipped. Hired a lawyer. Tried everything she could to get my sister's will deemed invalid. Didn't work, of course, but I still had to take the time to go to court and make sure it didn't. Sid was a mess. And she didn't care about the money, so she was ready to just sign whatever my mother wanted her to. But Hannah would never have been okay with that."

When the silence starts to rest in the air, I gently squeeze his hand. "You're a good brother, Riker. A good man."

He turns, and I'm shocked by what I see. The beast of his grief has been completely unleashed, tearing him apart from the inside out. And there's nothing I can do about it. Except continue to coax it out and set it free.

"What part did Miranda play in all of this?"

His gaze drops down to the frame again. "What part? I don't know. The villain, maybe? No, that was my mother. Evil cheating bitch, I guess."

"So that's why you two split? She had an affair?" He's still not looking at me, but I'm not taking my eyes off of him.

"That was part of it. Yeah. Not the worst part. But definitely a deciding factor." His gaze is still glued to the frame in his hands, and a tear drops down onto the glass. His heart is breaking all over again. Maybe he hadn't loved her when they first got married, but five years is a long time. Feelings change. Evolve. Clearly, he was devastated when his marriage fell apart. "After everything else that had already happened that year . . ."

"I get it. Then you lost her and it broke you," I whisper, trying my best to hide my own hurt. This isn't about me.

"It wasn't losing her that broke me." He hands me the frame he's been holding this whole time and starts to walk away.

Automatically, my view drops from the back of his shoulder blades to the picture in my hands. Two small faces are smiling up at me through shattered glass. A little girl with white, blonde curls and a little boy with the biggest blue eyes I've ever seen. This wasn't ever about her. It was about them.

CHAPTER FIFTEEN

RIKER

Of all the rooms in this godforsaken house, this is the only one Miranda left fully furnished. I haven't stood inside these four walls since the day I came home from the hospital and realized this room would never be lived in by the baby we'd both spent the last seven months waiting for.

I remember sitting in that rocking chair in the corner. The same one we'd had in Harlow's nursery and then again in Mason's. I'd spent countless nights in that rocker, swaying back and forth when Harlow was teething. And then again with Mason when he refused to sleep in his crib for more than thirty minutes at a time.

I brought the rocking chair into this room right after I'd finished painting the walls. Teal. Miranda's request. The rocker was the first piece of furniture in the room, and I placed it right beside the window, imagining the nights I would sit in it again, gazing out at the stars and giving the newest member of our family his or her first astronomy lessons.

The last night I sat in here, I spent all night staring out that window. Asking the stars. God. For some sort of an answer. Some reason I could comprehend. It never came. And I never stepped foot in this room again. Until today.

Quinn's standing in the doorway, scared to come in. I know I'm putting a lot on her all at once. But we're running out of time. The only way she'll ever feel truly safe with me is if she knows all there is to know. Maybe then she'll finally be able to trust me and let down her guard.

"You never talk about your kids," she whispers.

"I don't know how." I've tried. Countless times. I hate not talking about them. Never saying their names. Never remembering the funny things they said or laughing about the crazy things they did. It's like they never even existed. And maybe that should make it easier, but it doesn't.

"Do you ever see them?" She takes a tentative step inside, like the floor might give out under her or the walls collapse. It's not the room making her feel that way. It's me. I don't know how to stop it. These feelings have been buried since they first attempted to take me out. Forcing them down and locking them up was the only way I could even function. Unfortunately, now that they're seeping through, escaping and overriding everything, I have no idea what I'm truly up against.

"I'm not allowed to see them." I need to sit, but the only chair in the room is the rocker, and sitting in it might actually kill me right now. So I lean against the changing table. It's better than nothing. "Harlow was about to turn four, and Mason was one when Miranda found out she was pregnant with baby number three. Timing couldn't have been better, really. I needed something positive in my life. Something I could look forward to. And while other lives had come to an end, here was a brand-new one just beginning."

She's following my example and resting against the crib across the room. Judging from the way her knuckles are turning white, her grasp around the railing isn't just to steady her. She's holding on for dear life. So am I. I'm gambling. And I'm no gambler. But there's a fifty-fifty chance I'll either wind up with her—all of her—or. . . nothing.

"For a while, everything seemed to be looking up again. The pregnancy proved to be the perfect distraction from all the shit going wrong in my life. Then, when she was seven months along, we had a scare. Wound up in the hospital where we were told that Miranda was suffering from severe preeclampsia. When the doctor explained that we needed to consider the possibility of inducing labor, her first response was that she needed to inform the father of what was happening." I take a long breath and exhale again. After years of blocking this moment from my mind, it's hard to face again. "I was standing right beside her when she said it."

· · · ·

QUINN

"It wasn't your baby." As soon as I say it, I want to slap myself. Like he really needed to hear the words out loud.

"Nope." His sad eyes travel the walls of the small room. "Turns out neither was Mason. Or Harlow."

This time I keep my mouth shut. But, mentally, I'm screaming. Furious at this Miranda person. This phantom wife who took the man that I . . . that . . . the man he was and took everything from him that mattered. She was the reason he ran off to the desert to die. It was her.

"Apparently, when Miranda and I first started seeing each other, she was also dating this guy, Colton. Then she found out she was pregnant and decided between the two of us, I was the more reliable income source since Colton was two years younger and still going to school. So she married me. And had Colton's baby."

I still can't fully wrap my brain around all of this. It's probably a good thing. "She knew the whole time?"

He nods. "Yep. And he was in on it too. The whole time." He laughs. Probably because it hurts less that way. "See, he was going to pilot school. And lo and behold, she became a flight attendant. Maintaining their relationship became a piece of cake when he graduated, and they started working for the same airline. Meanwhile, I stayed home taking care of their kids."

"You never even suspected?" I've never been cheated on. Surprisingly. But I always wonder if cheaters are really good at hiding their secrets or if those being deceived have an instinct to look the other way. Sort of out of self-preservation.

"Not even once. I should have. Our marriage was far from perfect. If anything, it was practical. We got along well enough. Had sex just often enough for me to believe I conceived three children, and, other than that, we were getting what we needed elsewhere. Miranda with Colton . . . me with the kids."

Those last four words stay with me. Repeating themselves over and over until they're ringing loudly in the back of my mind, drowning out every other thought. Only I can't let him know. Not now. He can't see that the revelation of his past has just wiped out any chance of us ever having a future. Hope. That small, yet mighty, word. It's gone now.

"What did you do after you found out?" I'm forcing the words to come out. Making myself go through the motions so he can too. If nothing else, I'll see this through with him. I'll be there for every step as he faces the grief he so clearly still carries. Maybe then . . . maybe after me, he'll find someone who can make him happy again.

"I didn't do anything. I didn't know *what* to do." He pushes off from the changing table and walks over to the window. "In the end, I didn't need to. Colton was making good money by then, so there really wasn't any reason for Miranda to stick around here. She filed for divorce. Tried to have the prenup my dad insisted she sign to protect the family business thrown out, but couldn't because the judge wasn't an idiot. When everything was said and done, she got nothing. And she got everything. My name was taken from the birth certificates. Their names were changed to Colton's. The five years I spent as a father were completely erased. And so was I."

"I'm . . . so sorry." I stumble over the words as I walk across the room to meet him.

He turns toward me. "Don't be." He takes both my hands and kisses them softly. "No matter what happens between us. Don't ever be sorry, Quinn. These last few months with you have changed my life. Made the difference between existing and living. You did that for me. And that's not something I ever want you to forget." It's as if he knows.

"You don't know how much I wish I was someone else. Someone better. Someone who actually deserved to hear all the amazing words you say to me." Tears are rolling down my cheeks, but I don't stop them. I don't want Riker to let go of my hands. Not yet.

"If you were anyone else, I wouldn't be standing here right now, Quinn. I wouldn't be ready to let go of a past I thought I'd never be able to face again, let alone part with."

I start to tell him he's crazy for thinking that, but he stops me by devouring my mouth with his, drinking me in and draining me of every thought and emotion other than how completely consumed I am by him.

"Riker." I breathe his name against the softness of his skin because it's all I can say. All I can think.

"Stop. You're thinking too much. It's done. You. Me. Us. It's done," he whispers back. "So just let me hold you. Please."

And I do. I slide into his embrace, pressing myself to him as tightly as I can, until my racing heart meets his and finally slows itself to join the calming rhythm coming from his chest.

We stand there together. Both silently letting the tears fall. Both knowing this moment will change us. And neither of us is ready for it.

When we finally leave behind the wrecked remains of what was once a happy home, we're both quiet, hardly speaking to each other. Breakfast has fallen by the wayside. Neither of us is thinking about food anymore.

"I could call Sid. Tell her I'm not coming in today. We could just ... be. Lie in bed. Go for a walk. Whatever you want."

He sits on his mattress, already dressed and ready to go. He needs to show up to feed Nox this morning, just like he always does. He knows that. I know that. He's just scared to leave me. And that's something we both know as well.

"Sid needs you. Nox needs you."

He gets up and crosses the small room in two steps to get to where I'm leaning against the wall. He kisses me. "But I need you."

And I need him. God, I *need* him.

"Then stay." The words trickle out of my mouth before I can do anything about it. I have no business asking him to do something I can't do in return. I can't stay. I want to. More than ever before. But I can't. Not anymore. Not now that I know.

The day passes in a blur, both of us too wrapped up in the aftermath of our own emotions to verbalize anything that isn't completely necessary. By the time night falls, we're still not saying much, and even when we make love, the usual screams of ecstasy are replaced by hushed whispers and quiet moans filled with the intensity of our feelings and the ache of knowing it's really just a long, passionate kiss goodbye.

It takes forever before Riker finally falls asleep, and it's close to five in the morning when I'm tiptoeing out of his apartment with a small bag and Harley at my side. The door clicks shut behind me, and I'm walking out on him. Doing exactly what I always knew I was capable of. And I don't feel a single solitary thing outside of the cold hatred that fills me up entirely, nearly suffocating me as I begin the shameful trip back to Kirsten's. Of all the despicable things I've done in my life, this one will top the list as long as I live.

Since Kirsten isn't exactly expecting me back, the bed in the downstairs room is completely stripped. Not wanting to wake anyone at this unfortunate hour, I curl up in one of the recliners in front of the movie screen, and Harley does the same. I swear, even he's disappointed in me. He just keeps staring at me, and his disapproval rips at my conscience, which is already in shreds without his help.

I have no expectation of sleep. Not tonight. Maybe not ever. Well, that's crazy. Of course I'll sleep again. But sleep would be a kindness right now. And I don't deserve any. There shouldn't be any relief for me. Not even the temporary kind.

So I sit here and force my eyes to focus on the clock, watching the minutes pass me by one at time. No TV, no music, and definitely no sleep. Just my own thoughts to occupy me. Many of them I've had before. They recycle well. Especially now. Because if I hadn't done the things I did back then, I wouldn't have had to do what I did tonight. It's all connected. One massive chain reaction.

For a while, I allowed myself to believe that the past was really that—the past. Gone. Closed. Removed from my present. Uninvited to my future. I was wrong, but I'm used to that. I'm wrong a lot.

By seven fifty I hear people moving around upstairs. Part of me is desperate to be found. The other is hoping against all hope that no one will come down those stairs until after I've left for California.

Hope keeps me going until ten. Then the door opens and Kirsten's heels come clicking down the steps.

"Holy shit!" Her eyes nearly pop out of her head. "You scared me! What the hell are you doing here?" She's already pissed, and she hasn't even heard the story. Wasn't that long ago she would have assumed Riker was to blame. Then he landed in her good graces and she came to realize I was the solid fuck-up she could continue to count on.

"I'm moving back." I don't actually believe that she'll accept such a simple answer, but I try never to overshoot my offers. I'd rather she reject it and I counter, and we continue the negotiations until she has enough of what she needs and I have some of my privacy left too.

"No, you're not." She marches straight for me. "Get your ass up out of that chair and go back. Right now."

"You don't understand, Kirsten. I can't be with him. And staying . . . even the next two weeks . . . I can't do it." I stand up, but only because I feel like it will help me make a stronger argument.

"Why not? Why can't you do it? Because he makes you too happy? Makes you feel too loved? Too safe? Too cared for? What is it? Tell me!" She's gesturing at me furiously, and twice she makes a fist I think she might wish she could swing at me.

"Because I feel nothing! That's why. He feels everything, and I feel *nothing*!" I shout. "I slid out of his arms and crept out of his home in the middle of the night while he was sound asleep, and I felt *nothing*. I was completely numb. Who does that, Kirsten? What kind of monster does the things I'm capable of?"

I want her to keep being angry at me. I want her to keep yelling. But her furious demeanor slips away leaving behind a mixture of pity and heartache.

"You're so stupid," she whispers. She shakes her head, but her hands hang listless at her side. "You don't go numb from feeling nothing. You go numb from feeling *too* much."

I press my lips together, as if that will somehow keep everything sealed inside me. "No. You're wrong."

"No, I'm not." She takes a step closer. "You love him, Quinn. And what you're feeling right now isn't nothing. It's heartbreak."

"I can't love him." I hiss out the words, trying with all my might to keep the tears from falling.

She tilts her head and looks at me with a sad curiosity shining in her glossy eyes. "Why not?"

"Because. If I love him . . . and he loves me . . . it will make it that much more unbearable when we can't be together." I've lost. My own body has defeated me and now threatens to destroy what's left with the ache of a thousand heaving sobs desperate to burst from my chest.

"But why can't you be together? Did he say something? Did you tell him about Jackson? What happened?" Her arms wrap around me, cradling me like I'm a baby.

"It's not about my past this time. It's . . . about . . . his," I blubber through my tears.

"What are you talking about?" She almost sounds scared. I guess I would be, too, considering some of the conversations she's had to have with me.

"His marriage. His . . . kids." I lift out of her embrace to look at her. "They didn't get taken from him because he lost it. He lost it because they were taken."

The corners of Kirsten's mouth curve tenderly in a sad state of understanding. "Oh."

"I saw pictures," I whisper, slowly gaining control of myself again. "Pictures of him with his kids. He was happy. Really happy." I turn away because I can't face her or anyone else anymore. "How can I stay with him, even two more weeks, when I know *I* can never make him that happy again?"

Kirsten combs the hair away from my cheek and kisses it. "How can you leave him, even for a day, when leaving means sparing him from learning he can't have something he never asked for, and denying him the one thing he has? You."

Then she walks away, her heels click-clacking with every step. It's not until the door closes and I know she's gone that I collapse on the floor.

CHAPTER SIXTEEN

RIKER

It's been a week. One whole goddamn week. Every day I tell myself she'll turn up before the sun does. Then, when she doesn't, I go to work, convinced I'll find her here when I get back. I don't know why I tell myself such bullshit. I've never been much for denial. For some reason this time I just can't get a fucking grip on things. I knew it could happen. Actually, I was pretty damn sure she would bolt as soon as I told her everything. I don't even know why I knew that, other than she's a creature of flight who lives in constant fear of being the cause of someone else's pain.

Ironic, really. Considering how much she's fucking hurting me by being gone. Only she can't see that. Or maybe she does. I don't know. I just know she believes staying will hurt me more than leaving. She's fucked up in the head that way. Fucked up in the heart. Fucked up to her very core. And if I ever find the bastard who fucked her up, I'll kill him.

Her flight for California departs in less than five days. I'm guessing Kirsten will show up on day six to collect all the stuff Quinn couldn't carry on foot when she left here in the middle of the night. I had half a mind to offer her a ride, but she seemed hell-bent on sneaking out, so eventually I just faked sleep to make it easier on her.

But it's been a motherfucking week. And I'm done faking sleep and making shit easier for her. If she wants out, I'm going to make her tell me. To my face. And then I'm going to convince her she's wrong.

Feeling amped up from the self-motivational rant I gave myself on the way over here, I jump from my truck and slam the door shut. I practically run up to the front door, and I don't even give a shit if anyone sees me. I'm not here to play games. The whole damn household is welcome to know exactly what I'm here for. Quinn.

Kirsten answers the door. She's instantly annoyed when she sees me. "What the hell took you so long?"

"What the hell did you let her come back for?" I counter.

She drops the arm holding the door at bay, and it swings open. "I tried to send her back. Trust me." Then she turns and goes back in, leaving me to follow her and close the door.

"Where is she? Downstairs?"

Kirsten shakes her head. "Went for a run. And since you're here, I'm guessing she's actually running. For a second there I was hoping maybe it was just code for sex with Riker again."

Even as she's using the words sex and my name, I'm scanning the room uncomfortably for her husband and kid. Thankfully, neither seem to be around.

"You don't mind if I head to the game room and see if I can track her down?" Maybe I can follow her tracks in the sand from there.

"Go for it. But I'm warning you, it won't be easy. She's made up her mind. And her jacked-up little brain may be broken, but her determination is not." Then she gives me the go-ahead nod and I take off down the stairs.

Downstairs, the sliding glass door is wide open, so she's definitely not back yet. I'm not exactly wearing running gear, but that sure as shit isn't going to stop me from going after her.

• • • •

QUINN

I've listened to the same song seventeen consecutive times now. I don't know why I won't take it off repeat. It's a horrible song. All about falling in love and soulmate bullshit. And yet here I am, going for eighteen.

I'm just plugging along, keeping my eyes locked on the sand, avoiding any and all eye contact with the other people who are annoyingly out here as well. Then Harley turns on a dime and starts running back the way we came.

"Har—" I don't even finish calling his name. He's not running back to the house. He's running toward Riker.

I'm tempted to keep going without Harley, but ditching him feels wrong on a level even I can't fall down to, so I start walking toward them while they make their way over.

"What are you doing out here?" I sound snotty. I mean to.

"Taking back what's mine." He's got a brazen look in his eyes, and I'm scared to ask what he's referring to.

"Look, I'm sorry, okay? I shouldn't have left the way I did . . . but that doesn't change that leaving was the right thing to do. For both of us." I'm avoiding his gaze at all costs, until his thumb touches my chin and forces it up.

"Who the hell are you to decide what's right for me? Huh? I've seen the shit job you do with your own life. Don't you fucking go around trying to make decisions for mine," he warns.

"Trust me. If you knew what I know, you'd be thanking me. Not running after me."

His hand drops from my chin to his side. "Enlighten me, then."

"Fine." I can't take it anymore anyway. "You want to know. I'll fucking tell you." But not while I'm standing so close to him. If I'm going to get this out, I have to move. And keep moving. And close my eyes, because saying the words out loud is one thing, but facing him and seeing his reaction . . . and watching how everything he feels for me fades into the ether is something completely different. So I pace.

"The reason I have to go back to California next week is because I have to be in court."

"What?" I should have told him not to interrupt me. I don't have the strength to climb over hurdles of his shock and disbelief while I do this.

"It's civil court. This time. My trial starts next week. It's a wrongful death case, and I'm being sued for a few gazillion dollars, which will likely be awarded considering I was already found guilty in criminal court. Of manslaughter. That's where I was the last three years. In prison." I stop. I still can't face him, and my eyes are squeezed shut just in case I catch a glimpse of him walking away. I listen. Straining to hear over the wind and the waves, but I can't make out a single sound indicating whether or not he's moved even an inch.

The feel of his hands on either side of my face startles me into lifting my lids.

"I'm listening," he murmurs, concentrating his gaze on mine, leaving me no way to escape this time.

"Haven't you heard enough?" I gasp.

"You honestly think you've said anything that makes me want to turn away from you? What, you think I can't fill in the blanks on this one? Think I don't know you well enough to know you're not a murderer?" His tone hardens when he says the word. I don't think he's mad at me. Well, he is. Mad at me for implying that I am one. Or that I thought he would believe I was one. Not mad that I *am* one. Which I am. No matter how we twist and turn the words. I killed a man.

"You can't fix this," I whisper. "I know you want to. I know you think you can just come to my rescue and hold me until I stop screaming, but it won't work this time. My moments of peace with you were fleeting. And I knew it all along. I tried to tell you." I force myself to stop before I say anymore and start weeping into his chest.

"What's a gazillion dollars? Really. What's the real number?"

My eyes slant. Damn him. "Why?"

"I'll pay it. If your biggest fucking problem here is paying off the assholes who unleashed the beast who beat you, then yes, I *can* fix it. And your stubborn ass isn't going to stop me." He doesn't sound nearly as convinced as he'd like to. He sounds desperate. Scared.

"Even if that was the biggest fucking problem here, paying my debt is not yours to do. I am not your responsibility. And I don't want to be." I push back, freeing myself from him and those devastating eyes.

"If it's not the money or the trial, then what is it?"

I take a deep breath in and swallow down the fear threatening to take me out before I can finish what I set into motion. Then I let it all go. "The problem is that I don't have any feelings. Not for you. Not for anyone. I had feelings once. And I wasted them on the wrong person for many years. Until one day, when something broke inside me. Literally." I search his face and zero in on his black pupils and the empty abyss I crave right now. I let it pull me in, away from here. Away from everything until I'm just floating far off in the distance where I can barely hear my own voice anymore. "I killed him. And now I'm dead. You can't fix dead, Riker. You're just going to have deal with it."

"You're not dead. I've felt the warmth of your breath on my lips when you've kissed me with more passion than most people are capable of. I've heard your heart beat out of your chest after you've made love to me. And I've seen the way your body comes to life under my touch. You. Are. Not. Dead. And even if you were, it wouldn't change a damn thing. I am in *love* with you." His mouth charges at mine and stops short where he hovers, a raspy rumble coming from his lips. "Deal with *that*."

His kiss takes me so rapidly my head is spinning. Or maybe it's from hearing him say those words. The words I was hoping he would never say. Because now there's only one way out.

"Don't." I push his chest and break away from him.

"Why not?" He's not trying to kiss me anymore, but he's not letting go of me either.

"Because." I stare him down square in the eyes. "I don't love you."

He bites his lip, dropping his head to his chest. "Really? You're going to do this?"

I shrug out of his grip. "I have to. Not telling you the truth would be wrong. I've led you on for long enough."

When his head rises again, his mouth is one thin line, and his jaws are clearly clenched. "But you're not telling the truth. You're lying straight to my face."

"I'm not," I insist, my tone void of all emotion. "You just don't want to hear it."

"You're right. I don't want to hear it." And for the first time, he physically turns away from me. "I don't know what else I can do here, Quinn. I've given you everything you've asked for. I've respected your privacy. Did all I could to earn your trust. Shared with you the darkest, most devastating parts of my life. And did the one thing I swore to myself I would never do again: I gave you my heart. And yes, I know you didn't ask for it. And fuck, I get that you don't want it. But don't you dare stand there and tell me that you didn't give me yours too."

I clamp down on my own tongue so hard I taste blood, but it's the only way I know how to hold it together right now. By keeping my focus on something small. Simple. Like the sharp pain in my tongue.

I grind my jaw back and forth one last time, and I think I may need stitches by the time this is over. Then I do it . . . I say it again.

"I'm sorry this is so hard for you to accept. But I can't tell you what you want to hear. I am not now, nor have I ever been, in love with you."

His eyes narrow, and fury flares inside them. "Take it back," he snarls through gritted teeth. "Take it back, Quinn, or I swear I'm walking away and I'm not coming after you again. Because I can't . . . I can't keep doing this with you." Then his face loses all tension and he whispers, "Or did you forget, you're not the only broken person standing here?"

It takes everything I've got not to say and do whatever it takes to erase the hurt so clearly pouring out of him. But I can't. Not when I know it would only be temporary.

"I won't take it back. I can't."

For some idiotic reason, I expect him to continue to fight. To say something else. Anything to get me to change my mind. Because on some sick, selfish level I'm desperate for him to change it. Only he doesn't. He turns and walks away just like he said he would. And I have no choice but to stand here and watch him.

CHAPTER SEVENTEEN

RIKER

I don't think I've moved in twenty hours. After I left Quinn out on that beach, I just drove home, walked in, and sat down on the bed. And here I am. Still in the same fucking place. My phone rang several times, but I never bothered to check it. I'm pretty damn sure it was Sid anyway. She's the only person who calls me. Plus, I missed feeding Nox last night. And then again this morning.

I don't care if he starves to death this time. It's his fucking fault I've been sitting here for twenty hours. His fault I'm hoping a tsunami hits this house and takes me out to sea with the rubble. If he hadn't been so damn stubborn that day, running off and choosing her—her, of all people—to be the one to catch him, I wouldn't be in this mess now.

I'm about to start cursing him out loud when a knock sounds at my door. I watch it, waiting to see it open. Frankly, I'm a little shocked Sid knocked at all. Normally, when I go AWOL she's prone to just busting through doors.

Then, there's another knock. Well, that rules out Sid. And pretty much my desire to see whoever it is. Not that I want to see Sid either, but her I can't deny. Everyone else is open to rejection at this point.

Only, whoever the fuck it is is persistent because they're knocking again. And they're not letting up.

"What the hell!?" I get to my feet and stomp across the room. When I throw the door back, Kirsten's little fist nearly pounds me right in the nose.

"Oh. Good. You're home." Then she lets herself in, even though she has to squeeze past me to do it.

"All of her stuff is right there." I point at the boxes I stacked along the wall a few days ago. Then I walk straight for the bathroom. I don't need to watch her take the only thing that's left of Quinn.

"I'm not here for her shit."

I stop. "What?"

She nonchalantly takes a seat at my kitchen table. I guess she's planning on staying a while.

"I said, I'm not here to pick up Quinn's crap. She wanted to move out, she needs to figure out how to finish what she started. Even if it will be considerably harder now that she decided to leave for California four days early."

I'm not sure if I'm curious or scared right now. Part of me is still leaning toward hiding out in the bathroom until she leaves. The other part of me thinks I might die in there if I go that route. I don't know Kirsten all that well, but what I do know tells me she's not likely to leave until after she gets what she wants.

I walk back to the table and sit across from her. "Then why are you here?"

"To finish the shit *I* started." She places her keys and purse on the table. Yeah. She's definitely staying a while.

"What shit, exactly, are you referring to?"

She leans back into her chair and drops her eyelids, and I'm instantly unnerved. "Before I tell you anything, I need to get one thing straight. I love my sister. I would do anything for her. Anything."

Not feeling any better about this yet. "I had a sister. I get that. What I don't get is how anything you did plays into my relationship with Quinn."

She sighs. "Because. I'm the one who brought her here. And then, because that wasn't enough, I brought her straight to you when I had Sophie's birthday party at your ranch. But, in my defense, I did try to intervene the moment I saw sparks flying back and forth between the two of you."

I lean over the table toward her. "Kirsten, no matter what's happening right now, I'm not sorry I met her. I'll never be sorry. You really have nothing to feel bad about. You didn't really even do anything."

She nods. "You're right. I didn't. Which is very unlike me. I don't know if Quinn told you, but I'm a meddler. Major meddler. I pretty much believe I can fix everyone's life if I can just get in there and do it myself. Which is to say, I'm going to meddle right now, so hold tight. Shit's about to get bumpy."

"You know, you swear a lot for someone who looks like a human Barbie doll. You're definitely not for ages three and up."

She laughs. "Really? You want to talk to me about how contradictory my appearance is to my personality? Mister inked-up redneck who grunts more than he speaks, but is actually smart, kind, and—wait for it—in touch with his feelings."

"Point made. Get to meddling, woman." There's a twister slowly funneling in the pit of my stomach, and it's growing into some sort of anxious excitement. Maybe I'm not as fucking lost here as I thought. What had Quinn said about her sister? Once she locks in on a target, there's no avoiding that missile. Well, shoot away, Kirsten. I'm ready to be hit.

"I don't know how much you know about Jackson." She reaches for her key ring, and she starts moving the keys as if she's organizing them somehow, but really she's just sliding them around in circles. She's nervous too.

"I know he hit her. And I know she killed him. In self-defense." I kind of assumed that was the gist of it, but watching Kirsten trying to decide where to start suddenly makes me feel like I wasn't even close.

"Yeah. I mean, that's the short version, I guess." She tilts her head back and forth. "The really, really short version. More like the blurb, really. You know. Like on the back of a DVD?"

I know. I *don't* know why she's rambling on about movie summaries.

"Anyway, the more extended version started when she was fifteen. He was twenty-six."

The storm in my stomach rages, and my fists clench under the table. I'm pretty sure if I open my mouth to say anything right now, it won't be good, so I shut up and just nod.

"Quinn was friends with his baby sister, who was seventeen at the time. Ashley. The two girls met through barrel racing when Quinn was eleven, and over the years their paths kept crossing until a friendship developed. So, naturally, when she met Jackson and he started spending more time with the girls, no one really thought anything of it. He was a roper. And with the girls getting older and participating at bigger events, more often than not they were all at the same ones."

She sets down the keys again and lays her hands flat on the table. "We just . . . we never suspected anything inappropriate was happening. We knew the family. Our parents were friends. Jackson seemed like a good older brother who was just looking out for his little sister and her friend. I mean, we actually appreciated how much he watched over them at these events. You have to understand, men like Jackson have a way of hiding in plain sight, using their charm and permanent smile to cover up the beast that lives below. We had no idea." She shakes her head, guilt brimming in her eyes. "Wasn't until she was eighteen and moved in with him that we found out they'd been dating the entire time. She insisted they never slept together until she was legal, but we all knew that was bullshit. The second she turned of age, everything shifted. Suddenly he made no secret of his claim on her. It was almost like he was rubbing it in, that he'd stolen her right out from under our noses. And she was so young and so in love, she didn't even see it."

"Was he already hitting her?" I don't know why I'm asking. I don't need any more reasons to despise the man. No. Not man. Perverted piece of shit.

"Yes. I think so. She wouldn't ever admit it, but she'd turn up with bruises and broken bones and blame it on some accident while riding or working horses. At one point my parents were ready to sell her mare because of it, but she begged them not to. After that, she got better at hiding her injuries. Even later, during her trial, she refused to go into much detail. Her stupid-ass pride just wouldn't let her. But you've seen the marks. And I'm sure you've noticed how her left arm won't straighten completely. Or how she limps ever so slightly on days when it's overcast. He didn't just break her spirit. He literally *broke* her. Countless times."

"He's dead now." I'm reminding myself. But hearing her confirm it again wouldn't hurt.

"Yeah. He's dead." She wipes her eyes delicately with the tips of her fingers, careful not to wipe away any of her perfect makeup. "But she's still not free of him. Some days I wonder if he killed her before he went. If maybe the Quinn I see is just a ghost. An illusion I hang onto because I'm not capable of letting go. Because that's all she's been. An empty shadow of the girl she used to be. Until you. You don't know what it's been like, Riker. What it means to me to see her smile the way she has since she's met you. You brought her back. You did the one thing none of us were able to do . . . you saved her. From him." She clears her throat. "Now all that's left is to save her from herself."

• • • •

QUINN

It's surreal being back at my parents' house. I haven't lived here since before I was eighteen. And even back then I felt like I was hardly ever home, but here I am. Standing in my old room. Or what used to be my old room. My mom turned it into a guest suite somewhere along the way. She's apologized about a million times for doing so, but, honestly, the last thing I need right now is to be surrounded by all my old crap. The only piece of my past I wish was with me is Harley, but the flight here would have been rough on him, so he'll have to stay put with Kirsten a little while longer until I can figure things out. If I figure things out.

"I made soup burger." My mom stands in the doorway, smiling. "It's still your favorite, isn't it?"

I haven't had soup burger since I was about eleven. And she knows that. She's just desperate to see me eat something. So I nod.

"Soup burger sounds perfect, Mom." I even force the corner of my mouth upward. "Thank you."

Relieved, she walks from the room, and I follow her out to the kitchen, even though I have no idea how I'm going to force down even a bite. I haven't felt like eating anything in days, and now the thought of putting anything in my mouth, let alone something that's the equivalent of a creamy sloppy joe, makes me want to vomit. On the plus side, there's nothing left in my system to do so with.

"Is Devyn still coming by this afternoon?" she asks while she makes me a plate.

"As far as I know." I feel like I've been talking to her nonstop for days. Up until now she's handled everything without me, but now that the trial is actually starting, I can't bury my head in the sand any longer.

"I talked to Kirsten earlier. She said she and Sophie will be here tomorrow afternoon. She wanted to be here in time for the opening statements, but she couldn't get the flight she wanted."

She places the plate in front of me along with a tall glass of chocolate milk. I love my mom. I love her even more for trying to bring back some sense of normalcy. But then I kinda hate myself for making her revert to a time when I still wore pigtails and thought boys were gross.

"I told Kirsten she didn't need to come at all. I wish she wasn't putting Sophie through the rigmarole of all this—taking her out of her normal routine, and making her sit in the middle of all this crap right when her school year is starting. It sucks. At this rate, the girl is going to grow up thinking I ruin everything." My gaze keeps bouncing back and forth between the creamy ground-beef mess on a bun and my glass of chocolate milk. I can't decide which to tackle first.

"Don't be ridiculous. Of course she's coming. We're all coming." My mom pulls out her chair with a little too much force, causing her to hit the table and nearly knock over my milk. I catch it just in time.

"Mom." But she won't meet my gaze. "You can't keep doing this to yourself. I am so sick of everyone's life being put on hold on account of mine. And this time, you really don't have to be present. There will be limited testimony. Most of the evidence was already submitted during the discovery process. I just need to show up, go through the motions, and wait for them to tell me how much I owe. You all dropping everything to sit through the tedious trial with me won't be helping anyone. Least of all you."

Finally, she takes her seat, but it's like she completely tuned out the last thirty seconds when she declares a simple, "Eat."

I don't argue with her. I just scoop up the bun and whatever is willing to stay in it and take a hearty bite. With everything I'm putting her through, the least I can do is deal with a bout of nausea.

"Thank you." She sighs, then rests her chin on her hand. "You're scaring me, you know? More than usual. And between you and me, that's quite an accomplishment."

I gulp down some milk. "I'm sorry." I don't know what else to say. Saying I'm sorry doesn't even begin to cover anything anymore. I feel like a broken record every time I utter those hollow words, but they're all I've got, so I say them anyway.

"What happened in North Carolina? Kirsten won't tell me, which makes me think it's horrible. Is it horrible? Because you're not eating or sleeping, and you're . . . giving up. And I don't understand. Please, help me understand."

I take one last bite, mostly to buy myself some more time, but then I push the plate away. "I'm not giving up. I'm just . . . giving in." But I can hear myself. My monotone voice. I sound defeated.

"But why? You've come through so much. Why stop fighting now when you're so close to getting through to the other side?" I can tell by the way she keeps wiping the corners of her mouth that she's trying not to cry. It's her thing. Her telltale gesture that the emotions are getting to her.

"Because, Mom. There is no other side." And that's the ugliest part of it all. I'm twenty-two. My life should just be getting started, but the reality is some things are already over before they ever began.

"How can you say that? Of course there is. There is always light in the dark. Always something to hope for." Her voice cracks, and I loathe myself a little more.

"I met someone. In North Carolina. That's what happened, Mom." I close my eyes and take a deep breath. "I fell in love. And then I lied to him so he would let me go."

Her eyes widen. "Why?"

"Because. It was the right thing to do. Look at everything I've cost you and Dad. Everything Kirsten has had to do for me. You guys *have* to love me. Riker doesn't. And he shouldn't. Not when I would end up taking more than I could ever give him."

She stands from her chair and hurries over to me, wrapping her arms around my shoulders and kissing me repeatedly over my hair. "You are such a foolish girl." She clasps my face in both of her hands. "You give more to all of us than you could possibly imagine. Your strength and courage inspire me every single day. And not just because you faced your own demons and waged your own war, but because you took that experience and you learned how to fight for others. No mother has ever been prouder than I am of you. Maybe I have to love you because you're my daughter, Quinn, but that doesn't mean I have to like you. Or admire you. Or be in awe of you. Those things I feel because of what you do. Not because of who you are."

She crouches down beside me, still holding onto my face. "If this Riker person had a chance to see even half of what I see when I look at you, he already knows how much you have to offer. Even if you don't."

I want to shake my head. Want to tell her she doesn't understand. But I can't do either without bursting into tears. So I just suck it up and nod. "You'd like him, Mom. You guys think a lot alike." I smile. But I don't feel it. I don't feel anything anymore. Only it's different now. Before when I felt nothing, it felt empty, like a void tin shell of myself. Now when I feel nothing, everything seems tight, like I might crack and crumble at any given moment. I'm scared to think. Scared to focus my eyes on any one thing for too long. Scared to make any sudden moves. It's strange. And exhausting. This new not feeling.

Slowly, she stands up again, releasing my face but not until after she places one more kiss on top of my head. "Well, I really hope I get to meet him someday."

I should say "me too," but I don't hope that at all. I hope he does what he said he would and never comes after me again. Because I won't have it in me to lie to him again.

Thankfully, my mother isn't waiting for an answer. She's back over by the stove, putting up the leftovers while I pick at the food still on my plate. I had three decent bites, but there's still too much here for me to just toss, and if I wrap it up my mom will notice I didn't eat enough and the whole cycle of worry will start all over again.

Then, because the fates are feeling generous today, the doorbell rings, announcing Devyn and my easy out from finishing what's left of my heaping portion of soup burger.

"I'll get it." I rush out of the kitchen before my mother can intercept and tell me to sit back down at the table.

When I reach the door, I take a deep breath before I open it.

"You look like shit." Devyn walks past me into the house.

"Thanks. You look pretty fucking tired yourself." I follow her into the formal living room. Devyn's been to this house often enough to know her way around.

My mom pops in from the adjoining kitchen. "Hi, hon. Coffee?"

Devyn smiles at my mom with a genuine sense of gratitude. "That would be amazing, Julie. Thank you."

She doesn't bother asking me if I want anything before she disappears again, probably because she's avoiding hearing a no. This way she can just bring me whatever she wants.

"I'm serious, Quinn. You look like death warmed over. You can't show up to court like this tomorrow. You need sleep. And body fat."

I plop down on the couch and wait for her to do the same. "What difference does it make what I look like? Besides, looking too healthy and strong bit me in the ass the last go-around."

She snorts. "Yeah, well, looking like a strung-out drug addict definitely isn't a usable alternative."

"I'll see about getting a face mask and body suit for tomorrow, then." Annoyed, I look down at my lap. Then I notice my bony knee poking through my jeans and can't help but wonder if I really appear to be decaying at a rapid pace.

My mom comes back into the room boasting a large tray of coffee and baked goods. Clearly, she's on a mission to fatten me up as well. It's not like I've dropped a ton of weight in the last week. I just didn't have that much extra to lose.

"Here we go, girls. I'll get out of your way so you can get to work, but if you need anything, just holler."

"Thanks, Mom." I smile again, this time for real. She blinks her eyes in a silent "you're welcome," then scurries from the room.

Devyn starts to pull file after file from her briefcase. "She's worried about you. Everyone is. I've even been getting calls from your dad."

My dad's not a talker. If he's making the effort to pick up a phone, things are serious. "I'm trying, okay? I'm here. I'm conscious. It's all I've got."

She reaches for my hand and squeezes it. "Let's get you *more*."

Then she dives right in and doesn't let up again until its pitch-black out and she's certain I'm fully prepared for the battle ahead. She was the same way last time around. Even with a guilty verdict, things would have been so much worse if it hadn't been for Devyn. And it's no secret why. Devyn is a survivor of domestic abuse herself, but her mother wasn't so lucky. And she would defend me to the death for doing what I did, because there isn't a day that goes by she doesn't wish her mother had done the exact same thing I did.

CHAPTER EIGHTEEN

RIKER

It's been almost two weeks since Kirsten was here. By the time she left, I was determined to go after Quinn. I was all packed and ready to go when I realized what I was doing and unpacked again. She has enough on her plate. It doesn't matter how badly I want to be there for her if she doesn't want me there. Showing up, fighting her on this . . . it would only add to the turmoil. And I don't want to be one more asshole who brings her heartache.

So, even though being stuck here while she's fighting for her life again is killing me, I'm staying put. Waiting. Counting the seconds as they pass and hoping that I'm getting closer to seeing her again with every tick of the clock.

To keep me from losing my shit altogether, Sid's keeping me closer than usual, making long-ass to-do lists that I know I'll never finish, mostly because I keep redoing the same shit day after day. If she has me move that damn wash rack one more fucking time, I'll probably tell her to shove it, even though I know she's only doing it to keep me busy and distracted. It's not working. No matter what she has me do, Quinn is all I can think about. And it's not letting up now that Harley is staying with me while Kirsten's in California.

"You have a phone call." Sid's standing over me while I'm lying on my back, half under the tractor.

"Here?" I can't think of single person who would try to reach me at the ranch. Everyone I talk to has my cell number. And that list is short. Half of it is standing next to me.

"Yeah. It's some lawyer. Said she got this number from Kirsten."

I jerk up so fast I hit my head. "Shit."

"You okay?" Sid's leaning down, searching for me.

Holding my forehead, I slide out from under the tractor. "Yeah, I'm fine. Office phone?" I'm already on my feet and headed that way.

"Yeah. The one on my desk," she calls after me, and I give a backward wave to let her know I heard her.

A second later I'm in the office, rushing for her desk. I grab the phone lying on a pile of shot records for one of the horses. "Hello?"

"Is this Riker Shepherdson?" It's a woman.

"Yeah. Is Quinn alright?" I don't even care that I sound desperate.

"Alright might be a stretch," she says dryly. "My name is Devyn Hartley. I'm representing Quinn in the wrongful death suit brought against her by Jackson Murphy's family, but I'm sure you're already putting that together for yourself."

I close my eyes to focus my rapid thoughts. "Thank you."

"For what?" She sounds surprised.

"For taking care of her." It seems like such a stupid, empty thing to say, but I mean every word.

"I'm not sure I'm doing a very good job right now. Quinn's not making it easy." Of course not.

"What can I do to help? Please. You can't give up on her." I'm still rubbing my forehead where I hit it, but it's no longer from the pain. Just the anxiety of not knowing what's happening out in California.

"Trust me, I'm not giving up on her. Ever. But I do need your help."

I sit down, the sensation of relief moving in just from knowing there's finally something productive I can do. "Anything."

"Kirsten tells me you and Quinn were involved, and since that would make you the only other man she's ever had a relationship with, I need you to come and be a character witness."

I yank a pen from the old coffee mug Sid uses as a pencil holder and search for a piece of paper to take notes. "I'll be there. Just tell me when."

"Hold your horses, buddy. First, we need to discuss the nature of your relationship. I can't take you into court unless I'm sure you can actually help the case." I hear papers being shuffled on her end as well. She probably has a list of questions all ready to go. I only have one.

"Why do you think my testimony will help at all?"

"Because the last time Quinn was on trial, Jackson's family did a bang-up job of painting her as the aggressive one. Everyone, including her best friend, his sister, got up on the stand and told the jury about Quinn's scary temper. How she had mood swings that would turn violent and that it was actually Jackson who was constantly having to defend himself against her." She sounds pissed, like she's spitting the words instead of speaking them.

"That's fucking insane." Then I realize I just swore at her attorney. "I mean, how could anyone in their right mind believe that?"

"Because. It was her family against his. Quinn didn't have any other friends or boyfriends. Jackson made sure of that early on. Then the district attorney came along and pointed out how physically strong Quinn was. How she'd been wrangling twelve-hundred-pound horses from the time she was five. They showed pictures of her tossing hay bales around in the barn like they were pillows. Others of her hoisting multiple fifty-pound feedbags on her shoulder from the time she and Jackson's sister had a bet on who could carry more. Quinn was a tough girl. It was almost impossible to listen to them talk about her, see those pictures and then look at her in person and still believe that she would just take a beating from anyone."

There's silence on her end of the line, but I'm still trying to understand everything I've just heard, so I don't say anything either and just wait for her to continue. "Self-defense was even harder to argue when there were no weapons in the house. No proof she'd had reason to believe her life was in danger, as none of the abuse had ever been documented. All the jury had to go on was what the State was telling them. And our repeated insisting that the State was getting it wrong. But this time things are different. This time we have you. And I'm hoping that you'll be able to paint a different, more accurate picture of who Quinn really is. I would like you to come here and tell the jury about the Quinn you know. So they can see her the way you do. Not the way the Murphies want people to see her."

"I'll do whatever I can. But I should warn you. You may have another client on your hands if any of those assholes cross my path or say a single word against her in my presence." I know I sound like a macho douchebag, but I can't help it. I mean it. I'll lose it if anyone inflicts any more pain on her.

"Trust me. At this point, we'll all be going to prison. I don't think any of us can take any more of this shit than we already have." Then she hangs up without saying goodbye. She must have a lot of phone conversations with Quinn.

A little while later I get a text from Kirsten with my flight confirmation info. I'm leaving tonight, and this time I'm not coming back without her.

· · · ·

QUINN

I catch myself cradling my own stomach again. I've been doing it all morning. Ever since I saw the results. There's a baby in there. And that thought alone fills me with more joy than I ever thought possible.

A baby wasn't part of the plan. Not yet anyway, but now that it's happening, I just know it will change everything. This baby will save us. It will save Jackson. He'll finally have to get help. I know he will. He won't risk his temper getting the better of him with his own child. Not after what life was like for him growing up with his father.

"Abby?" His voice booms through the house the second he walks through the door. He's in a good mood. And it's only going to get better when I tell him the big news.

"Hey, handsome." I greet him with a long, deep kiss. He's the only boy I've ever kissed this way, but I can't imagine anyone else's lips feeling this good on mine.

He slaps my butt, his way of letting me know the kiss is about to come to an end. "Grab the cooler and fill it up. Mac and I are going fishing."

He takes off down the hall to change clothes. He's been working horses all morning, and his jeans are caked in dust and dirt. "I was kind of hoping we could spend the evening together. I was going to make chicken alfredo pasta." It's the only thing I know how to cook, but it's his favorite, so it's the only dish that matters.

He comes out of the bedroom already wearing his shorts and t-shirt. "Go ahead and make it anyway. I'll eat when I get back."

Since he's not really taking the bait, I try another approach and slink my arm around his neck, running my fingers through the hair on the back of his head while my other hand starts to undo his pants. "Are you sure you don't think you'd have a better time with me than Mac?" I murmur into his ear before I flick his lobe with my tongue.

"Abby. Come on, stop playing around. I really need that cooler packed. Mac's waiting at the dock already." He shoves me off him and I step back, tucking the fallen strands of hair behind my ear and trying not to show that I'm embarrassed.

"Sorry. It's just . . ." I bite my lip. This isn't how I wanted to tell him.

"What?" His brow is cocked, and he stops halfway to the kitchen. Only it's not curiosity that's etched on his face. It's annoyance.

I muster a smile. "I'm pregnant."

Suddenly it's like all the light is snuffed right out of him. His eyes narrow, and all the white in them seems to disappear until there's nothing but blackness. He doesn't say anything. Just storms past me, grabbing Harley by his collar as he goes by me and dragging him into the bedroom where he slams the door shut. And I know why. There's only one reason he ever locks up Harley.

I should run. I should scream for help. But I've never done either, so I'm not sure I know how. Except this time it's different. He's not going to hurt just me.

"You stupid fucking cunt," he snarls just as his fist makes impact with my abdomen and I curl over from the pain.

"Jackson." I try and breathe through the pain. "Please. Not my stomach. You'll hurt the baby. Your baby."

He laughs. An evil laugh, the one I hate. It doesn't matter how often I tell myself it's not the real Jackson. It's just the damaged, frightened boy still fighting back against the man he could never escape growing up. In the end, neither knows how to exist without the other, and I'm starting to think I won't be able to exist as long as they both do.

"Oh, Abby. My dumb little Abs. You really think I want you to have my baby? Why? So the stupid brat can suck up all your time? Never mind what it would do to your body! Fuck that. We're putting a stop to this mess right now." He throws another punch at my gut, and this time the force of it sends me down to the floor.

"Jackson. Don't, please," I beg. "I swear, nothing will change. You'll still be the most important person in my life, you know that. And I'll exercise. I'll watch what I eat. I promise, you won't find an ounce of fat on me. Just a tiny baby belly. And that'll be gone right away." But I know nothing I say will make a difference. It never does. And I won't cry. Crying only makes it worse.

"It will be gone right away," he promises with a smile. Then his foot lifts and swings in my direction, heel first.

I can't even scream. I used to. Years ago, when it first started happening. But I learned quickly that more noise meant more creative ways to shut me up. Gags. Disgusting things poured down my mouth until I nearly drowned. I've had to force my body into learning new ways to react. My mouth still opens from the pain. But now, nothing comes out.

Still gasping for air, I'm not prepared for the second blow. Or the third. After that, I lose count. Harley's growling and clawing at the bedroom door. In a sick sort of way, I like hearing it because it gives me something to focus on. A sound outside of Jackson's panting, or the material of his pants being rubbed together as his legs continue to move against one another with each kick. A sound far away from the blood rushing in my own ears or the cries I've learned to internalize. A distant sound. Almost like a place I can go so I don't have to be here.

Then, heat rushes over my thigh. The liquid makes my skirt cling to my legs, and I make the mistake and whimper. Not from the pain. Just the loss.

His hand rakes through my hair, catching the thick curls in his fingers and yanking me up to my feet. He leans in, hovering over my face, and his spit sprays when he speaks. "What was that? Were you saying thank you for fixing your little problem?"

My instinct is to nod, but his grip on my hair is so strong it's impossible to move. So I whisper, "Thank you." Another gush of blood runs down my leg. "Asshole."

For a moment, he's so shocked he just glares at me. But I know it's only temporary. I'm counting on it. I'm hoping for it. Desperate for another blow. A bigger one. This time aimed at me. One that will take me out so I don't have to feel what I'm feeling right now. Because knowing that I just let the man I love kill the baby I dreamed of is a new kind of hell even I can't bear.

Then it happens. Still holding me by the hair, he charges forward, slamming me into the wall headfirst. And because he's an extra special kind of pissed now, his hands alone aren't going to do it.

Blood is running down the side of my face and over my eye, but I can just make out the table lamp he rips from the desk right before it crashes into my skull and I collapse again.

Dazed from the pounding in my head, I don't even try to move. I just lie there in a pool of my own blood, waiting for the Grim Reaper to come and take what's left of me while Jackson proceeds to whip my battered body with the lamp's cord.

He works himself into such a frenzy he doesn't even notice when Harley manages to escape the bedroom and comes barreling into the room ready to attack.

Through blurred vision, I watch as the most loyal friend I have in this world sinks his teeth into Jackson's arm, temporarily forcing him to stop slashing away at my raw and mangled skin.

Panic strikes me at my core. I know Jackson. He'll kill Harley for this.

In a swirl of growls and shouting, chaos ensues as they both take their stance—Harley shielding me with his own body, Jackson preparing to lunge straight for him because I no longer matter in this equation.

"Harley, no!" I shout from somewhere inside of me I thought was already destroyed. But for the first time in his life, he completely disobeys me.

Jackson advances and gets a hold of Harley just long enough to throw him across the room, where he crashes into the opposite wall with a loud thud and heartbreaking wail.

He continues to whimper, but I can't hear anything else. No movement. Not from Harley anyway.

Jackson has a sickening grin on his face as he turns away from me and starts toward my dog.

Only he never gets to where he's going. Because I'm on my feet. I'm picking up the lamp. And I'm swinging it. Hard. And straight at his head.

I watch as he tumbles to the ground, total shock in his eyes. I swing again, smashing his face and waiting for the baffled look over my betrayal to shatter. I keep going. I can't stop now. I just keep swinging the lamp and letting it crash into some other despicable part of the monster. Long after it stops moaning. After it stops moving. Twitching. Breathing. I still swing. And I scream. And for the first time in years, I hear my own voice when I do.

"Quinn. Wake up, baby. It's okay. Mommy's here, baby." My mother's voice slowly gets louder over the sound of my own screaming, and I follow it until I can hear it clearly, calling me to safety.

It's not until I open my eyes that the screaming stops. I swallow. My throat feels hoarse, and I know that part wasn't just in my dream.

"I'm . . . okay. It's okay." I nod repeatedly. Mostly for my own sake. I'm drenched in sweat as usual, and I find myself checking my own hands over and over for any traces of blood. My mind is still convinced it's there, even if my eyes can't find it.

"No, you're not. You're not okay, Quinn. This is not okay." My mother is shaking her head, anguish in her strained voice. "What can I do? How can I help? Please, I just want to make this better for you. Tell me what you need."

I rest my head on her shoulder and let her rock me gently back and forth. "Riker. I need Riker." But he's not here to save me anymore.

CHAPTER NINETEEN

RIKER

"She doesn't know I'm here?"

Kirsten shakes her head but keeps walking up the stairs to the courthouse.

I hurry to catch up to her again. "No one thought it might be good to warn her?"

"No. You know Quinn. She's not particularly good at accepting help from others. That's not an annoying little something she reserves exclusively for you, you know."

We walk in through the massive glass doors, and Kirsten doesn't even hesitate. The gigantic hall is nothing if not intimidating, but she clearly knows exactly where she's going.

"How long ago did they start?" I glance at my watch for what's probably the five hundredth time this morning. I have plenty of time. I'm not due to take the stand for another thirty minutes.

"About three hours ago. Quinn had to give her testimony first thing this morning. Last I heard from Devyn's assistant, she was still being questioned by the Murphys' lawyer." Her tiny little nose twitches, showing her disgust. I've noticed it does that every time she says his name. Jackson. Murphy. What physical reactions have I developed as a result of knowing it now too? My fists clench every time I hear it, but that's a no-brainer.

She stops in front of a large set of double doors. "We're here." She eyes me up and down. "You may want to take a moment. Take a breath or something."

I frown. "Why?"

Her hand reaches up to smooth the collar on my dress shirt. "Because. It's murder in there." Then she pats my chest and nods at the security guy to open the door.

The room is quiet when we go in, not counting the booming voice of the attorney standing front and center, who based on his tone alone is in the midst of verbally assaulting the person sitting in the witness stand—Quinn.

Kirsten shoots me a warning look, and I unclench my hands, then slide into the seat beside her. Sitting right in front of us is an older couple. The woman's profile is almost identical to Quinn's. They've got to be her parents. And I ache, realizing these are the circumstances in which I'll be meeting them.

"Did you, or did you not, continue to attack Mr. Murphy long after he was already unconscious?" The man's oversize belly jolts with each emphasized syllable.

Quinn nods, her face void of any and all emotion. "I did."

"Now, Ms. Quincy. If it was really an act of self-defense as you claim it was—"

A woman at the table before us rises to her feet in an instant. "Objection, Your Honor. He's badgering the witness. She has explained multiple times here today why it was, in fact, an act of self-defense. Suggesting otherwise or trying to undermine her testimony with such a belligerent tone is not only objectionable but unconscionable at this point in the proceedings."

Judge Hanson, a woman who looks to be in her sixties, with silver hair draping her shoulders in large sweeping curls, moves her head curtly. "I'm inclined to agree, counselor." She turns toward the Murphys' lawyer, the unconscionable one. It's the nicest thing anyone could say about him as far as I'm concerned. "Please proceed, but keep your insinuations to yourself."

"Yes, Your Honor." He clears his throat, preparing to have another go at Quinn. "Ms. Quincy. Please tell the court why you proceeded to attack a man after he was unconscious and clearly no longer a threat to you."

"I didn't want to. I just . . . couldn't stop. I knew if he got back up, there would be no escaping him again. But I never intended to kill him. I realize that's hard for everyone to comprehend. In spite of everything he did to me, I still loved him." She's staring blankly ahead, and I wonder where she's really at. I want more than anything to run across this room and bring her back. To see the light shine in her eyes. To know she's present. Alive.

The Murphys' lawyer snorts, and I see Devyn about to shoot out of her chair again, but he catches himself and she does the same.

"You're right. That is hard to comprehend. Impossible, actually. Considering we've all seen the pictures. We know what you're capable of. The only question left now is how much do you think the loss of a life is worth? How much do you think you owe for what you took that day?"

"Objection!"

"Withdrawn." He tilts his head toward the judge. "Our side rests, Your Honor."

Her lips purse. "Yes, I should think so." She addresses Devyn next. "Counselor, would you like to cross-examine the witness?"

She's already walking out from behind her table. "Yes, Your Honor. I would."

She approaches Quinn. "I think opposing counsel brought up an interesting point. How much is the loss of a life worth? Is there a number high enough, in your opinion, Ms. Quincy? I ask because Jackson Murphy's wasn't the only life lost that day, was it?"

"No. It wasn't."

Devyn shakes her head. "No, it wasn't. As we heard earlier, during the altercation leading up to Mr. Murphy's death, he brutally attacked the defendant with the specific intent of terminating her pregnancy. Which he succeeded in doing. A life was lost. A life Mr. Murphy should have felt a God-given instinct to protect. And yet he snuffed it out in the most violent way imaginable."

"Objection, Your Honor. I'm not hearing any questions here."

Devyn raises her hand. "Oh, I have one. I promise."

"Then please get on with it, counsel." As of yet, I can't really tell if the judge likes one of them better than the other, but then I guess she's not supposed to.

"Will you ever be able to conceive another baby, Ms. Quincy?"

Quinn's jaw tightens, and the light that was missing comes back in a furious blaze. "What?"

"Please answer the question, Ms. Quincy," the judge directs her.

Quinn bites her lip, blinking several times. "No, I will not."

But Devyn doesn't let up. "Why not?"

Even from where I'm sitting, I can see her swallow hard like she's forcing down a spear that's painfully trying to push its way up her throat. "Because the repeated blows to my abdomen that day caused such severe internal bleeding that they had no choice but to perform an emergency hysterectomy to keep me from bleeding out and dying."

"So, essentially, Jackson Murphy didn't just kill his own baby. He killed every baby you had the potential to conceive and birth in your lifetime." Devyn spins around to face the jury. "How much do you suppose that's worth?"

Then, before the other side can even utter their objection, she quickly adds "Withdrawn" as she returns to her seat. "Defense rests, Your Honor. I have no more questions for the defendant"

And neither do I. I get it now. Everything. Those unborn lives he killed that day meant something now. Because they weren't just hypothetical babies anymore. They could have been ours.

• • • •

QUINN

I'm getting a tremor in my left hand. I haven't had them since I was on trial for Jackson's murder. Maybe they're courtroom related. Maybe they're Jackson related. Either way, I shake my hand to try and un-twitch whatever muscles and nerves are causing the spasm. But nothing helps. I want to cry. It's stupid. But this one little vibration is pushing me over the edge. Probably because it's just one more way the universe is letting me know that I don't have control over anything. Not my own life. Not even my own body.

"Ms. Quincy?" The judge's voice cuts through my thoughts, and I get the feeling this isn't the first time she's tried to get my attention.

"Yes, ma'am?" As far as I know the plaintiff's side is allowed to have another go at me. What with me being their star witness in the case against myself. I guess that's the downside to being the only person still alive after the altercation. That and the whole being labeled a murderer bit.

"You may step down." She nods toward my seat beside Devyn. "Counsel has declined to redirect."

I glance over at the Murphies and their attorney. They don't seem too happy about it. Now I'm kind of sorry I zoned out and missed whatever conversation led up to this.

Regardless, I follow her orders and hurry over to my chair. Any seat is better than this one.

As soon as I'm beside her, Devyn rises. "Your Honor, the defense calls James Shepherdson to the witness stand."

What? I immediately spin around and search the room. I don't have to look long. He's sitting two rows behind me. And he's staring straight at me because he knew I would look for him the moment I heard his name. He doesn't smile. He doesn't do anything other than stare back at me. It's the first time since I've known him that I can't get a read on what he's thinking or feeling. Riker's an open book when it comes to his feelings, which means he's making a conscious effort to hide them from me now.

"Counsel, before you call your first witness, perhaps you would like to make a motion?"

Devyn shakes her head like maybe she's misunderstood the judge. "A motion, Your Honor?"

"Yes. A motion." Judge Hanson leans forward. "You are familiar with court proceedings, are you not, counselor?"

"Of course, Your Honor." Devyn lifts her chin a little higher and squares her shoulders. "We'd like to make a motion to dismiss, Your Honor."

Then, shocking us all, the judge nods. "I should think so. Motion granted. This case is dismissed."

Jackson's mom and sister are visibly enraged by this unexpected turn of events while I'm just . . . here. I have no idea what to do or feel. It's too much. It's been less than ten minutes since I was asked to relive the most terrifying, most traumatic, most *devastating* day of my life. I can't just snap out of that and rejoice because the universe has flipped the script on me out of the blue. Besides. I don't trust the universe yet.

"Your Honor, with all due respect, you can't be serious." Not surprisingly, Harrold Sullivan, the other lawyer, is up on his feet trying to undo what's been done. "Mrs. Murphy's disabilities prevent her from working. Her son was the sole provider of their family. His death has caused them financial hardships they can't begin to overcome unless the defendant pays what they are owed."

"You're confused, counsel. Your talking portion has come to an end. So sit back down and be quiet unless you want to find yourself in contempt of court. It's my turn to talk now." Judge Hanson adjusts her seat and fixes the long flowing sleeves of her robe while Sullivan drops into his seat, completely flabbergasted. "I didn't choose to pick up this gavel or wear this robe to sit by and watch our justice system be misused in such a grossly negligent way as I have seen here since the proceedings began." She folds her hands and lays them flat on her podium. "However, after hearing testimony today from the defendant, I am more convinced than ever that we owe this young woman not only a not guilty verdict, but an apology. As members of this court, it is our duty to act with the utmost respect for human life, always. Unfortunately, at times we seem to forget that the defendants, however reprehensible they may seem, are entitled to that same respect. And when I see cases like this one, I am reminded time and time again that we are failing in this very important aspect of our jobs." She directs her focus to me and gestures for me to stand. Even though I can barely feel my legs, I do.

"You give me hope, Ms. Quincy. You give me hope, because your strength in spirit and your kindness of heart remain even after all you have endured. You give me hope, because I believe you will continue your work as you have done since your release from prison, and with your help, maybe society will stop asking women to be more preemptive in dealing with their attackers. Expect less mindful planning of their reactions to their attacks. And be more gracious and understanding of women who love their attackers in spite of how they suffer."

She turns toward the Murphies. "I am truly sorry for your loss. No mother should have to endure the death of a child. But no woman should have to endure the violence your son subjected Abigail Quincy to either. No human being should have to face the choice between dying and taking a life. Least of all the life of someone she loves. And no human being should ever have to face prosecution for surviving what should have killed them. Abigail Quincy owes you nothing. We owe her. We owe her the years of her life she spent in prison. We owe her for the months of public shaming she endured during her trials. We owe her for the undeniable pain and likely humiliation she faced every time she was asked to recount the times she was brutalized. And we owe her for never acknowledging her losses. For saying *it's your own fault*. For suggesting she deserved the sort of treatment she was given. Let me assure you one last time, she does not."

Her attention lands solely on me as she slams down her gavel. "This case is dismissed. Abigail Quincy, you are free to go. May no one ever be foolish enough to attempt to drag you back into my courtroom." Then she grants me an unexpected smile and stands to leave.

I still haven't processed any of it when Devyn throws her arms around me, jumping up and down like we're twelve and just got One Direction tickets. Kirsten's already piling herself on top of us. Over all the commotion, I can still hear my mother sniffling repeatedly while my father keeps clearing his throat. Then I remember. He's here.

"Riker." It's the first thing I've said since I was asked to leave the witness stand. As soon as his name passes my lips, it's like the sea of people surrounding me clears. Only he's not there anymore.

"Where did he go?" I break away from Devyn and Kirsten and take several steps toward the empty seat he occupied just a few minutes ago.

"I don't know. He was here a second ago." My sister's searching the room as well.

Then it hits me. "How long was he in the courtroom, Kirsten? When did he get here?"

"You were still testifying. The asshole was just asking you the last of his questions and then Devyn got up." She's smoothing the sides of her dress. She's anxious.

"He heard." My voice gets stuck somewhere in the back of my throat.

"He needed to hear." Kirsten steps up to move directly in front of me. "He needed to know. Everything. And I swear to you, Quinn, his reaction wasn't what you're thinking."

"Then why did he leave?"

Helplessly, she glances around one last time. "I don't know."

"Come on, honey." My mother drapes an arm around me, and my father curls his around my waist from the other side. "Time to close the door on this chapter and see what's on the other side." She smiles, and I know she's thinking about our last conversation about my life. Maybe she's right. Maybe there is something to hope for. I found light once in the black abyss I'd fallen into. And now that he's back, maybe I can come out of it for good. If he really is back.

My family shuttles me past the Murphies and their attorney, all of whom are out in the hall waiting to glare at me as I go by. I don't care anymore. Somehow, the words Judge Hanson said to me have changed things. It's like she took the power back from the universe and handed it back to me. For the first time ever, I am in charge of my own destiny. And now that I know what that means, I'm not screwing it up. Starting with the man I love. The man who made me want to be better. The man who found my heart when it was missing and gave me his until I found my own.

"He's handsome," my mother whispers as we walk outside. I smile. He is.

I rest my head on her shoulder and close my eyes to the bright sun. "I didn't realize you got to see him. He was sitting behind you."

Her hand squeezes my side. "I didn't, really. But I'm getting a pretty good look at him right now."

My eyelids fly back up in a flash, only now all I can see are black splotches while I wait for my eyes to adjust. Frustrated, I blink repeatedly. All I want is to see his face. See him grin that Riker grin and know that everything is going to be alright. That he forgives me. That he accepts me. All that I've done. All I'll never be able to give.

And then, finally, I do. He's got both hands placed in his pockets, his lips tucked up halfway in a tentative smile. It's like he pours strength into me just by being present, and I start to move toward him, getting faster with each step I take until I'm there, in his arms. Safe. And whole.

"Please don't tell me to leave," he whispers.

"I won't. Not ever again. I swear." I wrap my arms around him as tight as I can. I don't ever want to let him go. I just want to hold him. Kiss him. Tell him how stupid I was to push him away. The only thing I don't want to say is *I'm sorry*. I'm so fucking over *I'm sorry*.

I tilt my head back and find looking down at me. God, how much I've missed this. Missed him. Whatever convoluted ideas I had about love once upon a time have been completely eradicated and replaced with the magnitude of his fierce heart and what it has taught me.

"I'll never be able to give you what you lost." I need to say it. Now. I can't move forward wondering. Waiting to hear him change his mind about us. About me.

"I'll never be able to take back what was done to you." His lips brush my forehead.

"I never expected you to."

He lowers his lips to be even with mine. "Neither did I. All I've ever wanted from you was *you*. It's all I'll ever want." He kisses me, and I believe him. More importantly, I can give him what he wants. Truth is, he already has it.

I'm still clinging to him when Devyn begins to usher us all down the steps of the courthouse. "I don't know about you all, but I'm ready to get out of here and not come back for a while." In unison, five heads jerk around at her. "What? I'm a freaking lawyer. I *have* to come back. You"—she points at me—"are never to set foot in another courthouse for as long as you live, though. Unless it's for a good cause." She winks. "You know, like a marriage license."

"Oh, you know, we could just grab one now while we're here, and then you'll really never have to come back." Kirsten. Who clearly thinks she's being hilarious.

"Alright, alright. I get it. My man is hot, and you all think I need to slap a sold sign on him."

"Actually, I was thinking he needed to slap one on you. So you remember next time you want to do something stupid. Like run away from home and the best thing that ever happened to you." Kirsten nudges Riker as she passes him.

"You girls are so romantic." He laughs. "Seriously, though. Could you stop horning in on my proposal?"

My eyes widen, and I'm certain deer in the headlight doesn't even begin to cover it.

"Relax. I'm not asking you to marry me." He kisses my cheek. "Now."

"Huh." I'm not sure if I'm disappointed or not.

He notices and leans in close while we walk still wrapped up in one another. "Oh, don't you worry, Boots. It's going to happen."

"Promise?"

"Promise." And he doesn't make those unless he knows he can keep them.

I smile. My life is changing. And I'm finally ready to change with it.

CHAPTER TWENTY

RIKER

After we left the courthouse, we came straight here to Quinn's parents' house. Nate and Sophie were already here, ready and waiting with a makeshift banner welcoming Quinn to her new life of freedom. Apparently, Kirsten called ahead to give them the good news.

Quinn's mom's been on the phone since we walked in the door an hour ago, busy updating every friend and family member of the unexpected change of course, while Kirsten's been out on the front lawn sending off every reporter who dares to show his or her face around here. The civil trial didn't catch nearly as much media attention as the criminal one had, until today. But considering even Nate is opting to stay inside and let her handle things, I'm thinking Kirsten has it covered.

Meanwhile, Quinn is like a completely different person. The distant look in her eyes is gone and there's a new lighter way about her. I think we both know she still has a long way to go before we can seriously consider things like marriage and a family, but watching her sit with Sophie around the coffee table playing a game of Go Fish and giggling like she doesn't have a care in the world is all the proof I need that the life we'd both given up on is ours for the taking again.

Which means there's someone I need to talk to. Someone who needs to know more about me and how I feel about his daughter.

Mr. Quincy is outside, cleaning the grill. I kind of like that his idea of celebrating is firing up the barbeque. Reminds me of my dad. Family meant everything to him, and bringing everyone together over food he prepared was one way he showed it.

"Sir." I nod as I step outside to join him.

"Please, I'm wearing an apron that looks like a naked body builder with a tuff of pink fluff covering my crotch. I hardly think now is the time to be so formal." He chuckles, and I wonder how long it's been since he's done that. Really, truly laughed because he felt happy and carefree enough to do it. "Dave will do."

"Dave it is, then." I step beside him. "Can I give you a hand with anything here?"

He tips his head at the cooler sitting on the picnic bench. "You could grab me a bottle. And get one for yourself while you're at it."

I immediately do as he says. I'm not a big drinker, but a beer to take the edge off my nerves right now doesn't sound like a bad idea at all. I pop the top off his bottle and hand it to him.

"Thanks." He takes a swig. "So I'm assuming you didn't come out here just to watch me clean the grill."

"No, sir—I mean Dave." Fuck me. Why am I having a fucking meltdown about this? He's not even making it hard on me. "Thing is . . . " I put the bottle down. Maybe a clear head is the better way to go. "I know I'm probably not the man you had in mind for your daughter. There's the age difference. And I've been married and divorced. Not to mention I'm in my thirties and still haven't figured out what to do with my life other than handle the business of those no longer around to handle it for themselves." I glance down at my rolled-up sleeves and the ink covering every inch of my exposed skin. "I probably don't make the best first impression, all things considered."

Quinn's dad steps away from the grill, then takes my beer and heads over to take a seat at the patio table. I follow his lead, assuming he's about to give his side of the story and why he has reservations about my relationship with his daughter.

"Riker, my wife tells me you're a father."

I nod. Although most people wouldn't consider me one anymore, I sort of appreciate that he still does. "I'm not technically able to claim that title anymore. But I still feel like one. I don't know how to turn that off."

"It can't *be* turned off. Once that love starts, it flows freely until the day you die. It's not like any other kind of love. It can't be changed or stopped or affected in any way. It's true. It's unconditional, and often it's heartbreaking." He balances his bottle on its rim. "My daughters have endured more heartache than most. During the years young adults are meant to be exploring the various avenues available to them, making fools of themselves and enjoying the freedom to do so, my girls weren't so lucky." He levels his gaze with mine. "As a father, I've felt it all. Everything they feel, I feel too." He smiles. "I know my daughter is in love with you, Riker. And whatever preconceived notions you have about my expectations of the man who would hold her heart one day, I didn't have a single one you haven't met. You showed up here today to defend her. To stand by her. I can't think of a better first impression than that."

I laugh uncomfortably. "Thank you. That really means a lot to me, that you would say that. I love her too. More than I thought I could love anyone. And I want you to know I don't intend to stand by her just today."

He nods, then lifts his bottle to cheer, and I meet it with mine, clinking the glasses together loudly. "To Quinn."

"To Quinn." I grin like a total goof, all because I like the sound of my girl's name when it comes out of my mouth. Knowing I have her father's blessing to call her mine means something to me. And I suddenly understand why Hannah and Sid never made it down the aisle without my mother. It wouldn't stop me from marrying Quinn, but I get it now.

Satisfied with our little chat, her dad gets back to his feet and begins to undo his apron. "Now then, just to prove to you that I am not only accepting of this relationship but am happy to welcome you to the Quincy Clan, I'm going to let you wear this and man the grill." He hands me his gear and winks. "But when Nate asks, tell him you had to arm-wrestle me for it."

"What?" I laugh.

"He'll believe that. And even if he doesn't, he's a blue-collar guy. I can beat him if I have to." Then he chuckles again and starts pulling Tupperware filled with marinated steaks out of the cooler while I light the grill to take charge of dinner, naked guy apron and all.

. . . .

QUINN

I'm in my parents' bedroom searching for an old puzzle of a unicorn I know my mother saved, when my eye catches on one of the pictures on her dresser. It's of me and Sophie. Only Sophie was just a baby and I was a completely different person. I'm smiling in the picture. I remember exactly when it was taken. Sophie had just learned to crawl, and I'd taken full credit for it because I'd been the only one silly enough to get on the floor and lead by example. That's how I was back then. Silly. Fun.

I never doubted for even a second that Sophie would grow up calling me her favorite aunt. I had visions of her coming to me to talk about boys and clothes and every other trivial yet monumental thing a teenage girl needs to chat about for hours on end. I planned on being the one she came to. And then I left. And the aunt who came back was never going to be worthy of those moments.

Sophie would never remember the aunt she had back then. She'd never know how many hours I spent giggling with her. How often I'd played peekaboo, or the countless times I sang the ants go marching round and round because it was the only thing that kept her from crying while riding in the car. All she knew now was the serious, solemn aunt who hardly ever spoke to her. The aunt who had moments of joy, but more often than not opted to hole up in her room by herself.

I don't want to be that aunt anymore. I want to be the one she can count on. The one she can come to. And I want to be fun again. I'm ready to be fun again. And not just for Sophie's sake. For my own.

"Hey." Riker's standing in the doorway. He's wearing my father's apron.

"Hey yourself, stud." I walk over and tug at the naked guy covering his body. "What's happening here?"

"Your dad likes me." He's pleased with himself. "I'm in charge of the grill."

"Um, the grill is out in the yard." I point out of the room and down the hall.

He gives me a look like he doesn't appreciate my insinuating he's an idiot. "Yeah, I'm pretty clear on that. He sent me in here to get you."

"Oh." I reach both arms around him. "Well, now that you've got me, what would you like to do with me?"

"Nothing I can do in your parents' bedroom. Now back up before this pink ball of cotton covering my crotch starts to move into an awkward position."

I laugh. It feels good. All of this feels good.

"So, what happens next?" I ask as I loop my arm into his and we start walking down the hall.

"That depends."

"On what?"

"On what you want to have happen." He stops before we enter the living room to join everyone else.

"I just want to be with you." I reach up onto my tiptoes to reach his lips. "But before you agree, there's something else. Something I need to tell you. One last truth I owe you."

"Well, let's hear it," he murmurs, and I can't help but smile.

"It's pretty major," I warn, still moving my mouth over his while I whisper.

"With you, everything always is." His lips twitch playfully. "Now stop stalling and just say it."

So I do.

"I love you, Riker Shepherdson."

QUINN

It's been five years since Judge Hanson dismissed the case against me. Five years since I was set free. Five years since I said I love you to the man who has since become my husband.

As soon as Kirsten was able to stop writing checks to the Quinn's Legal Defense Charity, she found herself a new cause to sink her money into. Mine. Barks Against Battery has grown tremendously in the last few years, successfully matching nearly five thousand women with adoptable dogs in seven states, and we continue to expand every day. I no longer feel like I need to seek redemption for the things I did, but I know I'll never be satisfied when it comes to the number of women out there I want to reach before they find themselves in the same place I was. Or worse.

Riker has found his calling as well. He still runs the family business, but the bulk of his time is spent on the ranch where he and Sid have moved the focus away from lessons and onto equine therapy. I think it's the best decision he's ever made for himself. Nox still refuses to be cared for by anyone but him, but I think it's more out of spite than anything else. And I've even started riding again.

"You ready to get out of here and get some dinner?" Riker's standing in the stall eye to eye with the black stallion he still claims to hate.

"Yep." We still eat takeout more often than not. "Joe's tonight?" He comes out into the aisle, and we start walking, his hand sliding into mine automatically.

"Works for me." I whistle for Harley, and he comes cruising around the corner from wherever he was. He's getting older, and his arthritis slows him down more than it used to, but his spirit is still as young and free as it ever was.

When we get home, we take our dinner out onto the back deck. We've moved since the early days in his garage apartment, but our place is still tiny compared to the mansion he used to live in. All either of us really cared about was being on the ocean, and that we are.

"Kirsten call you about Nate's birthday party?" he asks between bites.

"Yeah. It's supposed to be a big surprise." I toss a fry to Harley. "But Sophie called right after she hung up and said Nate already knows."

He laughs. "You going to tell Kirsten?"

"Haven't decided yet. Waiting to see if she has some tedious job for me to do like last year when she made me the valet." It had its upside, too, though. I didn't have to deal with any strangers for more than thirty seconds at a time. I'm not as cranky as I used to be, but I'm still not what you might call a people person.

"Well, you better figure it out fast because she's making me the decoy. Apparently, I'm supposed to take him out for the day, and if I don't have to stress about the possibilities of having to dig out my dad's old golfing gear, I wouldn't mind knowing now."

I smile. "I'll tell her."

"Thank you." He moves the takeout boxes out of the way and leans over the table. "Now then, how about dessert?"

"What did you have in mind?" I ask, even though I already know the answer. A lot has changed over the years, but one thing is exactly the same way it's always been. We still can't seem to get enough of one another.

He doesn't answer out loud, but I follow his eyes with mine and land on the railing facing the ocean.

"Dessert with a view. I like it."

He chuckles, and my stomach still flips back and forth from the deep sound of it.

He leans forward, about to kiss me when he stops short. "You hear that?" He pulls back, leaning his head toward the house. "I think it's your phone."

I reach for his shirt and bring him toward me again. "So what?"

He smirks, and his lips softly sweep mine. And then he stops once more. "Seriously. I hear it again. Someone is trying to get ahold of you."

"It's probably just Kirsten," I whine.

He laughs. "Well, then you should definitely go answer it. We both know she won't stop until you do."

I groan. "Ugh. Fine. But don't you move!" I untangle myself from him and hurry inside to find my phone.

When I finally locate it, it's not ringing anymore, but I have seven missed calls from Devyn. Before I even have a chance to hit return on my screen, she's making her eighth attempt.

"What the hell is going on?" I'm instantly freaked out. Devyn doesn't call back to back unless it's serious. She's no Kirsten.

"I should ask you the same thing. Answer your damn phone, woman!" She sounds out of breath, like she's on the move. "I have an opportunity for you, but you have to decide right now if you want it or not."

"What?" I walk back out to the deck. "What are you talking about?"

"A baby."

Silence.

My mind draws a complete blank, and I can't think or move, or breathe, for several seconds.

"A what?"

"A baby. One of the lawyers in my firm was handling a private adoption. A beautiful baby girl was born three hours ago. She's healthy and *perfect*, but at the last minute the adoptive parents backed out. And now . . . her mom can't keep her. And she's too emotionally fried to go through the whole process again right now, so DCF will have to be called. Unless . . ."

Riker is standing right in front of me. His hands are softly moving across my skin, his face full of concern, but he doesn't interrupt.

"Unless what?" I don't want to assume. I definitely don't want to guess.

"Unless you guys want her. I already called Judge Hanson. She'll sign off on the adoption herself. I'll handle everything else. *No one* could get in the way of this."

I'm a felon. I was convicted of manslaughter. A violent crime. I'm not exactly a prime candidate for adoption agencies looking for potential parents, and forget the foster system. Honestly, Riker and I'd given up hope we'd ever be more than just us.

"You're sure?" I breathe into the phone. "They would let me be her mother?"

"I promise. I wouldn't be calling you if I had any doubts about this. I know what it means to you. What it means to both of you. Trust me."

I wipe my eyes. I didn't even realize I was crying. "I do trust you. Tell them we want her. Tell them we can't wait to meet her. Tell them we're on our way. Tell them thank you. Thank you. Thank you! *Oh my God, Devyn.* Thank you."

"I'll tell them." Her voice is just as choked up as mine is. "Call me when you land. I'll pick you up."

She hangs up, and I just stand there. Shaking. I can't believe this is happening.

"Where are we going? What is happening? Jesus, Quinn, you look like you're having a fucking seizure." Riker pulls me to his chest and holds me tight, trying to still my body. "Should I be panicking?"

"No." My teeth are chattering from the adrenaline surging through me. For the first time ever, I'm enjoying the experience. "You should be packing. We have to get to the airport. ASAP." I break away from him far enough to look him in the eye. "Because our daughter is waiting to be picked up from the hospital."

Riker's face twitches like he can't decide how to react to the news. "What?"

I can relate. I'm still processing all of this myself. "There's a baby. In California. For us." Forming sentences has never been so challenging in all my life. "You and me. We're going to be parents."

And then he totally loses it. His eyes get glossy, and he has to clear his throat several times, while he kisses me over and over until both of us are out-of-breath, sobbing, crying messes.

Still overwhelmed with emotion, he presses his forehead to mine and quietly says, "Let's go get our daughter."

"Hannah," I whisper. "Her name is Hannah. Hannah Hope Shepherdson."

THE END.

A Note From The Author

THANK YOU SO MUCH FOR going on Quinn's journey with me. While her story is not real, there are countless stories and women who are. Please consider joining me in supporting organizations that seek to help both the *Quinns* as well as the *Harleys* of the world in hopes of giving them a *real **Happy Ending***.

    **A percentage of the proceeds from sales of this book will go to local shelters supporting women and children in need, as well as those who save our four-legged furry friends. **

If you enjoyed TIN, you may also like Don't Fall.

Chapter
One

TESSA

If I hear that bitch giggle one more time, I may punch someone. Not really. Well, not *likely*. I've never actually punched someone. Even if I've thought about doing it. A lot. Especially in the last seven hours.

I've worked here for nearly three years, slinging beers and booze five nights a week, but after being gone all summer, it's been hard to find my groove again. Provided I ever had it here to begin with. I thought I did. After tonight, I'm struggling to remember how I ever made it through a shift without throwing myself headfirst into a brick wall.

It's not so much that I find everyone as annoying as I'm finding Nat and her damn high-pitched squeal tonight, it's more about how extremely inadequate I feel ten seconds after walking through the doors. I'm the only chick with dark brown hair in a sea of human Barbie dolls. I'm also the only one with my original boobs - my very own, much smaller boobs. Inevitably, this seems to directly relate to my tip jar always being slightly on the slimmer side at the end of the night. That, and I don't do the giggle. The giggle is where it's at. I know this. The more I think about this, the more I realize, I've always knowns this. And it's not like I look down upon the giggle. I don't. It's just that in this world where giggle is master, I am its bitch - its pathetic, incapable bitch. One who finds the sight of hard brick particularly inviting tonight.

"Natalie!"

I automatically look up from running my end-of-the-night reports at the sound of Burt's voice. He's the boss. He's also a lot like Grumpy from the Seven Dwarves. Unless he's drunk. Then he's a cross between Dopey and Sleepy. I like drunk Burt best. Grumpy Burt scares me a little. From the look on Natalie's face, right now, he scares her a lot. I notice she's no longer giggling either. In fact, her face is stone cold and red hot – contradictory but true – as she ushers the hot dude she's been letting grope her behind the counter for the last thirty minutes back out to where the customers are actually supposed to be during operating hours. Half an hour after closing, his ass is supposed to be out in the parking lot.

An angry jerk of Burt's thumb and we all know she's being summoned to his office. Things are about to get ugly. He won't fire her. Even Grumpy Burt is incapable of firing anyone. Unless they have a penis. Then he'll fire away. But Natalie doesn't have one of those, so she's safe.

It takes all of five minutes before she comes storming back out of the office. Tears are streaming down her face as she barrels her way through me on her way to her end of the bar.

"Hey!" I nearly eat it on the nasty floor mats and what is left of my fruit tray goes flying, red maraschino cherry syrup spilling everywhere in the process.

Natalie doesn't care. Nor does anyone else, until she drops a glass by accident and sobs dramatically, shoulders slumping in her state of complete and utter misery.

I'm down on my hands and knees still picking olives out of the holes in the mat when I see both bar-backs and three bouncers rush to her aid. Fucking unbelievable. What I wouldn't give to own the giggle for just one night.

The giggle is master.

The giggle keeps your ass from picking bits of pickled produce off the floor.

I've barely resurfaced with my mangled fruit tray and I find I'm standing face-to-face with Melissa, the assistant manager. "Can you help Nat finish up tonight? She's really upset because Burt got on her case for having that guy in here after closing." She leans in closer to whisper, "Apparently, he's a freaking cop. Off duty, but still. Burt is livid."

"I bet." I dump the disgusting fruit buffet into the nearest trashcan.

"Yeah." She nods, her hopeful eyes still waiting for me to confirm my desire to acquiesce to her request. Turning halfway until Natalie lands in my line of vision, I reach up to rub the dull ache in my shoulder. She really slammed into me when she came through. And she didn't even say sorry. Honestly, I'm not really feeling all that helpful right now.

"Dude, I don't know. Nat was a total bitch to me all night. She ignored half the customers when she was busy flirting with her cop boyfriend and then accused me of stealing her tabs when I picked up the slack. Not to mention, she about dislocated my shoulder five minutes ago."

"Tessa, come on. We all know what it's like to have a shit night. Just go help her out so we can all get out of here." This time she doesn't wait for me to agree. Probably because she knows she'd have to wait forever.

I mutter a handful of my go-to obscenities under my breath while I finish cleaning up my own station before I take a deep breath and visually attack the area I'm about to venture into. Nat's sitting on the beer cooler now, eyes all puffy and her pointy nose twitching as she sniffs loudly every two seconds. That may be even worse than listening to her giggle. Although judging by the way Tony, the bar-back, and Seth, the new bouncer, are still coddling her, I'm the only one who wants to dry heave at the sound of her snot traveling back and forth inside her sinuses.

"What still needs to be done over here?"

"Ice bin needs cleaning out. Liquor needs putting up, and glassware needs restocking," Tony answers for her.

"I still need to count out my drawer as well," Nat adds in a whimper, more to Tony than me. I guess we're not speaking. Fine by me.

"If you've got this, I'm gonna walk Nat out to her car so she can get out of here." Seth, the new guy, clearly isn't aware that we all walk out together on weekends.

"Nat can't leave until we all leave. Bar rule." Then I take a page from Melissa's book and avoid eye contact from this point forward to end the argument. I just want to get this done and over with.

It's after three a.m. when I'm finally getting into my car. I notice my escort left me one row over when he reached his own truck. I don't blame him. I'm pretty sure my biceps are bigger than his. He was probably safer walking with me than I was with him.

Regardless, I'm on the road and headed home. Home. Sounds almost strange now. It's the same place I've lived since I was twelve years old and first moved in with my great Aunt Edie. It felt like home the second I walked in and knew I was staying. Even after she moved up north three years ago to be closer to her children who insisted she needed more care than I could give her, it felt like home. She still spent the winters here with me, and on the summer days I missed her most, I could call and put her on speaker, just to fill the condo with her voice for a while.

But things are different now. There won't be any more visits. No more time spent listening to her fill me in on all the newest gossip going around the assisted living complex while I go about doing laundry or cooking or catching up on schoolwork. Aunt Edi is gone. And somehow, home feels gone too.

I exhale slowly, trying to steady all the emotions attempting to take me down again. Meltdowns and driving make for severely inefficient travel conditions. I know, I had about three on the drive back down here. The first time my speed dropped down to twenty-nine miles an hour for a good ten minutes. The second, a semi nearly took me out when I swerved trying to find a tissue (yeah, okay, so I nearly took out the semi, but size-wise, come on, who was taking out who here?!). The last one really did me in. It was so bad, I had to pull over on the side of the road and wait it out. Or, let it out, rather. The only reason I ever got a grip again was because my need to pee suddenly became a more pressing issue than my need to cry. Damn liquids turning my body all leaky.

Stupid tears and stupid sobbing are the reason I had to bypass stopping by the condo and instead go straight to work after an eleven-hour drive. I allow my gaze to dip to the right and take in the pile of bags. Unloading everything from the passenger seat alone is going to take at least three trips. And that's before I even tackle the back...and the trunk. Which will definitely have to wait until sometime tomorrow. Tonight, all I'm thinking about is what it will take to get me from point A to point bed.

If I don't hit any red lights, I can make it to the condo in thirteen minutes. With lights, it'll be seventeen. Yeah. I'm anal like that. I've timed it. I'll need another twenty (maybe thirty given the luggage trips) to get inside, get showered, pour a glass of water and climb into bed. I'll catch the end of Frasier. I don't really want to watch it, I just like the background noise when I'm falling asleep. And I need sleep. Almost more than I need that shower. And I reek of booze and stuff I don't care to contemplate, so if sleep is competing with showering, sleep is rating higher than usual.

I've barely got my key out of the ignition and the door open, when I hear Jules.

"Thank God, you're finally here."

I was thinking the same thing. I just wasn't expecting to hear it from her the second I step out of the car.

"Jules? What are you doing out here? Do you know what time it is?"

She reaches for my arm and misses. She's drunk. Fucking awesome.

"Come oooon. Drea needs you." Her fingers catch my elbow on the second try and she stumbles off, dragging me along. We don't get far before I see my best friend and neighbor sitting in a rumpled mess on the ground beside the staircase leading up to the third floor and our respective units. She's got on her favorite hot pink bejeweled hoodie, so she's impossible to miss, even in the dark.

"Drea, what are you doing down there?" At three thirty in the morning, I was hardly expecting a welcoming committee, even if I have been gone all summer long.

"She can't move," Julie explains dramatically as I crouch down to further investigate.

"You can't move?"

Drea bites her lip and shakes her head. Even in a drunken stupor with mascara running down one side of her face and smeared lip-gloss reaching down to the dimple in her chin, she's still beautiful. "I think I broke my leg."

I fight the urge to roll my eyes. Doesn't matter what sort of a state she's in, she'll notice, and she'll hold it against me tomorrow. Regardless of how ridiculous she acts; she expects to be taken seriously. Apparently, it's part of the best friend code. I just take her word for it. That's part of the code, too.

"Why do you think you broke your leg?" Meanwhile, I can't even find her legs under the fluffy skirt thing she's wearing. It looks like part of her old prom dress. *Wait a minute.* "Are you wearing the gown you wore to prom?"

"Yes! Stupid Scott dared me to. He said there was no way my new boobs would fit." By new boobs she doesn't mean fake, just that they came in after graduation. Surprised us all.

"He was right." I pull the zipper on her hoodie up higher. "Back to the leg." Which I've now found. Strapped into the same heels that nearly killed her on prom night. "Drea," I grumble, starting to piece things together. Her left ankle is red and slightly swollen. She must have rolled it coming off the last step. Wouldn't be the first time a pair of shoes nearly sent her to an early grave. Booze, stilettos and Drea just don't mix.

Placing both hands under her arms, I hoist her to her feet. We're barely standing when Jules reaches out in an attempt to help, and nearly knocks us all over.

"It's cool. I've got her." Her face falters slightly and I add, "Thanks, though. Really."

I line Drea and myself up with the stairs and peer up at the daunting task that lies ahead. I'm definitely off-schedule. Cheers'll be on by the time I get to bed. Because I really need more bar sounds for background noise after all of this.

"Oh, I better get Scott. He can carry Drea upstairs." Jules makes to rush past me, but I stop her.

"If Scott was willing and able to do that, why was she sitting on the ground when I got here?"

"That fucker," Drea mutters. "He's the reason I fell."

Oh, hell no. "What?"

"He was supposed to catch me." Her eyes glaze over as she stares off into the night.

"What were you guys doing?"

"Walking down the stairs!"

I hate when drunk people get exasperated with me. Like, really? *I'm* the problem in this conversation?

"Got it. You were walking. You tripped. He was supposed to catch you, on principle I'm assuming? And he dropped the ball, or rather the ballgown. Literally."

"Exactly!" Her enthusiasm does seem to bring back some clarity. "Then he had the nerve to try and help me up. *After* I already fell! I told him, 'Fuck off, buddy. Too little, too late.'"

"Fantastic." I shake my head and reposition my grip to make sure I won't drop her as well. "Alright. Let's get this done and over with. First step. Nice and easy."

It takes us at least twice as long as it would have if Scott had just carried her ass, but we finally make it to the third floor. At least her door is shut. Most nights when I find Drea out in the parking lot, we make it upstairs to find the door wide open and all of her worldly possessions free for the taking, not to mention the open opportunity for any potential creeper hoping to move up in the world of sex crimes.

"Hang on, I gotta get my keys." I turn to Jules for backup in holding Drea upright but she's nowhere to be found. Her condo is on the floor below us. Obviously, I was kidding myself when I thought she was on this mission with me for the long haul.

I'm struggling to balance keeping Drea on her feet and digging around in my purse when the door opens all on its own.

"You need a hand there?" Scott. Ney. *Stupid* Scott.

"You're still here?!" I practically throw Drea at him. He catches her. This time.

"Drea took my keys before she started playing dress-up." He bends down enough to reach his arm under her knees and lift her properly. Her head is already nestled into his shoulder, completely unaware of how much she hates him at the moment.

"You don't sound drunk," I point out the obvious.

"I'm not." He turns toward the living room, likely headed for the couch.

"Then why did Drea take your keys?"

"Because Drea was drunk."

I'm not finding this chat with sober Scott to be any easier than the one I had with drunk Drea. I should really just retreat now and pretend this whole thing never happened.

But I don't. Because Drea's my girl and even if Scott loves her, his standards still far short on occasion where her care is concerned.

"You staying here tonight?" Scott mumbles, eyeing the sofa as if he's wondering about its availability.

"No," I scoff, slightly more annoyed than necessary. Just because I want to make sure Drea doesn't land face first in a pillow where she might choke to death on her own vomit at some point during the night, doesn't mean I intend to babysit her until morning.

He shrugs and proceeds to place her on the wide cushions. I snatch an afghan from the recliner and hand it to him to cover her.

"Any reason she's not allowed to sleep in her bed tonight?" I ask, leaning on the armrest.

"You mean outside of her tendency to wake up throwing punches when she's hung over?"

Forgot about that. "Right."

Even in the midst of being a pretty straightforward jerk about things, I notice Scott still can't quite get past how much he loves the crazy, punching drunk girl lying on the sofa. A gentle sweep of his finger over her forehead to move the tangled mess of curls from her face. A subtle tuck around her feet to make sure her bare toes don't get cold. And lastly, a sweet kiss on her cheek and a quiet murmur of I love you, before he shuffles his feet lazily toward the bedroom still trying his best to portray a demeanor fit for a dude whose high-maintenance girlfriend never gets the best of him.

Drea giggles. Because she can. Even half asleep and wasted.

"Isn't he so cute?"

"Who?" I roll my eyes, knowing this time she can't see them. Guess she's back to being in love with Scott again.

"Hot New Neighbor Guy." She stretches her arms out above her head, a doofy smile resting on her lips.

"I wouldn't know." And I'm not all that interested in finding out. "Meanwhile, he's been living here for months. How do you still not know his name? I'm thinking it's not Hot New Neighbor Guy."

She attempts to make a *psh* sound but winds up blowing raspberries instead, spitting all over her own face. "You don't know. It could be."

"Yeah. Okay." I stand. This time, I'm really leaving. "I gotta go. If I don't meet with my pillow sometime in the next ten minutes, no one is going to be safe around me tomorrow."

"You're so traumatic." She goes to swipe a loose strand of hair from her face but winds up just swishing it back and forth from one cheek to the other.

"It's dramatic, not traumatic. Being friends with you, *that's* traumatic. For me. Seriously, Drea. Classes start back up tomorrow. It's our final year. Don't you think it might have made a nice impression to start the semester *not* hung over for a change?"

"It's just the first week. Nothing ever happens in the first week." She turns until the side of her face is in the cushions and she smiles. I can't help but imagine her younger self sleeping with her teddy mushed against her nose like this because she's got an oddly toddler-like expression right now.

"Yeah, I know. The first week doesn't count. That's the fourth year in a row I've heard that argument." But she can't hear me. She's passed the fuck out.

• • • •

HOT NEW NEIGHBOR

I wait until I hear the door close and know they're both safely inside for the night before I go back to bed. Nearly called the cops two hours ago when the party spilled out into the common area, also known as my front doorstep. Then I remembered, I'm not old enough to be that asshole yet. So, I went back to bed.

Until I heard shouting, which turned out to be singing.

And I went back to bed.

Until there was cursing and door slamming, which turned out to be the sober boyfriend getting irritated with the task of babysitting.

So, I went back to bed.

This last go around, I woke up because I had to take a leak (in hindsight, having a drink of water every time I was up, *just because*, was not a great idea). Since I *was* up, I figured checking in with the partiers was the responsible and nosey new neighbor thing to do.

I was just settling in at the peephole, located at a convenient angle to the door across from me as well as the stairs given the kitty-corner layout of entryways up on the landing, when I spotted two women struggling to get up that last flight of stairs. I was nearly out the door to help them before I decided that being the weird naked neighbor at three a.m. approaching drunk girls was not the lasting impression I was hoping to make around here.

Given how close they were to reaching the top, there was no point in trying to get dressed in a hurry. Instead, I opted to supervise. From a distance. And out of sight.

Now that I know everyone is safe and the party is definitely over, I have no plans to wake up for anything other than my alarm clock.

Except, my night is obviously not going in that direction.

My face has barely touched my pillow when I hear someone at the door.

"Goddammit." I push up and move back to my feet, grumbling the whole way, "Freaking drunk girls. Freaking college kid neighbors." And fucking Olivia turning my life into this shit.

When I hear what sounds like the lock clicking, I speed up. I turn the corner to the living room, just in time to see her walk in.

Our eyes meet.

Her eyes drop a little lower.

She screams.

Because I'm still naked.

A shitstorm ensues. I'm yanking the first thing I can get my fingers on into position in front of my crotch (the first thing turns out to be a throw pillow from the loveseat) meanwhile, she's shouting everything from four letter words to cries for help and requests for 911 calls as she makes a very calculated move for the umbrella tucked in the corner beside the coat closet and begins swinging it at me with full force.

"Whoa!" I duck just in time. "What are you doing?" But she just keeps on coming, leaving me no choice but to abandon my efforts to stay covered for an attempt at staying unclobbered instead.

Dropping the pillow leads to two things in my favor. One, she's temporarily distracted. Again. And two, I have two free hands with which to grab the umbrella and disarm my crazy attacker chick.

Stumped, the crazy chick glares back and forth between me and the door, clearly uncertain which to approach.

I help her out. "Get out. Unless you want to stick around while I make that call to the cops you were screaming for a second ago."

"Are you insane?!"

"Bold words from a crazy person who broke into my apartment and started swinging an umbrella at my head!" Now that I'm no longer under attack, I make the time to walk over to the kitchen table where I left the laundry basket and pull on the nearest pair of sweatpants I can find. I'm almost not surprised when I turn around to find she's followed me.

"I'm not the one who broke in," she screeches. "And I'm definitely not the crazy one here!" Though she does seem less convinced of this when she comes to a stop in front of me, taking in the whole room.

"You've been here long enough to do laundry? What are you? Some sort of a squatter?"

I close my eyes and count to three. I'd like ten, but three is all I have time for. "Look, I know you girls have been partying really hard tonight, and things get a little confusing after that much fun, but this is my apartment. Not yours."

She stares at me and I get the odd sensation she's silently counting as well.

"First of all, I'm not drunk, and while I'm exhausted enough to believe that I may have temporarily lost my mind and wandered into the wrong unit, that still doesn't explain why my key fit or why this place is filled with all of my shit." Her pitch rises even higher as she spreads her arms out to her sides, indicating that everything in sight is hers. "My shit. ALL. MY. SHIT. Plus, YOU! Why do I have you? You don't go with anything in here!" Exasperated, her flailing arms collapse at her sides.

Then, the front door swings open yet again, and the drunk girl from before comes stumbling in along with her sober boyfriend right behind her.

"We heard yelling," the guy announces.

"You're late," the crazy girl spats. "I could be dead right now."

"Hot New Neighbor wouldn't kill you," the drunk one points out, laughing to herself.

Crazy girl's eyes widen. "This is Hot New Neighbor?"

"Well, that's not what I'm calling him," the boyfriend chimes in. "But yeah, that's the dude you've been subletting your place to."

"I'm not renting from her," I interject, feeling the onset of a revelation coming for us all. "The woman I spoke to sounded a lot older. And frankly, saner."

"What the hell is going on?" the crazy girl whines, dragging her feet to the first kitchen chair in reach and sliding her small frame into it. She suddenly seems a lot less crazy and a lot more vulnerable. "Who would rent out my condo?" She buries her face in her hands and I have to fight the urge to reach out and comfort her. Instead, I march into the kitchen and retrieve my lease from the drawer below the coffee maker.

"Edith Dash."

Her head lifts and her glassy eyes peek out. "What?"

"Edith Dash, that's the woman I'm leasing from," I explain, coming back toward her to hand over the lease so she can see for herself. Only she doesn't take it. She just starts shaking her head 'no' over and over again.

"Not possible," she whispers.

"Why isn't it possible?" I ask, growing increasingly frustrated with the way this is dragging out for no apparent reason.

She wipes her face with the back of her hand. "Because Edith Dash died two months ago."

"What?"

"Edith Dash is...*was*...my great aunt. I've lived in this condo with her for the last decade. It's been my home from the moment she invited me in, I seriously doubt her dying wish was to steal it out from under me. So, no. It's not possible that she rented this place to you. And, even if she did, it wouldn't matter. It's mine now."

"This is your condo?" I ask, trying to clarify what has become confusing beyond my four-a.m. brain capacity.

"Yes. My condo."

I pull up a chair and sit down across from her. "Which your aunt sublet to me, *for a year*, before she died."

"Just to be clear," sober boyfriend interrupts. "No one is going to kill anyone tonight?"

I nod. "Yeah, I'm pretty sure we can rule out murder for the time being."

"Cool. Then I'm going to take drunky here back to the couch." He scoops her up into his arms and turns to leave without further ado, pulling the door shut with his foot on the way out.

I stare back across the table at the girl who now looks neither drunk nor crazy. Just exhausted. And heartbroken.

"Look," I start quietly. "It's late. There are two rooms here, two beds and two of us. Any chance we could just get some sleep tonight and sort all of this out tomorrow?"

Her jaw stiffens, and her lips turn into a thin streak on her otherwise soft face. "You want me to stay the night here with you? A total stranger?"

I can see how that sounds like a stupid idea. So, I extend my hand to her. "Michael."

She grudgingly lifts her own to meet mine. "Tessa."

"There you go." I smile, sort of. "Not strangers anymore."

Chapter
Two

TESSA

I wake up to a set of claws digging into my side.

Dick.

Drea's cat. Well, really, her boyfriend, Scott's. Two years ago, he asked me to cat sit while they went to Cancun for spring break, and I've been trying to get him to come and take him back home ever since. I've tried repeatedly just leaving him at Drea's, but inevitably, he finds his way back in through cracked windows or doors being held open a second longer than necessary. Doesn't help that Drea doesn't keep him locked in. Or that Scott seems rather disinterested in making the drive back home across town with him, but I'm not giving up hope on a Dick-less life yet. Even if I have taken him to the vet twice and bought cat food every two weeks since I ran out of the first bag he came with. Dick is not mine. He's not.

As soon as he feels me move, he switches positions and comes up to greet me, his motor-box running on overdrive. I laugh when his whiskers brush against my cheek, and finally, I open my eyes even though my alarm has yet to go off.

"Nothing like having a Dick in your face first thing in the morning," I mumble quietly, although I suppose sarcasm is lost on cats. He noses me several times, waiting for me to finally reach up and scratch his ears. As soon as I do, he drops down on his side and goes back to massaging my ribcage with his pointy little nail extensions. I don't even care. I'm actually smiling, his sense of contentment is so damn contagious.

Shit. Dick is mine. He is.

Slowly, I drag myself out of my make-shift bed compiled mostly of an old comforter and pillows stacked up in the rarely used and thus semi-empty dining room, and make my way out into the living room, cradling the cat like a baby while he curls into me. If only it was this easy with two legged men.

Drea's still on the couch where Scott left her, but she's awake and sitting up like maybe she's been that way for a while.

"Aw, look at you holding Scott's Dick in your hands." She snorts, she's so amused with herself.

"That joke never gets old," I grumble under my breath, because sarcasm is also lost on early morning Drea. "Speaking of jokes, where's Scott?"

She grimaces. She caught that one. "He took off a while ago. Had to get to work." That explains why he was so agitated about not finding his keys last night. Also accounts for his sober state of being given the firehouse is no place for a hangover. For all his lacking heroics last night with Drea, Scott's still a decent human overall.

"I take it you two are over your little tiff from last night?" I ask, slowly moving my way around the room, still slightly distracted by the quiet purr of my cat.

"We had a tiff?" Of course, she doesn't remember.

"You woke up in your prom dress. That didn't trigger anything for you?"

She shrugs. "Not really. Woke up wearing my grandmother's wedding dress last weekend. If that wasn't cause for concern, I'm not likely to be all that worried about waking up in much of anything else."

I take a minute to let her words sink in. "You ever think maybe you drink a little too much?"

"I'm pretty sure I do," she agrees. "But you and Scott make it so easy to be reckless."

I sigh, lifting Dick to mush his head to my cheek. Cat cuddles, man. "I'll have to talk to Scott about that."

"Be sure and tell him thank you when you do," she says, waving her hand at me like she just remembered something.

"Why am I thanking him?"

She smiles, the way only a truly proud girlfriend could. "He unloaded your car for you this morning before he left."

"He did?" Now *I'm* smiling. The way only the friend of a proud girlfriend could. "Scott is so nice. I don't know why we're always so mean to him."

She throws her hands up at me, dismissing the statement. "He has it coming. Every time!"

I laugh. They're a weird pair those two, but I can't even imagine either one of them with someone else. They just...fit.

"Meanwhile, do I smell coffee? Please tell me I smell coffee."

"You smell coffee." She nods. "But it's not ours."

"What do you mean?"

She shrugs. "I got up to open the door to the balcony a little while ago because it was so stuffy in here. Scent must be wafting over from your place." Despite the intruder's efforts to make nice, I rebuked his suggestion we both spend the night together on account of knowing someone's name not making them any less of a stranger.

"Is it? *My* place?!" I drop Dick in her lap and move on to the kitchen. I've got my hand on the door to the pantry when I hear her make an almost painful sound. "What?"

She makes a face to match the sound. "I forgot to pick up more coffee when I was out yesterday." I get it now. The sound. The face. It was in anticipation of the pain I'm about to inflict on her.

"Drea! It's coffee! Coffee should always be available for those who need it! It's coffee for God's sake!" I don't know why I keep referencing coffee as if it's a legally required beverage or something. Clearly, I'm the only one who understands and respects the importance of the coffee and one's need for it. "I can't believe you, Drea. I need the coffee. I need the coffee like I need the air. No air, no Tessa."

She laughs at my plight. "I get it; you need the coffee like you need the crack. Why don't you just go home and ask if Hot New Neighbor can spare a cup? Actually, that's totally what you should do." Her eyes light up and she's suddenly wide awake. Scheming does this to her.

"You're out of your mind. I'm not asking Hot New – Michael – for anything." I look at the curtains blowing in from the balcony. "I am going to go and stand out there to try and get high on the scent though."

"Get that crack, girl." She giggles and hurls the one remaining throw pillow from the sofa at me, I guess in lieu of cracking a whip at my heels? I don't know. I do know it hits me upside the head just as I reach the doorway, causing me to step outside looking even more disheveled than I did before.

"Good morning."

I yelp. "Holy shit. You scared me." I scramble to straighten my hair, or at least push it back out of my face. On second thought, maybe I'm better off leaving it there. I'm fairly certain last night's makeup doesn't look so hot this morning.

"Sorry. I don't mean to keep startling you." But he's grinning, so I'm thinking I don't buy that.

"Well, stop creeping up on me and that won't be an issue."

He laughs. It's a baffled laugh. Like he can't believe the things I'm accusing him of. "I was out here first. If anything, you're the one creeping up on me this morning."

"I smelled coffee." It's the truth. It's also the only thing I can think to say. It's pretty much the only thing I can think period. And not because it's the crack. Because he's fucking gorgeous. Ugh. Drea was right. Hot New Neighbor suits him way better than Michael. I must have been really out of it last night not to notice sooner. Well, that and the whole thinking he was a rapist burglar thing did sort of sway my perception of him.

He holds up his mug. Steam is still coming out of it. He must have just refilled it. Bastard.

"Would you like a cup?" God, he's so nice. Gorgeous and nice. That can't be right.

"I'm dying for one actually. Drea's pantry is deprived. Of coffee..." I'm rambling like a buffoon. If buffoons could talk. I think being around him is making me stupid.

"Deprived of coffee, huh?" I don't think he understands the importance of the coffee either. This helps. He's losing his appeal already. Plus, he's still holding a cup of the liquid life source and I'm not, which honestly, I'm starting to feel a bit resentful over.

"When you asked if I wanted a cup, were you just inquiring out of interest or were you actually offering to share?"

He chuckles softly, holding up his finger indicating for me to wait before he disappears inside his – *my* - apartment. When he comes back out, he's holding *two* big mugs.

Good God, he's hot.

For a moment, he looks as if he's contemplating the best way to hand it to me from one balcony to the other.

"May I?" I point over to his landing.

"Come over here?" He doesn't seem to think that's possible. Little does he know that before Drea landed this place, I was neighbors with *Always Locks His Keys Inside Lucas*.

Always Locks His Keys Inside Lucas was never comfortable with handing out a spare set of keys but had no problem with leaving his balcony door unlocked and asking me to break into his apartment on a regular basis. *Always Locks His Keys Inside Lucas* is in jail now. Broke into someone's house. Some nights I worry I gave him the wrong idea about things.

I wave my hand impatiently to get him to back up. I really want that first sip of coffee to happen while it's still piping hot. Holding onto the outside light, I step up onto the railing and then climb into the frame of the window separating our unit from his. If I had a fear of heights this would be problematic, as it is, I pause briefly to remind myself that this is smarter than walking through the apartment and out through the front door because this way Drea can't see me, then continue onto the neighboring window where I can repeat the steps I took leaving Drea's balcony to join Michael on mine.

I'm about to hop off the railing and into safety when his hand comes out to assist me. Out of habit, I reach for the light again, cursing myself and my stupid instincts as I do it. Holding his hand would have been nice.

"Impressive." He grins, retrieving the cup he set down when he thought he was going to help me down, and handing it to me.

"Back at ya." The words slip out before I can stop them.

His eyes narrow and an awkwardness creeps in. "Excuse me?"

"The coffee," I say, hurrying to actually have a sip. "It's impressive. I could tell just by smelling it." The coffee's not bad. But it's not leaving nearly the impression his naked body did last night. Which is somehow all I can think about, now that I'm standing here, looking at him fully clothed. I missed a lot of details during our first interactions. Many of which are coming back to me in a rush of blurred images, bleeding into my mind one after the other, making themselves far more comfortable than I'd like.

He's tall. I'm tall and I have to look up to talk to him. But, he's not lanky like most dudes his height. He's got sturdy, broad shoulders and an overall body that looks like it moves often and well. But he lacks the gym body bulk, which I sort of loathe. I always imagine gym bulk to be the equivalent to fake boobs. It's perky and big and perfect, but it's just not natural. Neither is the ink which, as I can attest to, covers the majority of his skin, but I can very comfortably call that art, and art is like a step up from natural. So, you know, it works.

It's not just the body though that earned him the Hot New Neighbor label. His face is pretty damn nice too. Strong jaw, slight stubble which blends in with the dark fuzz he's got growing on his head. He's not bald, or even balding, but he does seem to take a low maintenance approach to hair. It suits him. He's not a slick back or faux hawk kinda guy.

I'm still contemplating whether or not I've seen his full lips stretch into a real smile yet, when he takes a sip of coffee, his mouth disappearing in his cup completely. Automatically, my gaze shifts to his eyes, and stops. I can tell from the way the corners of his baby blues crinkle, he's laughing at me for some reason.

Some reason. Like maybe the obvious way in which I've been ogling him for the last few minutes.

Oh, God.

"Well, this has been...interesting." I lift my hand to catch the light fixture and pull myself back up onto the railing in a hurry. It's going to be slightly trickier now with one hand, but I can make it work. I have to. "Thanks for the coffee."

"It's the least I can do, considering."

I jump down – careful not to spill, landing safely on solid ground again. I notice he's still standing there watching me. "Alright, so...have a nice day." I do a half wave sort of gesture and hurry for the door. I've got one foot in when I hear him again.

"Let me know when you're ready to talk about our situation."

I shake my head and move out of his sight, scowling at Drea who's perched on the sofa anxiously awaiting a full report on my coffee escapades with Hot New Neighbor.

"Don't. There's nothing to smile about."

She doesn't believe me. "Um, hot new guy - living in your apartment. What's *not* to smile about?!"

"The list is long, Drea," I counter. "But while we're on that, how could you go all summer and never mention that the new neighbor moved into *my* apartment?!"

She shrugs. "It's *your* apartment. Kinda figured you knew."

"Yeah. Well, clearly I didn't."

"So, now that you do, what are you going to do about it?"

I frown. "Is that your subtle way of kicking me out already?"

She laughs. "I'm not subtle, Tessa. Ever."

"Point taken." I have another drink of my coffee. It's getting cold already. That's what I get for wasting all my precious time ogling. "I don't know what I'm going to do. He's got a lease. I don't think I can kick him out, even if I am his new landlord."

"Or roommate." She wiggles her brows at me.

"Don't do that, it looks creepy. Creepy and crazy. Both of which I think of when I consider moving in with a man I know nothing about. Who moves in with a perfect stranger? No one. No one sane anyway." Drea's up off the couch and attempting to take the mug out of my hands as I'm speaking. Apparently, the crazy has a strong hold on her this morning. "What are you doing?"

"I just want one measly little sip."

"Fine. I'll save you one." I turn away so my cup is out of her reach.

"Ew. I don't want the *last* sip. It'll be all grounds and backwash."

I shrug. "Hey, desperate times and all that. Take it or leave it."

She fakes gagging. "I'll leave it."

Thought so.

The clock behind her catches my attention in the middle of it all. Doing morning gymnastics to get my coffee took up more time than I allotted for coffee consumption today. My ass needs to hit the shower, asap. I've got my first class in less than an hour, and contrary to Drea's beliefs, the first week of classes does count.

I'm almost to the bathroom when I notice Drea is hot on my heels.

"What are you doing? If you don't walk away within the next ten seconds, you're going to see me naked."

Drea rolls her eyes at me and leans against the wall, just in case I didn't get that she was planning on sticking around despite the nudity threat.

"Why? Just...why? I know I did a striptease that one night during our freshman year, but that's not the norm. So, if you're sticking around for a show, you're not gonna get one."

"You're an idiot, and also, a mediocre stripper. I'm here for more dirt on the neighbor, not your titties. Explain yourself. Why are you so against getting to know him and just making this situation work?"

My fingers are gripping the doorframe impatiently. I don't like running late and having to rush. But I'm pretty clear on the fact that Drea isn't leaving until she's satisfied.

"He was naked."

Her eyes widen. "On the balcony?"

"No! Last night, when I busted in on him. He was completely naked. I saw *everything*."

"So?"

"So, now it's weird. I can't look at him and not see him naked," I hesitate to tell her the last humiliating bit. "And I'm pretty sure he knows."

She smirks. "Can't stop staring at his crotch, or something?"

"Drea!"

She laughs. "What?! You're the one talking about his nakedness being a distraction."

I sigh. "The whole thing is just too weird. And frankly, he would be nuts to agree to living together after what he's witnessed from me thus far."

"Because you're the scary stranger in this equation now?" Drea's tone of disbelief is only slightly hidden in her desire to keep up with this conversation and the winding trail of thoughts I'm taking it on.

"I tried to kill a naked man with Aunt Edi's umbrella."

Amusement twists her mouth up as she tries hard not to laugh again. "Man, I'm never drinking again. I miss all your best shenanigans when I'm passed out."

"This is serious, Drea. There's a stranger living in Aunt Edi's room. Sleeping in her bed. Using her old dresser. All of her stuff is still in there. I've spent weeks, dreading the moment I would have to come home and face all of it, knowing she would never come back to claim it, but to come home and find him? Invading her space, taking it over? If I take even a nano-second to truly think about what that means, I will lose it." I shake my head. "I can't live with him. I can't even think about him. I just want him gone and the condo back to the way it was before."

All laughter has died from Drea's face. "It's never going to be the way it was before, Tessa." She reaches her hand out to squeeze mine. "Maybe that was Aunt Edi's whole point for moving him in. Making it as non-like it was before it could possibly be."

"I don't think Aunt Edi did this, Drea," I say quietly. "I think it was Meredith. We all knew Aunt Edi was dying. It's the whole reason we all went up there, to say goodbye. Makes sense Meredith would lease out the place. She's the oldest, and handling assets falls to her. Just turns out, the condo wasn't one of them." That part surprised me as much as anyone.

Drea smiles sadly. "Well, jokes on her, I say. He's gorgeous and seems nice. I bet he'd switch rooms with you in a heartbeat if you asked." She shakes my hand back and forth trying to wiggle me out of my funk. "Just give this a chance, Tessa. Aunt Edi would be the first person to point out that everything happens for a reason. Even this."

"But it's *weird*. And he could be weird. And unstable. Possibly even dangerous. Although, he does make a solid cup of coffee. But that doesn't speak to his sanity. Plenty of crazy people are fond of the caffeinated brew. Probably aids them in their craziness. Gets them all wired and shit."

"Yeah," her eyes bulge out dramatically. "I'm aware."

"Fine. I'm crazy, he's crazy. We're clearly meant for each other," I release in a loud exasperated huff. "Now then, can I please get in the shower before I miss my first class completely?"

"Who's stopping you?"

Unbelievable.

• • • •

WEIRD. AND UNSTABLE….AND POSSIBLY DANGEROUS HOT NEW *NAKED* NEIGHBOR.

I like her.

That's going to be a problem. Especially since I've already offered to room with her once. What's to stop me from doing it again? And this time on a more permanent basis? It has bad idea written all over it.

For starters, she's young. Way young. And most importantly, she's female. And females are not included in my current life plan.

Then again, she's young. Way young. Even if we did decide to suck it up and deal with our current living situation as it is by rooming together for the time being, nothing would happen. Nothing.

"What are you looking at?" I demand of Mr. Grey Cat. He's not my cat, hence the really lame not really his name - name, but he's been coming around ever since I moved in here, and I let him, because, well, sometimes it's helpful to one's sanity to not technically be talking to yourself. He doesn't answer of course, but I still get the sense even he knows I'm lying to myself where Tessa is concerned.

Then, because he's a cat and cats don't give a shit, he lifts his snooty little nose and turns away, tail slinking along behind his lanky body as he makes his way out onto the patio. I probably won't see him for a while after he disappears out there. Wherever he lives, and whomever he belongs to, must be close by.

With my last cup of coffee having been donated to the cause for the sake of the greater good this morning, I'm out of reasons to procrastinate. Time to get this day rolling and face the next phase of operation 'New life and New Michael' - *The new job.*

By the time I'm showered and dressed I'm back to looking for ways to waste time. I guess that's what living alone is. Time. Time I used to be able to fill with taking turns or simply waiting. I never took into account just how much of my time was taken up through the basic dynamics of coexisting with another human being, and I certainly never expected how empty those moments would turn when alone.

I'm on the verge of heading outside and tracking down Mr. Grey Cat, just to have another living being to talk to, when there's a knock on the door, followed by a key turning just before the whole thing swings open.

"Sorry!" she calls out, passing me in a hurry. Her hair is soaking wet, and her body is wrapped in nothing more than a rose-colored towel that barely reaches beneath her ass. Practically running isn't helping her parts stay covered either.

Averting my eyes slightly too late, I retract my previous plan to converse with the neighbor's cat and opt for Tessa instead. She's already far more interesting than any four-legged furball will ever be.

When I find her, she's hunched over in the most dangerous position imaginable, searching her mountain of bags for something I'm hoping covers her more than that towel does. Well, I'm sort of hoping. Sort of not.

"I'd apologize more thoroughly for busting in on you twice within the last twenty-four hours, but this is partly your fault, so I'm not gonna," she mutters, digging through a large duffle bag.

"Wait. How is it my fault you keep breaking into my apartment?

She stops what she's doing just long enough to glare at me. "My apartment. And it's not breaking in when you have a key."

I can't help but chuckle at the insanity of this whole scenario. "First of all, if you're really that confused about whether or not you're breaking in, we can call the cops and ask them. I'm pretty sure that won't play out well for you though, what with my lease and all. And second, I'm still not clear on how any of this can be blamed on me. As far as I can see, I'm the only real victim in this mess."

A sage green shirt whips out from the depths of her bag as her hand flies up into the air in some sort of act of victory. It's short-lived, however, and she pursues her search for more articles of clothing in the next suitcase over. "Victim, my ass. I'm the homeless one here," she grumbles on, "and you might have mentioned that all of my possessions were delivered to you when I was here earlier for coffee!"

I shrug. "I figured you already knew that. It's your stuff."

She stops, adjusting her towel in a huff. "People really need to stop making assumptions like that! I'm not nearly as well informed as everyone thinks."

I lean my shoulder into the doorframe, crossing my arms over my chest and settling in for the duration of this chat. "I'm starting to learn that about you. What's up with that? Do you lack a healthy sense of curiosity? Too self-involved to ask a few questions every now and again?"

Her eyes widen and I notice the striking green of her irises has brown flecks near the pupils. I also notice she's pissed. And alarmingly close to bursting into tears.

"Are you kidding me with this?"

"Shit." I drop my arms and step into the room, squatting to be at eye level with her. "No. I mean, yes. I'm kidding. I'm sorry." I run both palms over my face trying to conjure up a clear thought that isn't in some way tainted by her beautiful eyes or the distracting way more of her skin keeps popping out of that towel. "It's been a weird night...and morning, for me. For both of us. I'm sure this isn't easy for you. Making stupid jokes is just my way of making light of it all."

I start to reach for her shoulders then stop short. I have no business touching this girl. And the last thing I want to do, is freak her out even more than I'm clearly already doing. "What can we do to make this work? For both of us."

She sits back on her duffle bag, sighing loudly. "Do you really think we could live here together?"

No. Definitely not. As a matter of fact, seeing her in her towel is all the proof I need to be completely certain it's the worst idea in the history or worst ideas. However, I find myself nodding and saying, "Sure."

"Have you ever had a girl for a roommate before?" she asks, like someone who thinks it's important to ask questions, but has nothing really specific they want to know.

"Yep." She wasn't technically my roommate, but close enough.

"And your name's not going to pop up on any sex offender list, right? Because I'm gonna check." Her pointer finger darts out as a warning as she says it.

"Clean record. Promise." I hold my hands up, demonstrating my innocence. "Had to pass a background check before my lease was even approved."

This information does seem to appease her.

Then a second wave of shadows moves in over her face. "There's something else."

"Name it."

"It freaks me out...you staying in my aunt's room."

I can see how that might be a bit much, given her current frame of mind after just having lost her. "I can move into this one." I take in the purple walls, remembering why I chose the other room in the first place. "Provided, I'm allowed to paint."

"You're allowed." She smiles. Briefly. It's sweet and innocent, combined with her flushed rosy cheeks and fresh, clean skin, there's no denying she's a natural beauty. I wonder if she knows. Probably not. She seems unusually unaware of herself.

"So, it's settled?"

She nods. "Looks like it, Roomie."

I grin. This is such a bad idea. But she's such an excellent distraction. And I could really use one of those right now.

Chapter
Three

TESSA

I'm practically running out the door for the second time today, my own mug in my hand, freshly washed. I'm about to ram my elbow into my front door to knock and wait this time, when it opens unexpectedly and formerly Hot New Neighbor turned Hot New Roommate is standing there, just as surprised by the sight of me as I am by him. I don't know why I can't get myself to call him by his name. Other than I don't like it and Drea started me on this stupid nickname thing I can't seem to stop now.

"Mug."

"Wow. That was fast." He smiles. I wish he was ugly. Alas, he's not, leaving me to only one defense. *Look away.*

"Okay, then. Have a nice day." I readjust my bag, now that I have both hands to work with, and make a dash for the stairs. He's obviously headed out as well and the last thing I want is some attempt at small talk while we travel down three flights of stairs. We've had enough awkward small talk to last us for months to come. And God knows, how much more we'll accumulate once we're living together for real. If these are my last moments of freedom from repressed, weird, and humiliating conversations, I want to savor them.

With the sound of his thundering footsteps following close behind, I skip the last three steps and lunge for the sidewalk, an easy feat considering I run track in exchange for my education.

I fumble at my car, unable to retrieve my keys fast enough. As luck would have it, the fancy new BMW parked beside me is his. I should have known. I thought it looked out of place last night, but I just assumed someone had company.

"Running late for class?"

I look up involuntarily at the sound of his voice. Damn my efficient reflexes.

"How did you know I was a student?"

He shrugs. "Lucky guess. The laptop bag and books helped, of course."

He's wearing glasses now. They completely change his look. I also notice he's paired his bland khakis from earlier with a blue button-up shirt complete with long sleeves which given the hot weather, can only serve to cover up his tattoos. It's suddenly very apparent that he's older than me. He's like, a legit grown-up. Somehow, that only makes him sexier.

"Aha!" I yank my keys out at last.

He smiles. I smile. Why? Why am I smiling at the man who hijacked my home?

"I gotta go." And I do. But I smile the whole damn ride to school. Maybe I really am the crazy one.

I'm so freaking late by the time I pull into the parking lot, I have to run across campus to get to class. I think I hear my name called a time or two while I'm zooming past the blurred faces but catching up with people will have to wait until after Psychology.

When I almost come flying out of my left sandal, I pause briefly and fix the straps. I'm still focused on my toes and trying to get them back around the stupid thong of my shoe when I hear his voice. Again.

"We really need to stop meeting like this."

"Oh my God! Are you following me?" Clean record, my ass.

He grins like he's amused, something I realize he does frequently when interacting with me, and I'm generally not all that funny. "Relax, Tessa. I'm just trying to get to my class on time like everyone else."

"Alrighty then." I practically take off at a sprint, mostly to keep my next thoughts from spilling out of my mouth before I can stop them. Like, how is he a student here? And how has this not come up before now? Then, I notice the distance between us isn't increasing. He's headed to the same place I am. So, I speed up some more. At the very least, I'm not walking in late *with* him.

At least I don't plan to. When his hand reaches the handle the same time mine does, I lose all hope of ever being rid of him.

As soon as I'm in the room, I spot the only seat available in the front row. I'm mentally preparing myself to wrestle him for it as I make a mad dash for the last chair – determined not to let him steal another thing from me. Only when I get there, my butt claims it without any interference from him. Shockingly. In fact, now that I'm turned around again, there's no sign of him anywhere. Maybe I missed an open seat in the back somewhere?

"Good morning, ladies and gentlemen. Welcome to Social Psychology."

Oh God.

This can't be happening.

"My name is Dr. Michael McMichael – yes, my parents were those types of assholes – and I'll be taking over this course for Dr. Cremer while she's on maternity leave. For those of you wondering, she gave birth to a healthy baby boy just last month."

Michael McMichael. His parents really were assholes. Not important. He's my Professor. *Hot New Roommate Michael is my professor.*

I spend the next fifteen minutes staring at my feet and wishing I could disappear. Considering I'm sitting right up front, he'd likely notice if I made another run for it though. I can't text Drea either. I can't do anything. Least of all pay attention to anything he's saying. It's not until I notice everyone reaching for pen and paper or whipping out their laptops and tablets, that I start to feel as though participating is a viable option again. Thankfully, we spend the rest of class taking notes while he gives an annoyingly insightful lecture on gender and the ways in which society is affecting how we identify ourselves, as well as members of the opposite sex. He's smart. And humble in a way that really makes you underestimate him. Made *me* underestimate him. He's not crazy. Or unstable. But I am. Of course, Dr. McMichael already knows that because he knows his stuff. It's clearly why he's always laughing at me.

I don't wait even half a second after we're dismissed to jet from the room. Any and all future humiliation will have to wait until we're home again. Home. It'll never feel sacred again.

Rather than sit out in the open where Michael could stumble upon me some more, I head for the library and bury myself in the biographies section. No one's coming to look for me here and the librarians have come to accept that my face is just part of the furnishings in that section. I have a weird sort of fascination with learning people's stories. I don't even care who they are, I just want to know their history. What made them who they became. Which experiences molded their lives in the most significant ways. I think maybe it's because I know so little of my own history. It's made me obsessed with people who know enough about theirs to write a whole freaking book about it.

"Back at it already, huh, Tessa?"

It's Carlo, one of the students who works here. He's been here seven years. I don't think he's ever graduating. I don't think he wants to.

"You know it." I flip my hair and give him a cheesy grin. It's not flirting when it's with Carlo, therefore it's easy.

"Who are you getting to know this week?" he asks, a genuine curiosity in his tone.

Holding the cover out for him to see, I answer, "Alexis Lane."

"Who's that?"

"This super rad photographer. I saw his work in some other biographies I read. He's got some sort of magic eye for capturing people's secret essence or something. I don't know how to explain it, but once you get to know his work, you recognize it instantly. Anyway, after seeing so many of his portraits, I figured it was time to find out a little more about him."

Carlo leans in while I start to flip through the pages. "Huh. They're all pictures."

Disappointed, I hum in agreement. "Yeah, not what I thought it would be."

"Well, you know those artist types, a lot of them are extremely private. Secret identity and all," Carlo points out.

"I guess." I let my gaze sweep the images on the open pages once more. Maybe there's more in here about him than we realize. "I'm getting it anyway. If his pictures tell so much about the people in them, they're bound to reveal things about him as well."

Carlo chuckles. "You're going to make a damn fine reporter one day."

"That's my plan." I grin, closing the book and pressing it to my chest. This one is definitely going home with me.

From here, the day seems to pick up the pace. After my last class, I grab a quick bite to eat and then head straight to track practice. It's almost six o'clock by the time I'm pulling up in front of our apartment building and I'm exhausted. For the first day of 'first week doesn't count' classes, I got my ass kicked. I wonder if Drea faired any better. Probably. She didn't have her first class until eleven and she doesn't run track, she's here on a music scholarship and regardless of what she claims, I seriously doubt playing the piano while sitting on your ass can be all that tiring.

I scan the parking lot for a minute before I get out. There's no sign of the silver BMW. Convinced that it's safe to proceed, I practically run for the stairwell. Exhausted or not, I find the energy to take all three flights two steps at a time, and I don't slow down until I'm inside Drea's place with the door locked and chained behind me.

Drea and Jules are sprawled out on the couch watching something Channing Tatum on TV. That is, until I come crashing in providing them with better entertainment.

"What's wrong with you? Were you being chased?" Drea seems genuinely worried which will make my real reason sound super ridiculous.

"Don't tell me. The Zombie apocalypse is finally upon us!" Jules is not worried. She's not even faking it. Mostly, she just seems annoyed I'm taking her attention away from the man candy on the screen.

"Even if it was, you'd be the last person I'd tell. I'd just let them get you and feast on your brains. Although, feast might be a stretch," I mutter, dropping my bag beside the door and squeezing in between them on the sofa. I avoid looking at the screen. I caught a glimpse when I first walked in and heard my internal dialogue. It was comparing Channing to Michael. Channing was losing. It's not a place I'm comfortable going again.

"You know you're all sweaty and gross, right?" Drea gives me a disgusted sideways glance as I lean in for the coffee table to examine the now nearly empty pizza boxes spread out before them.

"I do. But a girl can't ever hear that enough, so keep it coming." I settle on a slice of mostly cheese and sink back into the cushions, kicking off my stinky sneakers and socks on spiteful principle.

Drea stares at me a moment longer before she bursts out, "Are you going to talk about what's happening here, or what? Why do you look like you took a wrong turn on the track and just kept running? And speaking of wrong turns, why are you here at all? I thought you were all set to stay at your place again."

I swallow hard to get down a way too big bite of pizza crust. It's cold and dry and not at all worth it.

"Hot New Neighbor Michael, aka Hot New Roommate Michael, actually prefers to go by Dr. Michael McMichael. At least when he's teaching my psyche class."

Drea gapes and even Jules returns her attention to me and away from Channing Tatum, going so far as to mute the television.

"The hot dude next door is a teacher?"

"Oh, yeah." I nod, taking another bite of pizza. I don't know why I'm still eating it other than I'm starving and too lazy to get up and forage for something else.

"Get the fuck outta here!" I think Drea is still contemplating whether or not I'm telling the truth. We have a history of pranking one another, usually for properly motivated reasons, and while I don't currently have one, I can see why she's worried.

"I'm serious. And since we're on the topic of awkward and embarrassing experiences I've had today, I also accused him of stalking me seconds before we both entered the classroom."

Jules starts laughing. Drea, who values our friendship a little more, does her best to suppress the grin I know is desperate to escape. Hell, I'm about to start laughing at the whole disaster myself.

"What are you going to do? Drop the class?"

"No!" Though that clearly has occurred to me. "Truth is, he's really good. The lecture he gave today was insightful and interesting and even though I hardly took any notes, I remember almost all of it. Like, he taught it in a way that it just clicked, you know? Plus, I need the credit, so..."

Jules is clearly torn between wanting to get back to Channing and feeling the need to add to this conversation. "Um, that's really cool and all, but don't you think the school might frown upon a professor and his student rooming together? I'm just guessing they have policies against that."

Drea shrugs. "Would they have to know?"

Staring at my sad piece of pizza, I start thinking out loud, "I'm sure they already do, they just don't know they do. But we're both in their system. And we obviously would have put down the same address, even before we realized we both intended to live in the same place."

"So, now what?" Drea seems disappointed. Like, she thinks my fucked-up living situation has all the makings of a romance novel or something and suddenly this plot twist isn't giving her the ending she was hoping for.

"I know," Jules chimes in with an unexpected amount of enthusiasm, (well, unexpected until I peer at the tv out of the corner of my eye. No Channing in sight, just some tire commercial). "You and I can switch! You move into my place for the semester, and I can move into yours."

"Ha!" I can't even give it a real laugh. "That's totally not happening. But thanks."

I toss what's left of the marinara-soaked cardboard back into the box and get up. "I need a shower."

"Yeah."

I drop a hard glance on Drea.

"Not because you smell or anything," she tries to cover. "Because you need to clear your head or whatever."

"Nice save," I say dryly as I walk away. I know she's right. I smell so bad I can freaking smell myself. It's appalling.

Tiptoeing for no real reason other than it seems safer, I make my way across the landing to my own front door. Unlocking it as quietly as I can, I start by sticking only my head inside and listening.

"Hear anything?" his voice rumbles from behind me.

My body slams into the door, the door slams open until it hits the wall, and to top it all off, I whack the crap out of my pinky toe. "Oh my *God*, man!"

Jumping around on one foot, I bounce around my foyer still holding all of my crap from the day, caught between wanting to escape and not wanting to hop the streets aimlessly with a load of books, a gym bag, and a laptop, since I have no real place left to go.

"I don't suppose you think it's a coincidence that the harder you try to hide from me, the more dramatic our interactions are becoming?" he asks dryly, setting down his bag along the wall (like he lives here!). "Also, why aren't you wearing shoes?!"

"I left them at Drea's," I whine, in hindsight a bad idea.

Given his expression, I'm inclined to think he agrees. Regardless, he keeps his mouth shut as he takes my stuff from me, places it on the coffee table, and starts moving straight for the kitchen.

"Interesting reading material you've got there. You studying photography too?"

"No," I say far snottier than necessary. "I just like learning about different types of people, and I happen to think the photographer who took those is very talented."

He doesn't say anything, just nods as he opens the freezer and retrieves a bag of frozen lima beans. Briefly, I berate him mentally for thinking of food while I likely have a broken bone in my foot, and mocking may also be taking place, because, lima beans?! Gross. But then, that jackass comes back over to where I'm still doing my busted toe-dance, takes my elbow to gently guide me backward toward the sofa where he helps me take a seat, before kneeling down to cradle my foot in one hand and hold the frozen beans on my smashed pinky with the other.

"How's that?" His voice is quieter than normal. Careful almost, and I notice he's not looking up to make eye contact the way he usually does. He's a stickler for eye contact, he is. Makes me all sorts of uncomfortable. Except now because he's looking at my feet. Which as it turns out, is way worse.

"Good," I mumble. "Thank you." Heat is surging through the top of my head and I can feel myself break out in a cold sweat. *Sweat.* Jeez, now I know why he's not looking at me. I'm disgusting. He's probably breathing through his mouth right now just to keep from passing out being this close to me.

Embarrassment makes for a convenient adrenaline replacer, and I jolt upward so fast, I nearly forget not to put weight on my right foot.

"Oh, look at that! All better already." I force a smile. My foot is killing me. Well, maybe it's a combination of things, but something – everything - is *killing me.*

"Tessa, your toe is the size of a small cucumber."

"Uh-huh," I squeak, doing my best to walk without hobbling.

"You should keep ice on it for a little while longer. And put it up. And, you know, maybe get X-rays," he calls after me, but I'm far enough down the hall to pretend I can't hear him. Just a few more feet and I'm in the bathroom, completely out of reach.

As it turns out, showering results in more than eliminating the stink. After mulling everything over until the steaming hot water turned icy cold, I've concluded that moving forward as if the previous twenty-four hours never happened, is my best possible plan of action. I'm not entirely sure how I'll convey my plan to him without acknowledging the lineup of disasters leading up to it, but maybe feigning complete obliviousness will work. He doesn't know me that well. I could be a total airhead.

I'm even fairly certain pleading ignorance is my best bet on the whole roommate - professor debacle. Seems like that's more his problem than mine anyway. Unless he decides it *is* a problem, in which case it *becomes* my problem because I'm thinking his lease will hold up over my desire to deny he has one. So, he likely won't move. And I, well, I have nowhere else to go.

Drea's place is supposed to be a two bedroom just like mine, but the spare room has long been converted to her music room slash recording studio, hence my sleeping over in her dining room. And with Scott spending more time there than at his multi-bachelor bachelor pad, it's already on the cramped side most of the time. Of course, there's Jules and her generous yet totally selfish offer to switch condos, and while I do like her super pimped out pad more than my own most days, I tend to think I'll like it drastically less when her fifty something sugar daddy shows up expecting, well, ya know, rent.

Finally clean and in my most comfy sweatpants, I walk back into the living room feeling like a sparkling new person. Or at the very least, a person instead of a grotesque beast. My toe is another story. It still looks like it belongs to a grotesque beast. But, I'm oblivious, so I don't care.

"You got a present while you were in the shower." Michael is standing behind the breakfast bar, making a sandwich. No, *two* sandwiches.

"I did?" I'm not sure I'm up for presents. Given the way my life is going, it's probably something like cat puke in a place Drea really doesn't want cat puke, and I'm really not in the mood to have my new sparkle besmirched with cat puke two seconds in.

He slides one of the sandwiches in my direction and gives a nod toward the living room. "I assume that belongs to you."

My eyes follow his nod and land on Dick. I notice they do that a lot around here lately. "Drea bring him by?" I ask, doing a weird skip walk thing, as if that could possibly hide my limping, to get to Dick and give him a proper hello.

"Nope. Just slipped in through the open balcony door and refused to leave this time." Michael grins, coming around the counter to take a seat at the breakfast bar beside the second sandwich. The one he made for me. I haven't really had a chance to take that reality in just yet.

"Yeah. That pretty much sums up how he became my cat in the first place." I sigh and back it up as smoothly as I can until I reach the bar stool beside Hot New Sandwich Making Roommate.

Nope.

Too long.

Won't stick.

There's an awkward moment where he's staring at me while chewing. Finally, he swallows. "What? You don't like turkey?"

"Turkey's good." I nod.

"You're not hungry?"

"Starving." That shit pizza at Drea's hardly curbed my appetite. Mostly, it just made me miss real food.

He places his half-eaten turkey on wheat back onto his plate, brushes the crumbs from his hands and leans sideways into his elbow to get a better angle at me. "Is this one of those moments where I shouldn't assume that you know I made a sandwich for you?"

"I mean, I sort of figured," I admit, climbing onto my own stool. "But given my poor conclusion drawing process the past twenty-four hours, I think it's best if we both just agree to spell everything out for one another until we really have a grasp on this new arrangement. And each other."

He smirks. He's amused by me. At me. I don't know. Whatever.

"I present to you, turkey, Swiss cheese, avocado, tomato and a little mustard, layered neatly between two slices of fresh whole wheat bread. It's yours. Because I was hungry. And eating in front of someone is rude." He picks up his sandwich again. "And also, because eating alone sucks. Which we'll both be doing if you don't hurry up and take your first bite before I take my last."

He doesn't need to tell me twice. One ginormous bite later and my belly and taste buds are equally impressed with my new roommate. Michael. Mike? Professor McMichael?

I can feel my lip curl up involuntarily. And it's not even for a good reason, other than I'm entertained by my own silly contemplation of his name and why it's so clearly *not* his name. "What is it that people really call you?"

He doesn't laugh. Or smirk. But his eyes light up with something new. Intrigue? Surprise? I don't know, but it's a new version of the usual steady gaze he keeps on me that makes me feel like I'm a caged animal in his personal lab somewhere. "What do you mean?"

I take another bite, to stall. Now that I've opened this can of worms I kind of wish I hadn't. "I just figured you had a nickname."

He chews way longer than he needs to before he swallows. "Like Mike?"

I shake my head. "I think we both know you don't go by Mike."

He holds the last of his crust within an inch of his mouth, and for a moment I think he's going to eat it, chew for five minutes and really make me sweat it out. Then he grins and the crust drops back down an inch. "I don't look like a Mike?"

My nose and mouth scrunch up before I can stop them. It really bothers me that much. Now that I'm thinking about it, I'm not even sure I'm buying that his last name is McMichael.

"You don't have the right hair for *Mike*."

This time he laughs. Loudly. Delightedly. A pleased laugh. Which would be odd if this conversation wasn't already so dumb.

"I don't have the right hair for Mike? Wow. Well, then. Do I have the right hair for Max? Doug? Or maybe Jason?"

"You're just throwing names out there now." Annoyed, I abandon ship and jump face first into the sandwich in front of me, resigning myself to calling him Michael for all eternity.

He's still staring at the side of my head. I can feel it, but I refuse to acknowledge it.

"Well, if I don't have the right hair for any of those names, I guess I better stick with Lane then."

Lane.

Slowly, I turn back to face him. "You totally have Lane hair."

He grins broadly, all of his shiny white teeth peeking out. "Apparently. Who knew?"

. . . .

FORMERLY HOT NEW SANDWICH MAKING ROOMMATE...NOW SIMPLY KNOWN AS *LANE.*

So much for making changes and taking time out from being me. It should have been so easy. Middle name out, real name in. Voila. New me. While I've never used my first name around friends or family, no one professionally has ever questioned it. Not once. Not even given the ridiculous combo of Michael and McMichael. But then along comes Tessa. Tessa the crazy girl with the umbrella. The flustered chick in nothing but a towel. The coffee addict with all the grace and strength of a circus performer.

My new roommate.

My student.

"So, weird coincidence this morning, huh?" I point out, sliding my plate out of the way and reaching for my water instead.

"I don't know. Can anything between us still be categorized as weird? Haven't we graduated past that yet? Onto something else, like...what's weirder than weird?" Her left brow arches thoughtfully as she continues to contemplate the answer to her own question. "Kooky? Freaky? *Ominous?*"

"Ominous? Are we headed for danger? Is one of us still planning to kill the other with an umbrella when they're naked and unarmed?"

She's so caught off guard, she nearly spits avocado across the room. Fighting her way through laughing and choking she somehow manages to put words together. "Maybe ominous was a bad choice."

"Maybe." I smirk. She's funny. And, I'm back at the beginning of my original train of thought. "Anyway, if you're not too busy planning my murder, there is one small hiccup in our current plan to room together."

She nods. She's figured it out as well. "The whole student – teacher thing."

"Exactly." I spin my seat around to face her full on rather than twist. "How comfortable are you with secrets?"

She frowns. "What kind of secrets?"

I'd thought that part was obvious. Apparently, we're still doing the spelling things out bit. "The kind where neither of us tells anyone that we're living together."

Her confusion only grows from here. "Not telling isn't exactly going to hide anything. I'm sure someone, somewhere in admin will notice eventually that we share the same address. Provided there isn't some sort of search engine already in place to pick up on such things."

She's a wee bit on the paranoid side, but that's not necessarily a bad thing. For me. In this case in particular. "Our addresses aren't the same."

"Come again?"

"I got the job before I got the condo. And I never updated my info."

Her eyes narrow slightly. "You don't feel like this may become an issue at some point down the road? You know they only forward your mail for like six months. What are you going to do after that? Just hope they don't mail you anything important? Like your W2's for example?"

"I bet you get told to relax a lot."

Her jaw stiffens. Her mouth all but disappears and I now know what she would look like should she ever decide to grow a unibrow. "You're right. I don't know why I even care. Not my job on the line. Not my mail getting lost. Not. My. Problem. AT ALL."

There's a zip of her stool spinning and the breeze she leaves in her wake as she makes every effort to stomp off in a huff. Only she can't quite pull it off because she's polite and considerate, and takes the time to clear both our plates, rinse them and load them in the dishwasher before muttering a 'thanks for the sandwich' and continuing her dramatic exit.

This is the point at which I stop her. "I'm not going to lose any mail because I still own the house it's being sent to. And, frankly, this job is...just a job. I have no intention of building a career around it. So, if it doesn't pan out, oh well."

Her exit successfully halted, I've topped my initial expectations and managed to stump her. "Huh?"

I release a long, worn-out breath of air. When I took this job, and found this condo, my intentions were to keep things simple. To create a disconnect. To change course abruptly and not look back until I was so far ahead, looking back didn't fucking hurt anymore. But those plans clearly only applied to life in a bubble. Blissful solitude which didn't include people or their prying questions. All of which disappeared the second she came crashing in, swinging her dead aunt's umbrella at my head.

Relenting to the situation such as it is, I get to my feet and approach her.

"I was supposed to get married end of May. The date was set two years ago. The wedding was paid for. Everything was ready. Except the bride."

Her eyeballs sweep from one side to the other, presumably in search of an escape. "Oh."

"Yeah. That's pretty much what I said too when I found out she wasn't as keen on getting married to me as she was ready to trek through Europe with my best man."

Her jaw drops and her eyeballs stop scanning the room, freezing instead. Directly on me. "Wow."

"Uh-huh." I hate telling this story. Which, I figured I would. This is the first time I've had to tell it. Considering it's September, I guess I held it off for a pretty long time. "With the wedding being canceled, it kind of put a damper on our other plans as well."

"Your other plans?" Fear. Definite fear in her voice. Hell, I'd be scared to ask as well. Curiosity though, it's a killer.

"To buy a far greater house than we could possibly need, directly on the beach so we could use it as a home office and combine our practices to run a joint couple's therapy center."

The corners of her mouth jerk briefly as she wards off the instinct to laugh. "I can see where having your marriage be a bust could sort of cast a shadow on couple's therapy." I have to commend her for keeping a straight face through that one.

"Yep."

Silence sets in as I give her time to piece the rest together for herself.

Eventually, her expression turns neutral. There's a softness in her eyes when she nods and says, "I'm pretty comfortable with keeping secrets."

Find more Lane and Tessa at www.authorksthomas.com

Acknowledgments

NATURALLY, NO BOOK would be written, let alone published, if it weren't for a great deal of amazing people. Like my daughter, who patiently accepts that there are times when I am completely zoned out, my mind wrapped around fictional people and imaginary conversations, and I need a minute to readjust before I can carry on in the real world.

Or my friends and family, who have come to understand that deadlines I set for myself are taken as seriously (or more seriously) as they would had they been set by a publisher...other than me. And that this means I may be sleep deprived, cranky and less social for large chunks of time. I am thankful they not only understand and accept this, but continue to love me in spite of it.

Then, of course, I have to thank those who bravely show up to beta read my first drafts and offer feedback I appreciate beyond measure. Tin's betas included some lovelies, old and new! So, here's my official THANK YOU:

Stephanie

Tawnya

Stephen

Rachel

Alyssa

You're all totally awesome and drenched in awesome sauce!!

My editor, Angela. Thank you for making Tin shine and giving me a chance to continue to grow as a writer. I can't wait to see what we create next!

A special thank you also goes to Tami at **Magic of Books Promotions**, for handling all of the marketing involved in the release. It is by far my least favorite task and I am so thankful to have found someone who loves my book babies as much as I do and goes above and beyond in finding them new homes with loving readers ;-)

Now, my thank you to you. And a little something I want to share with you …

When I first sat down to write this book, I had a very basic idea of what it would be, but no real direction. Then, once I got going, there was no stopping it. The story just flowed out of me as if it'd been waiting for a long time to be set free. Maybe it had been. Some stories are like that.

Quinn will always be near and dear to my heart, and I know not everyone who reads this story will feel that way. And that's okay. Maybe that's better even. It's hard to want people to understand her when it makes my heart ache to think about what it means for many people who do.

While her story ultimately came together through research and the usual dose of imagination, it was also founded in a place of personal experience. Experience I'd never expected to have. That's life though. And, I've learned that not all aspects of pain are bad...

In the end, I'm grateful to be the person I am today. To know what I know. Even if the journey wasn't always enjoyable, I'm quite pleased with the current destination and have great hopes for future travels.

~ K.

Did you love *Tin*? Then you should read *Don't Fall*[1] by K.S. Thomas!

2

When Tessa Harrison meets Michael McMichael (Yes - his parents were THOSE people) her first instinct is to clobber him on sight. He's naked and standing in the middle of her apartment, clobbering seems sensible, and Tessa is nothing if not sensible.

But that sensibility begins to wane as the two continue to be thrust together, and before long, there's no denying their increasingly intense connection, even if it is just physical.

It has to be.

Because it's all he's offering.

And it's all her guarded heart knows how to accept.

---

1. https://books2read.com/u/3k0OvN

2. https://books2read.com/u/3k0OvN

Tessa's convinced she's got everything under control but does she?

It doesn't take long before the rules get blurred, feelings are revealed and hearts are on the line.

Just as Tessa's about to take that last big leap, everything could end in one final crash. And it's all she needs to remember the lesson she learned years ago...

You fall, you go under. You don't get back up.

So you simply...don't fall.

Read more at www.authorksthomas.com.

Also by K.S. Thomas

A Finding Nolan Novel
Lost Avalon
Secret Hudson
Fallen Angel
Forever Francis

A Once Upon a Wedding Story
Save The Date
With Whom We Spend Our Lives
The Men Write in the Sugar
An Untwist of Fate

Don't Tell Mom
Don't Tell Mom She's Not A Rock Star

PINK
Nine (A Pink Novel, #1)
Eight (A pINK Novel, #2)

The Rock Star's Wife
Chasing After You
Coming For You

Standalone
Unhurt
I Call Him Brady
It's Kinda My Thing
I Think About You
Bittersweet
Tin
Last Girl
One More Chapter
Forget Me Not
EverAfter
Don't Fall
Love At First Sight
Fruit Punch Kisses
Trading Favors
One Moment at a Time
A Cinderella Twist
No More Love Songs

Watch for more at www.authorksthomas.com.

About the Author

Originally born and raised in Bremen, Germany, I currently reside in sunny Florida with my teenage daughter, our coyote, a three-legged roo, and a tamed wolf (AKA, our dogs). I like to think we have a bit of a Gilmore Girls thing going, except my kid is obsessed with dance not books, and I'm (much to my increasing disappointment) appropriately aged to have a teenager.

I love coffee and yoga and the ocean and cooking and asking 'none of my business' questions whenever possible.

While I spent my childhood certain I could be a Disney princess, sitting here, surrounded by my crystals, smudge sticks and tarot cards, eager to get out to my garden and walk on the earth in my bare feet and chat with the lizards about not eating my plants, I'm pretty sure I grew up to be the witch. The good sort.

And, obviously, I write romance novels.

That is, after all, what brought us together. Our love for...well, love. And who can blame us? Love has the power to bring out the best and the worst in us. It can make us strong or be our greatest weakness. It can make us move mountains or make us do some of the dumbest shit in the history of dumb shit. In short, love is entertaining as hell.

Read more at https://www.authorksthomas.com/.

Made in the USA
Columbia, SC
23 May 2023

16617653R00188